The Redemption
of
Don Juan Casanova

A NOVEL

Lloyd Lofthouse

Publisher's Note

This book is a work of fiction. Names, characters, places, events, incidents, organizations and dialogue in his novel are the product of the author's imagination or are used fictitiously. Any resemblance to actual persons, living or dead, events, or locales is entirely coincidental.

Copyright © 2015 by Lloyd Lofthouse

Published by Three Clover Press, California, USA

ISBN: 978-0-9860328-2-0

Chapter One
New Year's Eve
1989

"Have you ever felt God watching you, Jonah?" she asked. If a crimson Lincoln rose had a voice, it would sound like hers.

They were below deck in the great room of the Aphrodite, an 83-foot schooner moored to a boat slip in California's King Harbor marina.

Jonah shared the Aphrodite with a dozen bikini-clad vamps who had all gone to New Year's Eve parties much louder than the private party he was hosting with this one beauty who put the rest to shame.

Jonah liked his seductions to take place with music playing softly in the background. The first song drifting through the Aphrodite tonight was *Fun, Fun, Fun* by The Beach Boys.

He poured Beringer white merlot into a tall-stemmed goblet of foggy amber glass and sniffed the wine's sweet cherry aroma.

Her hands slipped around his waist from behind and worked to unbutton his blue, Hawaiian-flowered, short-sleeve shirt. He could feel her heat through the cotton. "Wasn't your mother Amanda a gambler?" she whispered, her warm breath caressing the back of his neck. "Didn't she play cards in speakeasies during the twenties to win this boat?"

Jonah stepped away from her, and her fingertips lingered briefly on his hips before they were gone.

Amanda had done more than play cards, Jonah thought. She started the family fortune in New York when she was seventeen in 1910.

Jonah turned and held out the glass of wine. It was difficult to keep eye contact with her, because a master carver had chiseled her butternut body into sculpted perfection. Though he wanted a visual feast before sleeping with her, drooling over a woman's body was against his rules of seduction because he knew it made most women nervous.

This one was decades younger than his eighty-seven. Like Picasso, Jonah wasn't attracted to women over thirty. When they were young, their smooth skin smelled of the sea and wind. Once the bloom withered, he lost interest.

"Take us out to sea, Jonah," she said. "Just like your mother did with the whores and gamblers." Her eyes were blue with green flecks of light dancing in them. She put the full goblet of wine he had handed her on the bar.

He sipped his wine, thinking that the last time the Aphrodite had been away from its berth had been the week before Pearl Harbor was bombed and that Amanda's prostitutes had probably elicited enough sperm here to sink the ship.

"Didn't you sail with Amanda when you were a boy?" she asked, and the tip of her tongue ran seductively along her lusty top lip. She wore tight, frayed, cutoff jeans. A shoulderless halter top barely covered her breasts, but not the smooth, muscular surface of her flat, naked abdomen. He thought, maybe I'll call this girl Butternut because of the color of her skin.

"Would you prefer something stronger." Jonah reached for a bottle of aged Glenlivet Scotch whisky. He poured an inch into a tumbler, hoping this would stop the questions about Amanda.

He didn't like distractions from foreplay. Hundreds of seductions had taught him that more than ninety percent of the enjoyment of sex was the game that led up to the orgasm, and he loved touching a woman's naked body more than he enjoyed the orgasm. Besides, with age, he couldn't get as hard or last as long as he had when he was younger.

She sipped the tumbler of Glenlivet dry and watched him over the rim of the cut crystal like a cat watching its prey.

"How many bedrooms on the Aphrodite?" she asked. "Have you had women in all of them? I heard that your mother produced pornography on this boat. I understand she even owned a high-class escort service at one time before she built the club. Is it true that she stopped producing pornography because she didn't want the attention of the Meese Commission?"

Jonah peered at her suspiciously. He couldn't remember her name, and he wondered if she was a reporter attempting to trick him into giving away the family secrets. "Amanda liked Scotch," he said, and poured her another inch of the Glenlivet. "Every morning when we docked and the clients went ashore, she would drink a full tumbler before going to bed." He recalled those nights fondly. After all, he had been Amanda's bed warmer before and after he married her oldest daughter. Amanda never married, and she had a different handpicked man for every one of the half-dozen children she gave birth to in her thirties.

"I want to make you happy," she said, and slipped the zipper of her jeans down an inch, revealing more of her trim, muscular abdomen. "Why do you call her Amanda and not mother?"

He didn't tell her it was because he wasn't Amanda's son, but rather her son-in-law. He'd changed his last name to Casanova because Amanda wanted her two daughters to have children with the family's last name. Besides, Amanda had taken him in when he was ten in 1913, and no one had ever discovered she wasn't his real mother. He'd been homeless, and she had wanted a son without going through the pregnancy. But, as far as the world knew, he was one of Amanda's children. Later, she decided to have her own.

"Meet me halfway for a kiss," he said.

A moment later, they were on the floor and her cutoff jeans and halter top had been cast aside. With Butternut naked, Jonah's hands explored all of his favorite places.

"I want to surprise you, Jonah," she said. "So close your eyes."

He watched as she pulled his pants down around his knees and left them there. He wore no underwear. She leaned down, and her long, straw-colored hair tickled his stomach as she took his soft pecker in her hand.

He watched, savoring the moment.

"No peeking, Jonah," she said as she pulled away. "Or there will be no surprise."

He wanted to touch the throbbing pulse of excitement he could see beating wildly in her neck. It reminded him of a baby bird ready to fly. She leaned down to kiss him, and her lips and tongue had the smooth, velvet taste of the Glenlivet.

He gently caressed both of her breasts, and felt her nipples harden. She leaned back, stretched her torso tight, and tossed her head to clear away the long hair that had covered her eyes.

She discovered he was feasting on her perfect body with his eyes, and she pursed her lips and wagged a finger at him. "What did I say, Jonah?"

He closed his eyes and waited, anticipation holding his breath hostage.

"No cheating," she said, and she stepped away from where he lay on the floor toward her purse on the bar.

She reached inside for the foot-long marble dildo, the one she'd stolen from a long-dead Greek god. The god's immortal dildo was going to be Jonah's final gift, to pay for Amanda's sins and his own.

Learning over him, she said, "Open your mouth, Jonah."

When he did as she asked, she shoved the marble shaft down his throat, shattering his teeth and destroying the inside of his mouth. His eyes flew open in shock, and he struggled to free his arms, which were pinned to his sides by her long, strong, tanned legs.

She shoved the dildo deeper into his throat.

Pain roared through his body like a tornado. One of his hands fluttered toward the security camera hidden in the bulkhead across the room, seeking help that wasn't there, because, wanting privacy, he'd turned it off before she'd arrived.

Once she was sure he was dead, she pulled the marble dildo from Jonah's throat and washed away the blood and saliva in the sink before putting it back in her purse. Then she dressed, slipped on latex gloves and cleaned everything she had touched. She found a vacuum and went to work. When she finished, she took the bag out of the vacuum and put it in a trash bag. She put her purse inside the bag, too, and then sealed the bag with a double knot.

She inspected the room once more before she went out on the aft deck of the Aphrodite and looked across the boardwalk at the nightclub, with its pulsing magenta walls singing *God Only Knows*. The music created an illusion that the nightclub was a throbbing heart, while the ocean glowed from phosphorescence as if heralding an army of horny aliens about to invade from the sea.

With her lips pressed tight, she reached in the back pocket of her shorts and took out a black business card with flaming Gothic letters across one side that read, "'Men in the last days shall be lovers of their own selves, covetous, boasters, proud, blasphemers, and he that killeth with the sword must be killed with the sword' — 2 Timothy 3:2 & Revelation 10:13"

She went back inside and placed the card across Jonah's gaping, bloody mouth. With regret, she caressed his face with her fingertips. She enjoyed sex, and this fit old man had aroused her interest. "Happy New Year, lover," she said, and blew him a kiss.

She checked the time on the clock behind the bar and saw that fifteen minutes remained until the new year. She tied the plastic trash bag to a belt loop on her shorts and slipped over the side of the Aphrodite and into the salty, cold water. She didn't have that far to swim, and the Glenlivet was still keeping her warm.

Chapter Two
New Year's Eve
1989

He hated the allure of Debbie's wavy, honey-blond hair cascading over her naked shoulders.

She said, "You look sexy tonight, Peaches."

His smile was automatic. Don had been trained to radiate smiles from an early age and to never frown around beautiful women, but he hated his nickname. Why couldn't she just call him Don like almost everyone else did?

The loud music vibrated through the walls and the floor and up into his legs, torso and brain, giving him a headache that distracted him from enjoying the eye candy in front of him.

Dancing was another way to escape. Ignoring Debbie, he walked around the front desk to the closed glass door that separated the restaurant lobby from the nightclub. Through the glass, he watched a thousand worshiping pagans writhe around a giant, stained-glass dildo protruding from the ceiling above the dance floor. From the dildo, twirling, swirling, multicolored lights sent off hot, flashing beams of psychedelic sperm that splashed off the dancers' faces.

A dozen bartenders sweated behind three cheery wood bars. The club was packed, and, to cross the room, Don would have to walk across people's shoulders and heads. He'd done it before to break up a fight in the middle of the dance floor.

Don decided the crowd wasn't for him, so there would be no dancing tonight. He hated crowds like this, anyway. Always had, ever since the war.

Returning behind the front desk, he finished examining a dinner receipt and carefully set it on the finished stack. He sensed Debbie still watching him before he glanced up past her bare navel and feasted briefly on her ample breasts to watch her nipples harden and push against the elastic fabric of her almost-transparent halter top. His eyes moved higher to study the freckles spread across her chiseled Nordic features. He managed to keep his expression innocent and naïve while suppressing his lust.

He'd had Debbie before—more than once. Sex with her was a great experience. Better than any roller coaster. But not tonight. Maybe never again.

"I'll buy you breakfast when you get off," she said.

"I'm going jogging."

There was a brief pause in the loud music from the club before she replied, "Yeah, sure, jogging after midnight in the cold and dark." Her lips puckered in disappointment, and she tossed her hair in a misty neon cloud around her shoulders.

"I'll talk to you next time I'm in town," she said, and spun on her high heels to walk briskly back to the glass doors to the club, where she stopped to flash the back of her right hand so the bouncer could see the stamp.

Satisfied, the bouncer opened the door to let Debbie through, the roaring music escaping momentarily into the lobby with the harsh scent of male and female sweat and pheromones.

Don had to admit, as she slipped through the narrow opening and into the packed humanity, that Debbie's legs were worth lusting after. They were long and muscular—the legs of a professional dancer. She worked in a chorus line at the Rio in Las Vegas and visited her older, overweight sister in Manhattan Beach often.

He'd dated Debbie several times, and, by the second date, he knew he could've seduced her on the floor behind the front desk of the lobby if he'd wanted to.

He was tempted to go after her, because he knew exactly how good her body felt under his hands, but he forced his lust back into the fireproof safe he'd built for it. To give in to the candy that Debbie offered would turn to guilt and remorse later.

The glass door closed, sending the tidal wave of lusty music back toward the dancers. With regret, Don returned to auditing the waitresses' receipts from the three dining rooms. When he finished, he walked from behind the cherry wood of the front desk of the Aphrodisiac Academe, and down the hot-waxed brick ramp, past his great-grandmother Amanda's clock and into the first of three dimly lit dining rooms. Most of the tables in this room still had customers. A lone light glowed from the nearest busboy station.

"You free?" Veronica asked. She was the best waitress in the club and could serve a dozen tables without missing a beat. Her people skills were so sharp that she easily earned more in tips every shift than all the others combined.

"Of course," he said.

"Good!" She sounded relieved, and Don felt alarmed. Something must be wrong, and, as the *maître d'*, he was the fixer.

Across the dining room and through busboy station was the kitchen, with men and women from south of the border mopping floors, scrubbing pots and washing dishes. Veronica was older than Don, but not by much, and she had a stocky, Eastern European figure—or, at least, what he thought was one. Her Honduran husband Javier was one of the cooks, and they had three kids, who were watched over at night by a grandmother from Poland.

Years ago, before her marriage and after he'd returned from his third tour in Vietnam, Don had taken Veronica to breakfast, and they'd kissed between bites of pancake and fried potatoes. The fling that followed lasted for three months before she woke up to the fact that he wasn't the marrying kind.

"What is it?" he asked.

"Norman," she said.

"Shit! Where?"

"Off the lobby."

"Tell Ben to join me there." Don retraced his route through the dining room to the bathroom off the lobby where he found Norman.

Normal was tall and thin as a pole. He was young, but looked as if he were on his way to becoming petrified. He was sitting on top of the counter with his long legs sprawled across all three sinks, staring at the mirror in deep concentration, as if he was willing the Wicked Witch of the North to appear from the mirror and weave a spell to make him handsome instead of butt-ugly.

"Norman, what have I told you about this?"

A stubborn defiance swept across Norman's toasted, leathery face like a filthy mop. He leaned closer to the mirror to pop one of his host of zits, and a white gob of pus with a spot of blood in its center splattered on the mirror.

Don counted at least a dozen more spots as he struggled against the angry pressure building inside his head. He couldn't let the anger out. It was its own breed of tiger—something he'd carried home from 'Nam.

In a forced, calm, paced voice, Don said, "What did I say?"

Norman rolled his eyes and picked up a sweaty bottle of Coors from the counter. The avocado seed in his pencil-thin neck bobbed up and down as he chugged.

"Do you need help in here, Don?" Benedict Wallace asked. Ben, the head bouncer for the club, was a lean man who Don knew well. They'd been a two-man Marine sniper team in Vietnam for three tours, and Ben stayed for two more after Don returned to the states. After Ben came home, he worked as a male stripper. He bragged that he was half Chinese and half Viking, and he had the face to match. He looked like an Asian demon, with wide flaring nostrils and a thin-lipped mouth that ran like an evil, wicked slash across his face. The right side of his face, behind the eye and mouth, was scarred and deformed from a burn he'd received in combat on his last tour. He also had dark, curly hair and piercing, almond-shaped, icy blue eyes that he claimed came from his Viking half. He loved to travel and had visited China soon after it opened in the early 1980s. He was married to one of Don's cousins who didn't like to travel, so Ben traveled alone.

Ben knew Don well, and the look in Don's eyes said it all.

"I understand," Ben said. He turned to Norman. "You won't be back."

"That's not fair, you faggots," Norman said. "You two are bastards."

Don felt the tiger stirring in his gut.

"Get out of here," Ben said to Don. "I'll handle this snot." Ben didn't need help to deal with the likes of Norman. In fact, Ben didn't need help to deal with anyone.

As Don left the bathroom, he remembered Ben in

Vietnam calmly filing his upper and lower front teeth razor sharp—he said they were the one weapon he could always rely on in close combat. He also had a fourth-degree black belt in Korean Karate, having worked closely with elements of the South Korean 2nd Marine Brigade known as the Blue Dragon on their first tour. South Korea sent more than 300,000 troops to fight in Vietnam.

⧗

As Don emerged from the restroom into what should have been an empty lobby, a familiar voice said, "My main man!"

Don stopped and deliberately looked in the direction opposite the voice. Oily, vomit-colored sewage flashed in his mind, and he could smell its stench. Before he turned, he composed his face into empty innocence his grandfather had drilled into him. Grandfather always said, "Never reveal what you are thinking, especially to women and pimps."

And the man he faced was a pimp. Teddy spent a lot of money in the club, but he usually came alone. Tonight, he was with three women—black, Asian and Caucasian—who were dressed in identical long, slinky, skin-tight dresses that revealed every curve of their Victoria's Secret bodies, each a different color. Amethyst for the brown-eyed blond, ruby for the black woman and neon citrine for the Asian.

Don had never seen any of Teddy's women in the

flesh. Glittery makeup swept lightly across their flawless features. It looked as if Teddy had ordered them from a factory, and they had just rolled off the assembly line of female perfection. Don had heard that Teddy's whores specialized in dominance and submission and the starting price was $500 an hour.

Teddy himself always dressed in hand-tailored, silk suits, and this one was all white. He was a Beverly Hills pimp with serious enemies. He'd earned an MBA from USC on a full scholarship and graduated in the top five percent of his class. His father was a white Russian, and his mother escaped from Somalia before being circumcised by some old woman with a chunk of broken glass.

Twenty years earlier, Teddy had also partnered with Amanda and directed some of her B-movie skin flicks when she attempted a comeback in film. The pimp porno director lived in San Marino, California, in a multi-million-dollar mansion.

Because of said enemies, when he wanted to party, Teddy drove his Jaguar out of Los Angeles to the beach and the Aphrodisiac Academe. Don also knew that Teddy considered himself a member of Amanda's inner circle.

Ten minutes remained until 1990, and the club was already crowded beyond the legal capacity.

Don held out a hand, and they slapped skin.

"Teddy, why are you coming to my house this close to the New Year? I thought you were going to a private party tonight."

Teddy smiled. When he spoke, his voice was soft,

like a feather duster gently moving across a hardwood floor. "A change of plans," he said. "If you know what I mean." Don knew. His wealthy customers and the pimps who wanted Teddy's girls were turning up the heat.

Don guessed that these three young women would cost a customer at least one thousand an hour. For the night, well … There was no discount. Teddy only dealt in the highest-quality female flesh, and Don didn't want to know how he recruited them.

"You know," Teddy said, "if Amanda has stayed in the film industry, we'd still be partners. She'd produce, and I'd be directing." Teddy held out a fist with the tip of a hundred-dollar bill peeking between two fingers and more hidden in the palm of his hand. Don freed the cash, wadded it up and dropped it on the floor, where he stepped on it and ground it into the bricks.

"Don't insult me, Teddy." Amanda was ninety-seven, and she'd retired into seclusion when she turned ninety.

For an instant, a hard look of anger flashed in the pimp's eyes. It vanished just as fast. Then Ben came out of the lobby restroom, towing a cursing Norman behind him. Once out the front door, Ben shoved Norman toward the parking lot. The door closed behind them and muffled Norman's curses.

When Teddy stepped closer, Don could smell his chemically controlled breath, and expensive cologne, the kind that stuck to oxygen like sticky, burnt rice.

"I'm begging you, Don," Teddy said so his girls couldn't hear. "Don't embarrass me. I promise you I'm strictly here to have a good time."

"If I hear the slightest hint that you are peddling flesh in my club …"

Pain swept across Teddy's face, as if his mother had just caught him lying about not taking a bath. "Didn't I say we were only here for pleasure, and haven't I been good to the club for years? How's Amanda? She's a fine lady. Next time you see her, tell her I miss her."

Don knew he'd been defeated. "I'll see what I can do," he said, and moved to the closed door between the club and the restaurant's lobby. It was a thick crowd, and he didn't see room for more bodies. He nodded to the bouncer, who opened the door and let a roar into the lobby that made Don's bones ache.

Teddy's face glowed as he ushered his women into the human crush. Before the door closed, Teddy turned and mouthed, "I owe you."

It was time to retreat, so, with an inch of Grand Marnier in a cut crystal glass, Don went through the still-busy Lady Chatterley room and into the empty and dark D. H. Lawrence room. There was a booth in the farthest corner, lost in shadows—the perfect place to usher in the New Year alone.

Chapter Three
January 1, 1990

As the drunken party people packed in The Aphrodisiac Academe cheered, groped each other and kissed to celebrate the beginning of another New Year, the D. H. Lawrence Room held Don in its empty embrace while he took one of his journeys back to Vietnam—one of many unwanted memories locked in his head for life.

On an even more depressing note, he had seduced Susan in this booth an hour after the dining room closed for the night.

That called for another sip of his orange-flavored cognac. After the conquest of more than a hundred young women, Susan had been his first virgin, and he'd married her three months later and divorced her before their first wedding anniversary.

Veronica's husband appeared from out of the dark and slid into the booth. Javier set a bottle of Cacique Guaro on the table—a drink they'd shared before. It was clear like vodka, but sweeter and with a little less alcohol in it.

"Looks like you need more booze," Javier said. Don finished the cognac in his glass and watched Javier refill it to the brim.

For the next few minutes, while they drank in silence, Don thought about his failed marriage to Susan. Before the marriage, she'd been a fascinating, unpredictable party girl—a passionate, flirty woman. After the rings went on and they said their vows, she started to turn frigid, until she wouldn't let him sleep in the iceberg their bed had become. Several months later, she accused him of only marrying her for her body and sex. He packed a suitcase and left their apartment the same day. It was because of the failed marriage that Don joined the Marines and ended up in Vietnam in 1969.

He finished the Guaro and slid the empty glass toward Javier, who lifted a questioning eyebrow but filled the glass again.

Then Don stood. "I'll be back." He walked through the dining room, checking to make sure the empty tables were clean and that all the side work had been done. Satisfied, he stepped inside the busboy station and dimmed the lights for the D. H. Lawrence room.

The kitchen had shut down service to the dining rooms at midnight, but one cook remained to prepare appetizers for customers in the nightclub. One-thirty was last call.

Don took a shortcut through the kitchen; nodded at Carlos, the closing line cook; and slipped into the busboy station for the Lady Chatterley room, the largest of the dining rooms and the one closest to the lobby. There was one couple left in that dining room, holding hands across the table and looking like they were in a trance.

Veronica leaned against the wall outside of the bus station next to her busboy.

"When the second hand hit midnight and everyone in the club went wild, he asked her to marry him," Veronica said. "She said yes, and they've been sitting there like that ever since. I hope they didn't turn to stone."

"Comp them a bottle of champagne to drink in the club, and it might snap them out of it," Don said. "And mention that we rent out one of our dining rooms for a packaged wedding and reception. Offer them a discount."

From there, he went to the front desk in the lobby. When he saw Teddy's white silk shirt emerge from the mass of humanity in the club and come through the glass door into the lobby, Don stepped back to watch from the darkness behind the front desk, where he couldn't been easily seen.

Teddy dragged his black girl behind him, and she was having trouble keeping up on her wobbly high heels. The cleaning crew had propped open the lobby's front door, and, after Teddy was outside with the girl, he yanked her toward him and hooked an arm around her waist.

"Teddy, please don't," she pleaded, and her words were cut off as he dragged her out of sight.

Against his better judgment, Don followed. The Aphrodisiac Academe's front door faced the parking lot. To the left was the Pacific Coast Highway entrance, where cars hissed by.

The shadows under the building eaves hid Don, and it was from there that he watched Teddy drag the girl toward his moss-colored Jaguar. The shadows of the Palm trees and shrubs that ran along the back of the parking lot, separating it from the boardwalk that ran beside the beach, looked menacing. Teddy stopped between his Jag and the palm trees. Don jerked at the sharp sound of Teddy slapping the girl across her face with an open palm. The girl whimpered, and her legs folded as she collapsed to the pavement. Teddy bent over and slapped her again.

"Listen, bitch, when I tell you to suck a dick, you do it."

Subconsciously, Don's legs started to move, and soon, he was standing by the corner of the Jag, right behind Teddy, who didn't notice.

"Please don't hit me again, Teddy. I'll do what you tell me. I promise."

Don watched Teddy pull a skimpy dress strap off the girl's shoulder until one of her small breasts was exposed. He grabbed the nipple and twisted it. She choked back a scream, folded at the waist and vomited on her lap.

The child whore from the Well of Purity in Vietnam appeared in Don's mind, asking him to help the girl, and he grabbed the back of Teddy's shirt and yanked him off balance. Teddy twisted like a corkscrew and came up in a crouch. Don slid to one side and, with little effort, sent Teddy flying through the air in an arc until he landed hard on his face and right shoulder. Recovering, he rolled over with a small .25-caliber automatic in his hand.

"You better make the first shot count, Teddy," Don said, staring into the pimp's eyes without blinking. "Because once you pull that trigger, it will be your last act on this earth." Don's personal demons watched and kept score for the child whore, Susan and every other abused woman he'd known.

Don didn't care if Teddy shot him. Maybe if he did, Don's demons would go away for good.

When Teddy recognized Don, his eyes widened in shock, and the barrel of the .25 wavered.

Don knelt so he was level with Teddy's face. "I'm very angry with you," he said, so the girl didn't hear him.

"It was just business," Teddy said with a trembling voice. Their eyes were pinned now, and Don could smell the man's fear. He knew it wasn't a good idea to corner a wild animal, especially one with a .25-caliber automatic aimed at your gut, but caution wasn't one of Don's strong points. He didn't give a damn if he died, because he thought maybe he deserved it.

"I wasn't selling her services," Teddy said. "I just wanted to give a New Year's gift to a good repeat customer." He started to stand.

"Don't move," Don said.

Sweat beaded on Teddy's forehead, and he gave off a sour, wild animal scent from the fear that had him by the balls. "What can I do to make it right?"

Good question, Don thought. "Give her to me," he said, surprised at his demand.

The surf beating on the sandy beach was the only other sound besides their harsh breathing. Someone rollerblading along the boardwalk flashed by on the other side of the palm trees. There was a snapshot of long, lean, tanned, muscular legs pumping hard, and then the girl was gone from sight.

"Sure," Teddy said, relief flooding his voice. "Keep her for the next twenty-four hours."

"Forever," Don replied without hesitation.

The next moment was long as Teddy decided between using the .25 and losing one of his high-priced, reusable products.

"Sounds like a good idea." Ben's voice floated out of the dark like a vampire bat searching for blood. He was standing in front of the Jaguar. "That way, you will get to see the sun rise in the morning and watch the Rose Parade on TV." Don thought about Ben's trusty 1911 Colt .45 pistol—the one he slept with and always carried.

Clacking heels on the parking lot broke up the standoff. It must have been after two a.m., because people were oozing out of The Aphrodisiac Academe. Don saw Teddy's other two girls in the growing crowd.

"You got a deal," Teddy said.

"You can stand up, then," Don said.

"Am I still welcome in your place?"

"Only if you come alone. Don't bring any of your girls with you."

Teddy brushed his pants with trembling hands. His .25 had vanished. He unlocked his car and ushered the other two girls in. His car was the first one out of the club's parking lot.

"What you goin' do with me?" the black girl asked with a brittle voice.

Don held out a hand, and she flinched. When she realized he wasn't going to hit her, she took his hand, and he pulled her to her feet. Don studied her eyes and then took hold of each arm to examine them.

"I don't do drugs, if that's what you thinkin'." She dropped her final g's when she spoke, and some heat had returned to her voice as her fear evaporated.

"How long have you worked for Teddy?"

"This my first month," she replied. "I've been trainin'. Teddy likes us to know etiquette. He brought me out tonight to test me."

"Why did you say no to the blow job?"

"That man was a fat, ugly peckerwood. His nose look like a blob of pink bubble gum. I ain't never goin' let trash like that touch me."

"A whore with a pimp has no choice when it comes to who she sleeps with," Ben said.

She ignored Ben as her smoky eyes studied Don.

"Now that you got me, what you goin' do?"

An average man could easily be swallowed by eyes like hers. "I'm not going to be your pimp," Don said, and he pulled a handkerchief from a pant pocket and tried to clean the front of her dress. In the process, he discovered that her body was hard under the thin, silky fabric. There wasn't an ounce of fat on her fit and muscular torso.

"What am I goin' to do without Teddy? I'll starve. I don't know nothin' and can't get no job, except maybe cleaning floors, toilets and making beds in some hotel. I already done that and don't like it. I don't want to work the streets. Never have, because I don't want to catch somethin' like HIV."

"Shut up and let the man think," Ben said.

Her eyes filled with fear. "You thinkin' of lettin' Teddy have me back? He'd beat me another shade of black and burn the bottoms off my feet. I see him do it to one of the other girls. I can't go back. You know another pimp that will take me?"

Don shook his head and started to walk away. Except for a half dozen cars, the lot had emptied.

"Where you goin'?" she asked. "You can't leave me. You responsible for me now."

The little girl from the Well of Purity spoke inside Don's head. "You think I'm going to forgive you if you don't save this one? You should have saved me when you had the chance."

Don looked over his shoulder. "You're going to do what I say." There was a rustling noise from behind one of the palm trees. A low-voltage warning ran down Don's back, and he stared at the palm tree and the shrubs around it. When he didn't see anyone, he decided it was just the breeze off the ocean.

She nodded.

"Come on," he said, and the whore followed him and Ben back to the Aphrodisiac Academe.

Chapter Four

Don still didn't know what her name was—the hooker who slept in the front passenger seat on the drive home.

Often, while driving alone, Don reflected on the life of his ancient ancestor, Giacomo Casanova. Most of his life, the Venetian had been on the move from one place to another—usually on the run from trouble, only to end up in another mess. For instance, Giacomo's torrid affair with an innocent-looking courtesan of sixteen, called Marianne de Charpillon. On their first meeting, she flirtatiously promised to make him suffer for loving her, and she kept her word. For years, she teased, tormented and exploited Casanova for everything she could squeeze out of him.

Knowing all about Casanova's life, it was safe to say that, even though Giacomo had seduced more than 200 women, at times, he was sinned against rather than sinning. It didn't help that he also thought that women were equal to men.

With trouble as his constant companion, Giacomo died a lonely man in 1798 at the age of seventy-three.

Don wondered if this black beauty he'd inherited would be his Marianne. He glanced at her. Her head lolled to one side and leaned against the passenger door window. Her mouth hung open—not very sexy—and her breath gave off a nauseating sour stench.

When the car's tires started rolling over acorns and the engine worked harder to power up Don's steep, hillside driveway, her eyes opened and she sat up.

California oaks standing guard on both sides of the narrow driveway made it feel like they were driving to the hotel in Hitchcock's *Psycho*. But behind the oak trees were only avocado trees.

Once in the garage, Don helped the hooker out of his maître d' car, a fire-engine-red, 1968 Ford Mustang Shelby GT 500.

Next to the Mustang sat a restored, 1945, four-wheel drive military Jeep with a canvas top and open sides. In the far stall was the banged-up, rusty, 1980 Dodge van Don drove to his day job as an English teacher in a public high school.

Working two jobs was how he held his demons at arm's length, and it also helped him stay out of a Giacomo Casanova-style mess with women.

With that thought, he wondered why he had played the knight in shining armor to this hooker. Sometimes, he didn't trust his own motives.

With a hand on her elbow, he led her into the house through the connecting door. The hands on the kitchen clock said 3:45. He moved her through the kitchen and across the great room with its wall of glass and ocean view.

The house sat on top of a hill. Access to the driveway was through an automated gate at the end of a winding road lined with costly homes. The concrete drive led to the back of the house and the garage.

"How does a guy with a job like yours live in a place like this?" she asked.

"This way," he said, ignoring the question and taking her hand to pull her away from the view and into a hall to one of the bedrooms that had been used by his grandmother's servants—one on the other side of the house from his bedroom. He wanted this temptation as far from his bed as possible.

Her room was a suite with a bathroom and a separate den, which had its own wall of glass facing the urban night lights and dark ocean. He pulled back the bedspread and helped her undress, only to discover that she wore no bra or panties. Her bikini-worthy body sucked the air out of his lungs, and it was all he could do to not eat her alive with his eyes. His hands twitched with the desire to touch and explore.

He was relieved when she slipped between the sheets and he pulled the blanket up under her chin, but it was too late. His pecker had given him away. He pointed to the bathroom and told her where she could find towels. Before he left, he closed the blinds and plunged the bedroom into total darkness.

In the kitchen, he washed his shaking hands and stared out the window at the view before filling a glass with distilled water from a water cooler next to the double-door Sub-Zero refrigerator.

On the way to his room, he stopped in the laundry, stripped and added their clothes to the dirty laundry.

Once the washing machine was busy, he went straight to the shower in his room at the end of the hall, where he turned the water to steaming hot. After he soaped up under the stream, he turned off the hot and gasped as the frigid water rinsed away the foaming suds. He seldom took artic showers, but he had to do something about the images of the hooker's body that flooded his mind with lust. If he were to join her in bed, he knew she would let him take her any way he wanted.

Out of the shower, dry and shivering, he slipped into his bed. It took a moment before the warmth returned. The last time he glanced at the clock, it was five in the morning.

⧖

The house was silent when the hooker walked, barefoot and naked, into the great room. It was cold inside the house, but she'd taken a hot shower, and her skin still glowed from the warmth.

In the kitchen, she stopped and looked at the clock on the wall. It was barely seven, and the early dawn light was already trickling into the room. It didn't take her long to find his bedroom, where she discovered him facing away from the empty side of the bed—her side.

She went to his wall-length window and stared at the view, but the cold was stealing her warmth and she closed the blinds before she poured herself into his bed like spilled ink.

She wondered why he hadn't brought her to his bed in the first place. Saving her from Teddy like he had meant only one thing. It was what all men wanted. Why else would he risk his life and spend his time on her? At the club, Teddy had talked about him as if he were some kind of legend out of an adventure movie. To her, he looked like a younger Clint Eastwood with better skin— the Eastwood from *Bronco Billy*, *Sudden Impact* or *Firefox*.

Thinking about Don knocking Teddy down aroused her, and she slid a hand over his right hip, where she discovered the jagged callus of a scar. Later, she'd find the other scars from wounds he'd collected during his combat tours in Vietnam and other faraway, dangerous places.

When she reached her desired destination, she took hold of it and felt it stiffen in the palm of her hand. Once hard, there was a gentle arc to it—like a banana. She'd never had one with that shape before and wondered what it would feel like inside of her.

⧗

Still half-asleep, the lusty dream was three-dimensional, and one of his hands felt as if it were touching a real woman's leg. He didn't want to wake up. Instead, he kept his eyes closed and explored the length of the leg to a hip and then to a breast and shoulder.

His imagination was working overtime this morning, and he didn't want to get up, anyway.

He had abstained from sex for six months and often had erotic dreams that woke him in the early morning hours, and, considering who was sleeping at the other end of the house, this time, instead of another cold shower, he decided that he'd play this lusty dream to its end.

All of the sensual sensations that followed blended into a collage of warm, smooth, silky skin. He'd never had fantasy sex like this before. Having a beautiful woman in the house did wonders for the imaginary sex life of a man who had sworn off real women.

But this was too good to be a fantasy. It wasn't anything like his usual early morning erotica, because, this time, there was the musky scent of sex, a smell that had never played a role in any of his wet dreams before.

Half-awake, sweaty, exhausted and spent, he went back to sleep.

⧗

The next time he opened his eyes, the glowing

numbers on the bedside clock told him that it was early afternoon. He had a slight hangover and attempted to rub the dry grit from his eyes. Failing, he slipped out of bed and made his way across the dark room to the bathroom, where he rinsed his face at the sink with cold water. He drenched a washcloth in cold water to rinse and cool his toasty-warm body. When he finished, he dried off with a towel and returned to the darkness of the bedroom, feeling somewhat refreshed.

When he slipped between the sheets, his legs touched the warmth of another person's smooth legs, and that was when he discovered he wasn't alone. Shit! That erotic dream had been real. The hooker was in his bed. The musky scent of sex had been theirs. He turned on a dim nightlight and rolled over to stare into her sleeping face.

She must have closed the blinds, which explained why the room was so dark. He usually slept with the blinds open.

Asleep, her features were filled with the innocence that must have been part of her before her life led her to Teddy and prostitution. Asleep and out of that sexy gown, she looked much younger than the age on her ID. If that ID was fake, it was a good one, because the face he was looking at didn't belong to a legal woman.

She opened her eyes and smiled at him.

"It would be nice to know your name," he said.

"You got a crooked dick," she said.

"Your name."

"They call me Cut."

"Cut?"

"When I was born, my momma said my color was like fine, dark crystal, but she didn't want to name me Crystal, so she called me Cut."

She was Cut candy then, he thought. She squirmed under his gaze as he explored her high cheekbones; narrow, delicate chin; and wide, oval eyes that stared back at him.

"My momma was a whore, too, but she was also a crackhead. That's why I had so much trouble learnin' in school. I was born a crack baby. They put me in a special class, but it didn't do no good."

"Tell me more about your momma," he said.

"She dead. By the time I was ten, I was in foster homes till my momma's younger sister came and took me to Chicago, where I turned thirteen." At the mention of Chicago, the innocence fled from her face and tears filled her eyes.

"What happened in Chicago?" Don asked in a tone of voice that said they were sharing intimate secrets that no one else in the world would ever know.

A pearl of a tear slid out of the corner of one eye and down an ebony cheek to drop on the pillowcase. "At night, my aunt worked as an exotic dancer in a strip joint. That's when her boyfriend came to my bed ..." She started to cry, and Don pulled her into his arms to comfort her. He wondered how long this abuse had gone on.

Her muffled voice continued from the space between his shoulder and neck. "By the time I was seventeen, I'd had enough, so I left. I hitched rides across the country with truckers, and those rides didn't come free, but they made the next step easy. In Los Angeles, I worked the streets, and, after a few months, a Mexican pimp made me one of his girls. He worked us hard—sometimes five to ten tricks a night for each of us. He carried this photo album around and used it to sell us to mechanics and truck drivers for a fifty-dollar blow job or one hundred to go all the way. Before I turned 19, Teddy found me after one of the tricks beat me and one of my eyes swelled shut. The Mexican said I was damaged goods and sent me back to the streets, but Teddy said he saw somethin' special in me that would make us both a lot of money from his wealthy clients. He promised me that none of the men I would be with would hit me again. He didn't say he'd do the hittin'. Teddy started to beat the gutter out of me. He said I wouldn't be any good for his clients until I had class."

"And tonight, when he asked you to give someone a blow job—"

"That was goin' to be my first trick workin' with Teddy. He lied about it being a gift for a good client. The man told Teddy he'd pay two hundred for a blow job from me, and Teddy told me to crawl under the table and suck it."

"You don't have to be a hooker if you don't want to," Don said.

"Am I goin' to be your woman now?"

"That would be against my rules."

Worry invaded her eyes, as if someone were trying to steal her dreams. "You married or somethin'?"

Don shook his head. "What I am is like a drug addict or alcoholic around women. Until you slipped into my bed, I'd been sexually sober for six months."

This thinking was a game Don played, just like Giacomo's off-again, on-again desire to be part of the Catholic Church. In the back of Don's head, there was this idea that maybe he could purify himself and wash away his perceived sins by being sexually sober and helping abused women.

Cut stared at Don with eyes like pure mountain pools with a look in them that maybe she had met someone she had never met before—a good and kind man—and, knowing this, Don felt like a fraud, because he wanted to touch her, and once his hands found her silky skin, there would be no stopping them.

He sighed. "You may be too young to understand this, but we are products of the world our parents raised us in—a world we had little or no control over." He reached out to touch her nose with the tip of his index finger, and then stopped an inch away. His hand, as if it had a mind of its own, jerked back, circled, moved closer and then pulled back again— indecisive, tempted.

Don rolled away from her, turned over and sat on the side of the bed. "I'll cook us something to eat," he said, and, not bothering to dress, left the bedroom. On the way to the kitchen, he stopped at the thermostat and turned the heat on.

A few minutes later, when he was mixing eggs in a bowl for a mushroom, asparagus and avocado omelet, Cut joined him, also naked. She stood beside him, and, since she was at least a foot shorter than him, rested her head against his shoulder and slipped her right arm around his waist. Right away, he realized he'd made a mistake not putting on at least a pair of shorts, because her touch aroused him. There was no way he could hide it.

"Here," he said, and handed her the wire whisk. "Keep mixing the eggs. I'm going to put some clothes on and find something for you to wear."

She looked down, and, before he took the first step, Cut reached out with her free hand and took hold of him. Shit, he thought. I'm a goner. He felt helpless when she led him back to the bedroom.

⧗

Two hours later, they were both dressed—she in an one of his older t-shirts and nothing else, and he in blue jeans and a white Henley shirt—barefoot and back in the kitchen, sitting on stools next to each other at the breakfast counter and eating the omelets, along with whole wheat toast covered with almond butter. Somehow, she managed to move one of her bare legs so it was touching his.

Looking at Cut walking around in that t-shirt aroused him all over again. How in the hell was he going to have the strength to let this delicious candy go?

"The first thing we are going to do—if you will let me out of this house," he said, "is drive to the Brea Mall and buy you some clothes so I can think again. I mean, you can't run around here dressed like that all the time, or I'm never going to get sober again. For you, with that body, we'll have to visit Nordstrom's."

A flirtatious smile played across her lips, and she washed another bite of her omelet down with a sip of coffee. There were also two smaller glasses with fresh-squeezed orange juice in them.

Wearing her clean, shrunken and wrinkled dress—it should have been dry cleaned—they spent the rest of the day shopping together and ate dinner out before returning to the house with her new wardrobe.

He had planned to sleep alone that night, but, once inside the house, she took his hand and led him to the bathroom, where they ended up in the shower together. Out of the shower, when she wrapped a towel around her torso and started to leave the bathroom for the bed, he knew he'd lost another battle.

The towel started below her arms but was too short to cover her hips, and what was exposed looked too good to resist. It turned out to be a long and sleepless night, and he had to teach tomorrow.

Before they finally fell asleep early in the morning, he said, "I think we are the same. There's something broken in me, too." Then, at three a.m., knowing there was no way he was going to work on Tuesday, he called the district's hotline and requested a substitute teacher to take his place. No one at the high school would question his absence. He hadn't taken a sick day for several years.

Nine hours later, it was the ringing phone that woke them both up.

Chapter Five

It seemed that Don had something in common with his eighteenth-century ancestor. At the age of 36, in 1761, Giacomo fell in love with Leonilda, the seventeen-year-old mistress of the Duke of Matalone, and wanted to marry her. Soon afterward, he discovered from her mother, Donna Lucrezia—a former lover—that Leonilda was his daughter. Even though he didn't marry his daughter, it didn't stop him from sleeping with both mother and daughter at the same time.

Don's problem with women who enjoyed sex as much as he did was that he kept going back for more—a weakness he was convinced he'd inherited from Giacomo.

It was easy to conclude that keeping Cut somewhere else was the only way to get back to a life of sexual sobriety. His close friend, Mandy, a leggy cocktail waitress at the club and one of the few women he was attracted to whom he'd never had sex with, was the perfect person to take Cut from his lusty hands.

⏳

Leaving Cut sleeping, he drove to the club thinking of ways he could convince Mandy to let Cut live with her, but images of a nude Cut still sleeping in his bed kept sabotaging his plans. In fact, concentrating on anything was a challenge, and he almost had an accident on Interstate 90 when traffic suddenly came to a quick stop.

When he arrived at the Aphrodisiac Academe, a half-dozen cars sat in the parking lot, along with three police cars and a van from the coroner's office. The police lieutenant waiting for him was a woman who cut her hair like a man, wore men's clothing, walked like a man and had a look in her eyes that said she regretted that she couldn't fuck like a man.

She introduced herself as Jane Eyre Patton, and Don wondered if her parents had cursed her with the name of the famous fictional character.

"You look like you're Irish," he said. She had piercing blue eyes and natural blond hair. She also had the shoulders of a linebacker and a face that would have been beautiful, if not for the dry, leathery skin. She was probably ten years younger than she looked.

"Call me Eyre." She held out a hand with skin that felt like an emery board. When they shook, she started to squeeze, and Don realized this was a macho contest to see who had the stronger grip. When he squeezed back, the lines radiating from her eyes deepened. When Don eventually relaxed his grip, she let go first. Her hand, which was swollen and red, went behind her back.

"Where do you live, Mr. Casanova?" she asked.

"Call me Don." He smiled and gave her his address.

She opened a pocket notebook and wrote it all down. "You look like you're in your early thirties," she said.

"Almost forty," he replied.

Her thick, unplucked, unruly eyebrows arched, and the skin on her forehead wrinkled into a spider web of lines that said she didn't believe him.

"Lieutenant, the club's chief of security called me at home and said that someone had died, but didn't say who. He said he'd leave that up to the police. Since you are the police, what happened?"

"I'll check your date of birth." She inspected his arms and chest. "What do you press?" she asked. "You look like you lift weights on a regular basis."

Don glanced past her and noticed that most of the police activity was taking place in the nearby marina where the Aphrodite was moored. He looked past the palm trees to the beach and saw that there weren't many people on the beach and the boardwalk appeared deserted.

"What do you do when you aren't working?" she asked.

"I exercise. I hike in the mountains with a few close friends. I like to do things with my hands, and I have another job." His second job was a secret from his family and most of the people who worked in the club. The only people who knew about his teaching were Ben and Mandy.

"Really," she said. "Why would you want to work another job? I'm sure you get paid more than enough as the Academe's maître d', especially seeing as how you belong to the family that owns about half the property along the local coast."

"Why the interest?"

"I heard you served in Vietnam. Did you kill anyone over there?"

"I don't talk about that." He didn't like where this was going.

"She ignored him and went on. "I ran a check on you and the other family members who work at the club, and you came up clean. My information says you served three tours in Vietnam from 1969 to 1972 and earned a Purple Heart with a cluster and a Bronze Star. It's obvious that you keep in good physical shape. After Vietnam, you sort of vanished for a few years before showing up here again. Even your tax records show nothing—no earnings of any kind. Where were you during those missing years after Vietnam?"

"Is this how all cops interrogate suspects?" he asked. Even if he wanted to tell her about those missing years, he couldn't.

"Who said you were a suspect?"

"I'm really sorry, Don." It was Veronica, whose arrival offered him a welcome escape from Jane Eyre, but when he turned and saw a face full of concern, his stomach flipped and his fingers and toes tingled. He knew who was dead. He should have figured it out after seeing all the police activity in the marina, but, due to his bedtime marathon with Cut, his mind wasn't functioning at peak potential.

"You work mornings now?" he asked.

"I'm standing in for Betty. I'm sorry about Jonah."

He felt the blood drain from his face, which brought on a wave of dizziness and a strong urge to return home to his bed and Cut. Sex always distracted him from reality's harshness.

Then the guilt arrived like a freight train, heavy and ponderous. The first layer of guilt focused on his wanting to return to Cut for more sex. The second layer was for avoiding Jonah as much as possible since returning from Vietnam. The layers swirled together to create a mix of bitterness that he resented.

Poker-faced, Don turned to Jane Eyre. "Are you married, lieutenant, and why did you become a cop?"

The lieutenant's eyes appeared to shrink into her skull, and her shoulders stiffened. "What puzzles me," she said in lieu of a reply, "is what would cause anyone to serve three tours in Vietnam. Are you a violence junky?"

"Why didn't you tell me my grandfather was dead?" There was a sharp edge to his voice laced with enough pain to garner some sympathy and possibly get this cop off of his back. "I don't like being played," he said.

She looked uncomfortable. "I'm sorry. I was just doing my job." She touched his arm briefly in a pacifying way, and he wanted to jerk away from her.

"If we are done here," he said, "I want to see him.

How did it happen?"

The coroner's van started its engine, and they all turned to look.

"That will have to wait," Jane Eyre said, and they watched the van glide by them and leave the parking lot.

Chapter Six

As funerals go, this one was exactly what Don's grandfather had always said he wanted. The police didn't want to release the body, but, after the coroner finished his investigation into the cause of death and filed the report, Amanda had pulled strings. Even at 97, she still knew VIPs from several state legislatures, four-star generals at the Pentagon, high-ranking members in the State Department, and members of Congress in Washington, D.C.

Once, when Don was ten, she'd mentioned her affairs with three of the Kennedy brothers before and after John Kennedy was President.

Jonas's stainless steel coffin had a high-impact, clear Lucite cover screwed on tight, and the coffin stood at attention center stage while a popular, regional band that often played the club performed his favorite music.

Don half-expected his grandfather to come back to

life, leap off the stage and start dancing with one of the scantily clad women crowding the club. All three bars were open, and drinks were on the house. An alcove to the right of the stage served a buffet of free food.

The band's lead singer, who had told Don she was from Singapore, was Lexi Yu, and she moved about the stage belting out vocals that always impressed him enough to wonder how a voice so powerful could come out of someone so petite.

Over the years, Don had shared wine and tea with Lexi. When he first met her, it didn't take long for him to develop a crush, and he lost a lot of sleep thinking X-rated thoughts about her. That had been a few years ago, right before her first single came out and she went on a bus tour of the country as a backup act for popular bands, but nothing came of it, and her career never took off.

Before Don met her, Lexi had been a friend of his grandfather's, and Don had always wondered if she'd been one of his many bed warmers—there were already a dozen of them in the club that night.

Lexi was worth watching. From where Jonah was situated inside his coffin, he could easily see over the heads of the band and watch everyone in the club, especially the sexy singer. The undertaker had dressed him in a Hawaiian muscle shirt that exposed his weightlifter arms and chest and tight, see-through spandex pants. Don was sure Jonah's bulge had been enhanced to twice its normal size.

"We've got a problem," Ben said from behind Don's

left shoulder.

"Did you think I expected tonight to be different from any other night?" Don turned and indicated to Ben to take him to the problem. It turned out to be Norman, who had failed in his attempt to crash the private, invitation-only funeral party by climbing over the ten-foot wall that surrounded the club's empty outdoor patio. A row of black, cast iron spikes ran along the top of the wall, and Norman was stuck on them. One of his legs hung on the inside of the wall, and his testicles looked as if they had been speared, too. His complexion was so pale that his zits looked like glowing embers on a sheet of white paper. His mouth hung open in shock, and he was gasping like a fish out of water.

"What are we going to do with this idiot?" Ben asked.

"Let him hang there."

"Nooo!" Norman managed to say, and then groaned in pain. "I ... know ... who ... killed ... Jonah."

"Now, that sounds interesting," said a voice from the other side of the wall.

Don pulled over a chair, climbed on it and looked over the wall to see who was talking. From the inside, the top of the wall was only six feet from the floor.

Jane Eyre's eyes met his. "Is he coming or going?" she asked.

"Going," Don replied.

"Norman was eighty-sixed from the club on New Year's Eve," said Ben, who was standing on another chair.

"I've seen this kid at the station before. We already closed down two bars along the beach that let him in on a phony ID. Before you kicked him out, did you let him drink any alcohol?"

"Help!" Normal squeaked through pasty-white lips.

"Shut up," Ben said, "or I might pull you down on those points and leave you there until sunrise."

"I'm interested in hearing what he has to say," Jane Eyre said.

"Let him say it from there," Don replied.

"Nooo!" Norman moaned.

"I can't let you do that," she said.

"Oh, come on, officer," Ben said. "This kid is trouble, and we didn't put him there. He put himself there. I've caught him trying to sneak into the club so many times, I've lost count."

"I'll push his foot on this side," she said, "and you two lift him over; then I'll join you in your upstairs office to hear what he has to say."

"It will probably be a dump truck full of bull shit," Don said.

"You might be right, but my job requires me to listen to douchebags like him."

⏳

"She was a mermaid," Norman said. He sat in a chair, holding a bag of ice to his swollen testicles. The melting ice had already drenched the crotch of his tight pants.

"A mermaid?" Jane Eyre shook her head, clearly disgusted.

Norman's free hand came up, and he jabbed a finger at Don and Ben. "It was after these two cocksuckers threw me out of the club, right before midnight. It's their fault I'm a witness to a murder."

"Did this mermaid have a tail like a porpoise?" Ben asked.

Norman looked like a dashboard bobblehead as he nodded. "And she had long seaweed for hair, too. I saw it floating behind her as she was swimming."

"How much did you have to drink last night?" Jane Eyre asked.

The upstairs office was almost soundproof, and it muted the music from the club to a muffled murmur. There were three desks with phones and computers on them. A second door led into a bedroom with an attached bath that management used for sleepovers and showers on long shifts. It was possible on the busiest days to start at six in the morning and get off at three the next morning, so having a comfortable, private place to crash for a few hours was a luxury.

Ben held up Norman's fake ID. "This is too good to be counterfeit. I think someone working for the DMV must be selling these on the side."

"We're working on it," Jane Eyre said. "There's someone at the Department of Motor Vehicles earning a hundred a pop selling these things, and I've already tried to squeeze the information out of this fruitcake, but he always says he doesn't remember."

"That might be true," Ben said as he handed the fake driver's license back to the police lieutenant. "I think he boiled away most of the mush between his ears by huffing glue when he was in grade school."

"Let him go," she said.

Ben escorted Norman out of the office and left Jane Eyre and Don alone. After the door closed, she said, "I didn't come here to deal with the likes of that idiot. I came here to get a look at the people who came to your grandfather's wake and talk to you."

"Have fun, lieutenant," Don said. "Everyone here was invited. Jonah left a long list with his last will and testament. He was a total social animal, and he knew every one of those several hundred guests by name. The food and booze is free, so help yourself."

"What did you do in Vietnam to earn that Bronze Star?" she asked.

"I can't talk about that. If you want to know, you'll have to get the defense department to declassify the file."

"There's something about you that doesn't ring true." She studied his face while rubbing her chin. "I checked out your day job. What's a former Marine and Vietnam veteran with Casanova for a family name doing teaching high school English to gangbangers in the San Gabriel Valley? That was a surprise. The more I learn about you, the more I want to know. Do your students give you a hard time because of your last name? Do they know about your night job?"

"Most of the kids I teach aren't literate enough to know anything about Casanova. If you don't mind, I have to get back to work." Don went to the office door and held it open.

Jane Eyre stopped in the doorway and looked up at him. "Another thing I learned is that, when you eventually came home after Vietnam, you had a falling out with your grandfather and whatever it was you two argued about didn't get resolved. You've hardly spoken to him for years; yet I understand he raised you instead of your parents. What was the argument about?"

"Lieutenant, if you think I killed Jonah, arrest me, but it won't stick. I worked New Year's Eve and didn't leave the Aphrodisiac Academe until after it closed early in the morning on January first, and there are a lot of witnesses who will account for my every move."

"I also heard you had an altercation in the parking lot and that you didn't go home alone."

"That's correct, and if you want to ask me any other questions, I want my lawyer present."

Chapter Seven

It was Mandy's complexion that had attracted Don to her the first time he saw her. Frosted light glowed from her iridescent skin as if she were a firefly, and that glow attracted men to her as if they were mosquitos hypnotized by the scent of blood.

Don had seen black and white photographs of Amanda when she had been Mandy's age in one of Aunt Eleanor's albums , and, even without color, it was obvious that Amanda's complexion has been the same as Mandy's, which helped explain how Amanda had been the mistress of several wealthy and powerful men before she had turned 25. Amanda said she started as a Ziegfeld girl and had her pick of men. One was Sherman Billingsley, who took his fortune from bootlegging and invested it in real estate. He was the founder and owner of New York's Stork Club.

His grandmother said that Billingsley collected

showgirls like some men collected butterflies, and one thing he liked to do was name his businesses after his girls. He named one of his drugstores after Amanda, who opened her first speakeasy in the basement of the drugstore and kept a few card games going in addition to some busy beds crammed in small rooms hidden behind a false wall. She recruited streetwalkers by offering them a safer place to do business in exchange for a ten-percent cut.

Billingsley died in 1966 at 70, but, by then, Amanda was long gone. Before the end of Prohibition, she'd sold the speakeasy and moved to California, where she used the money to buy the Aphrodite. The yacht served as a floating gambling hall and whorehouse. Her trick was to sail her clients outside the three-mile legal limit before she opened the bar, card tables and girls for business.

Using what she'd learned from Billingsley, she invested her profits in undeveloped property along the Southern California coast from Santa Barbara to San Diego. Her first legitimate business had been a Mexican restaurant with a takeout window for hot dogs. When Billingsley died, he left her some money, and she used that to tear down the restaurant and build the Aphrodisiac Academe.

⧗

Mandy shared no other traits with Amanda and lived in a two-bedroom bungalow near downtown Torrance, California. She'd been an important and tragic part of

Don's life for almost as long as he'd been an English teacher.

When Don turned off the Mustang's engine, Mandy appeared on her porch.

"How's she doing?" he asked as he left the car and climbed the steps.

"She's eating everything in the house," Mandy replied. "I think you're going to have to double her room and board."

She studied his face and touched his arm. "How are you feeling about losing your grandfather?" She had a genuine look of concern, but that was Mandy.

Taking two steps back, he inspected her from head to foot. "You look great," he said. Mandy was dressed in a knee-length black skirt and white blouse, with a string of black Tahitian pearls around her neck—one of Don's many gifts. She held a black satin sun hat in one hand. "Thanks for going with me to the burial," he said.

"Jonah was my friend, too," she said, "although it frustrated him no end that he couldn't add me to his long list of conquests. Every time I rejected him, he looked like a long-lost waif."

"Looking lost and helpless was his way to break down challenging women. He knew that seventy percent of communication is nonverbal and took advantage of it. Every woman he was attracted to was a target, and, to tell you the truth, I don't think Jonah had a depressing or frustrating day in his life. He could lose at the game of seduction with a hundred women in a row, and then score once and be on cloud nine until the next conquest.

He never went without, though. There were always the girls who lived on the boat with him. Their bodies were their rent."

Cut appeared in the doorway on the other side of the screen. At the sight of her, Don's heart leaped into his throat and blocked his ability to breathe. With the shorts she had on, she was almost all leg, and the halter top revealed a mouthwatering abdomen. Even her belly button was sexy.

He asked himself why he had been such an idiot to give her up for celibacy, and he briefly considered moving her back into his house and bed.

The screen door squeaked as she came out of the house and hugged him, which aroused him, and he knew she would notice because this was a total body hug.

"Lunch and dinner are already in the fridge," Mandy told her. "Don't eat it all at once, or you'll go hungry before we're back with more."

⧗

"It's nice to have someone staying in the house with me," Mandy said after they were on the road. "I think she's sweet."

"Don't let yourself be naive. Cut has had a rough life. She may be sweet, but under that angelic exterior is one tough girl who has made some hard decisions."

"I already figured that out, but I'm still curious about her. And I want you to know that you are the only person in the world I would do this for. What do you plan to do with her? She can't live with me forever."

"I think I'll start her as a hostess at the front desk of the Aphrodisiac Academe," he said.

Mandy burst out laughing. "You're kidding me, right? I don't think it's in her DNA to work a job like that. Do you really think giving her a job as a hostess at the club is a good idea? How long do you think it will take until she's back turning tricks in the bathrooms or in the back seats of cars in the parking lot?"

He instinctively knew she was right. "I'll think of something else," he said.

Mandy's father was an electrical engineer, and her mother was an accountant. She had a younger brother and older sister. Her family was the kind that sat down and ate dinner together every night without distractions to stifle family conversation around the table. Mandy earned a master's degree in English literature, and, after that, a teaching credential. They first met at the same barrio high school where Don still taught.

After they met, they started to eat lunch together in their classrooms, and, after a few weeks, he asked her out with the intention of seducing her. That invitation almost got her killed.

Their first date was on a Friday night, and she stayed at school late to correct papers. Don left the campus as soon as school let out and drove to the club for an hour or two to make sure his hostesses were ready to run the front desk without him for the night.

On the way back to the high school to pick Mandy up, he was caught in gridlock, and it took a half-hour to move one block. It was hot that May, and Mandy had her classroom door open because the school had shut off the air conditioning as soon as the students left.

It was 7:00 and dark out when three gangbangers found her alone in her classroom. She couldn't remember what they looked like. Her shrink said she had locked that memory and their faces somewhere inside of her head. Don understood that, because he, too, had some pretty bad shit locked up in his head that he wasn't sure he wanted to remember.

From her injuries and the damage to her hands, it was obvious she'd put up a fight, but they'd beat her senseless and raped her one after another.

When he got there an hour later, the door to her room was locked, but Don had a master key one of the custodians had given him. The room was dark, and he thought that she'd gone home, thinking he'd stood her up. But he knew the smell of blood, and that alerted him. Instead of leaving, he flipped on the light switch.

The doctor said if he'd arrived a half-hour later, she would have been dead. When she came out of the coma at three a.m. a week later, it wasn't her mother or father she saw first. It was Don sitting in the chair beside her bed holding her one good hand. The other hand had several broken bones and was in a cast. The rape changed both of them, and, instead of becoming her lover, Don became her best friend and found her a job working as a cocktail waitress at the club after she swore off teaching.

Don felt responsible for what had happened to her, and he didn't know how to fix it.

Chapter Eight

A breeze rippled the eucalyptus trees scattered about the cemetery. The fresh scent of earth and cut grass mixed with the sweet, clinging perfume of flowers saturated the air and hinted of death.

Don drove the Mustang past the long line of cars parked behind a black hearse before he pulled to the curb and parked.

As they walked up the slight incline toward Jonah's grave, Don reached for Mandy's hand, and her slender fingers slipped between his in a perfect and comfortable fit.

He felt his expression stiffen into its opaque combat mask. That meant his forehead would be lined with deep, angry creases—an intimidating look that served him well in the classroom but was seldom seen at the Aphrodisiac Academe. He may have come home from Vietnam resenting how his grandfather had taught him the art of seduction as a child, but Don had still loved the old man. Jonah had always been there for him when Don needed someone to listen—something his mostly absent father and born-again, Scripture-quoting mother had never offered.

The coffin was suspended in a cradle of webbing above the freshly dug hole. Only one woman stood close to the casket—someone Don didn't recognize. The other women, looking fearful—many with moist, red eyes— stood in silent pairs or small clusters a few yards from the grave, as if the grim reaper was waiting to pull them in if they got too close.

Don suspected their grief was more from losing their free room and board on the Aphrodite.

After walking up to the other side of the coffin, Don noticed the stranger's hair, which reflected subtle shades of red, auburn, brown or blond, depending on how the sunlight hit it. He'd never seen any woman with hair like that before. Even the brown strands were variegated. She wore a tight, black, one-piece dress that accented a head-turning figure. The hemline ended a few inches above her knees, revealing long, lean, muscular, million-dollar legs, similar to the pair that belonged to a young Ann Margret.

The graveside service was what Jonah had wanted. He didn't want any poetry or sermons. Instead, there was a honky-tonk piano sitting on the level ground above the crowd and grave, and, as the sun set and kissed the earth behind the dark silhouette of the piano, Lexi—dressed in black from foot to chin—started to play and sing Whitney Houston's "I Wanna Dance With Somebody."

While Lexi's rich voice filled the air, Don scanned the bereaved and spotted his mother standing next to a tree about twenty yards away. Jane Eyre Patton hovered near her with Don's younger brother, Dion, between them. Dion was the nightclub's assistant manager.

Squeezing Mandy's hand, Don let go and stepped up beside the woman with the incredible hair to discover that she was stunning, with sharp features and piercing, blue-green eyes. Becoming aware of his gaze, she glanced his way and smiled. Then she looked back at Lexi and the piano as the sun's rays surrounded the singer like a ball of fire and sent flaming beams of light skipping across the manicured grass toward Jonah's polished, stainless steel coffin.

Lexi's voice equaled Houston's—she hit all the notes without flaw. When the first song ended, she moved on, without pause, to "Didn't We Almost Have It All," and finished with "Where Do Broken Hearts Go" as the last light of day slipped away like a thief in the night.

The silence and darkness that replaced the music was startling.

Don felt an urge to finish the evening sitting in his favorite corner booth in the D. H. Lawrence Room, sipping merlot from a tall stemmed glass. But he didn't want to drink alone. He wanted to share that moment with the woman standing beside him. He turned to introduce himself and ask her to join him, only to discover she was gone. In her place stood his maternal, older half-brother, Ricky the Horse. It was as if the woman had been transformed into this tattooed, fifty-one-year-old man with half of his teeth missing.

His mother had given birth to Ricky while she was still in high school, before she met Don's father. Knowing their mother, Don suspected that Ricky's birth had been an immaculate conception, but his brother was no Christ child. He had dedicated his life to making sure he never made it to heaven.

"I heard about Jonah, little brother, and thought you might need a strong shoulder to cry on." He grinned, exposing his surviving teeth. Don turned and held out a hand to Mandy. She knew Ricky well and joined them.

"Any time you're ready to ditch this limp dick and spend the night with a real man, you let me know, babe," Ricky said. She punched his shoulder, and they both laughed.

"I see Amanda made it," Ricky said, and nodded toward a stretch limousine with smoked windows parked in another lane away from the hearse and the other cars. One of the back windows was down and—even from this distance—Don recognized his grandmother from the glowing tip of what he knew was one of her favorite, smuggled Cuban cigars reserved for special occasions.

Chapter Nine

Don could easily recognize a killer from the look in his eyes, and he had one standing in front of him now. If he hadn't stayed at school to work late, he wouldn't have been on campus with these four gangbangers confronting him.

It was Friday afternoon, about four o'clock, and the gangbanger closest to him weighed maybe thirty pounds more than Don. Much of the boy's weight was fat, even though the bulk of his arms extending from the rolled-up sleeves of the black hoodie said he lifted weights.

Don had all four of them cornered between two portable classrooms that backed up to a ten-foot block wall with homes on the other side. The other three boys, wearing gray hoodies, had shaved heads and baggy pants with waistlines hanging below their ass cracks to reveal green boxers.

The gray hoodies signified one gang; the black

hoodie, another.

"Hey, faggot, what you going to do if we jump you?" Black Hoodie asked. The boy lowered his head as if he were going to charge and gore Don with hidden horns.

"You're coming with me to the office to see the assistant principal for the fight I just broke up," Don said.

"What fight? There ain't been no fight here. You're a liar. We didn't do nothing wrong. You're nothing but a faggot who disrespected us by getting in our business," Black Hoodie said.

He should have felt fear. Instead, Don felt a calm glow of anticipation, and he was actually looking forward to a fight. Maybe Jane Eyre was right about him being a violence junkie.

Don smiled and said, "I never called you a faggot, because it takes one to know one."

After digesting those words, the gray hoodies broke out laughing. Black Hoodie looked confused and sensed the joke was on him. He shoved his chest out and pulled his shoulders back before he moved toward Don, who saw the black-inked jailhouse tattoos on the boy's neck, revealing his gang affiliation.

"Out of my way, cunt face," Black Hoodie said, "or I'm going to walk right through you and hurt your skinny ass." The three grey hoodies started forward, too.

Don looked like a tall, skinny nerd in his loose-fitting black jeans, blue shirt with a tie and pens sticking out of his left breast pocket. He looked like he weighed a lot less than his one hundred eighty-five pounds of muscle.

He could easily bench press his weight two dozen

times and squat three times his weight without breaking a sweat.

He held up a hand. "Hold it. I want you to know that I'm not a fighter. I've never started a fight in my life. I was not trained to fight. The Marines taught me how to kill, and the way I have it figured, whoever reaches me first is going to die."

Black Hoodie snorted, laughed and gave Don the middle finger with both of his hands. "We got rights, asshole," he said, "and you ain't got no right to touch us, or we'll sue you and get you fired." He reached in a pocket and took out a knife that he opened to expose a five-inch blade.

Excitement raced through Don's body, and he felt the urge to laugh. A lot of good that knife is going to do, Black Hoodie, he thought to himself. He'd read that about five thousand teachers were assaulted annually by students, but he knew with certainty that he wasn't going to be one of the victims.

"You didn't give me no respect, fuck face," Black Hoodie continued, "So now I'm going to cut you." He shoved his knife hand out in front of him and waved the blade back and forth as he closed the distance between them.

A second away from contact, Don pivoted and shifted his weight and feet to move out of harm's way, reached for Black Hoodie's wrist, applied the right amount of pressure, bent the hand up and back more than ninety degrees at the wrist, and slid the knife out of Hoodie's numb fingers before the gangbanger even registered that Don had moved.

With the knife in Don's hand where all four could see it, Black Hoody charged, swinging his fists. Don dropped the knife behind him, shifted his weight and pivoted out of the way. As he did so, he grabbed one of the boy's arms, twisted, and used the gangbanger's own weight and momentum to send him flying in an arc out to the concrete walkway in front of the portables, where his head hit the concrete like an egg cracking and he collapsed to lay still.

With a high-pitched ringing in his ears, Don turned to the other three and waited.

"Hey, man, you can't do that," one of the three grey hoodies said. This one had a pinched nose and small, close-set, rat eyes.

Don knelt and retrieved the knife. With a stiff arm, he sent it flying toward Rat Eyes and nicked the top of his right ear before the knife ended up stuck deep in the plywood wall of the portable behind him.

Rat Eyes squealed like a stuck pig and slapped a hand to his bloody ear.

"What's this?" exclaimed a voice behind Don, who twisted and stepped to the side so he could keep his eyes on the three grey hoodies. The voice belonged to one of the campus police officers, a man the students called Gunny because he was also a Vietnam veteran. Gunny had red hair and a face sprinkled with freckles. Occasionally, Gunny would come to Don's room after school to talk.

"The one on the ground was in a fight when I

arrived," Don said. "He also pulled a knife on me, so I disarmed and neutralized him. There were several others who escaped, and I didn't recognize any of them."

Black Hoodie wasn't moving, and there was a spreading pool of blood around his head.

"On the ground, now!" Gunny bellowed to the three grey hoodies, who looked startled before two obeyed. Gunny wore a Marine Corps drill instructor's Smokey the Bear hat, and he was on his portable radio calling for backup as he pulled out his eighteen-inch, wooden policeman's baton.

The grey hoodie still standing looked defiant, and Gunny started toward him. "Come on, Freddy," he said. "Make my day. I know you want to see if you can take me. I see it in your eyes."

Gunny handed the baton to Don.

"Today is your lucky day. Just you and me with no one to witness you getting your ass kicked." He nodded toward Don. "He won't say a word, and I promise that if you beat me, I'll let you walk."

Don knelt to check Black Hoodie for a pulse, only somewhat relieved to discover that the boy would live.

Freddy decided not to fight and went down on all fours.

"Put your hands behind your head," Gunny said as he snapped a pair of handcuffs on Freddy's wrists.

Another campus police officer appeared on a ten-speed black mountain bike and skidded to a stop. Leaving the bike on its side, he hurried to handcuff the remaining two grey hoodies.

Don heard a siren approaching, and, a moment later, a black and white sheriff's car came down the walkway and stopped near the ten-speed bike. The county had one sheriff's officer assigned to the district day and night, and that officer patrolled the schools on a regular basis. At lunch each school day, two extra squad cars were dispatched to sit in each high school's quad and watch the students, who could easily see the dash-mounted shot guns in the cars.

A few weeks earlier, a fight had broken out between two rival gangs at one of the Saturday night football games, and a dozen squad cars had responded to break it up.

Gunny squatted beside Don. "You a black belt or something?"

"Something," Don said, who learned hand-to-hand combat in boot camp and karate lessons from another Marine during the years in Vietnam.

Gunny said, "Hitler won't like this if you are involved."

Hitler was the staff's code name for the high school's idealistic principal who had stripped most of the teachers of any power to limit the poor behavior of students in their classrooms. He also wanted to fire all of the campus police officers and close down the Saturday school, but the parents on the PTA had protested to the school board, and Hitler had backed down.

Teachers who were tough on discipline and wrote too many detention slips were often called to Hitler's office to be accused of having no control over their students. When students didn't do the work, it was the teacher's fault. If too many students failed a class, it was the teacher's fault for not motivating them. It didn't matter that half of the students didn't bring their textbooks to class or do any work; it was always the teacher's fault.

Gunny raised an eyebrow. "What kind of something?"

"All the hand-to-hand stuff I learned in boot camp, like you did, and any karate moves I know I learned in Vietnam from another Marine in my platoon. My hands are not licensed, if that's what you're asking."

"Hitler don't like you. Nothing would make him happier than to accuse you of sending a student to the hospital. You let me take the heat for this. Keep your mouth shut."

"I can't do that."

"Like fuck, you can't," Gunny said. "You can't fool me. I saw the look in your eyes when I got here, and it's a good thing I showed up before you took on the other three, or one of them might have ended up dead. You're one stubborn, mean son-of-a bitch, just like me. We need teachers like you who won't take shit off these little bastards and know what it takes to teach them. You get your ass out of here and let me handle this."

Don started to open his mouth to protest.

Gunny's eyes narrowed. "I'll have none of that. If you don't get out of here, I'll hit you upside your head and blame it on him." He pointed at the still-unconscious Black Hoodie, who now had a paramedic working on him. Gunny took back his baton and smacked it in the palm of one hand, but the grin on his face told Don he didn't mean it.

"I owe you," Don said.

"You don't owe me shit. What I'm doing is what any Marine would do for another Jarhead. Go!"

Don, grateful but guilty, walked to his car and drove home to the house the family company leased to him for a dollar a year. He'd been teaching for more than a decade but still earned more money working half the number of hours as the maître d' at the Aphrodisiac Academe than he did as a teacher.

At home, he had time for a quick shower before he went to work at the Academe until midnight, and tomorrow was Saturday, so he'd sleep late.

Chapter Ten

"Where's your usual glass of wine?" Lexi looked like a cat studying its prey as she watched Don over the rim of her glass of green tea. The way her lips caressed the glass was seductive, and he imagined her singing "Need You Tonight." She had never looked at him like this before. What was up?

About nine hours had slipped by since his run in with Black Hoody, and he was sitting with Lexi at a table near the Academe's crowded dance floor.

"I'm determined to change my lifestyle," Don said, "and I've decided that drinking any alcohol lowers the odds of my success with giving up women. I'm going to drink tea like you do."

"I didn't believe Debbie when she told me you turned her down. Correct me if I'm wrong, but haven't we known each other for about eight years?"

"Something like that." He stared past her at the

dance floor and the stage where she would soon be singing her last set of the night. Looking into her eyes was enough to cause him to break out in a sweat. "I love to listen to you sing. Your voice is dark chocolate—much better than wine."

She was mostly Singapore Chinese but also Irish, Thai and French with a splash of Ethiopian. Her racial heritage was in her eyes, her cheekbones, her unique complexion, her hair and her size. It was obvious that she'd inherited the best genes from each of her ancestors. When she had first started to perform in the club, he'd lost a lot of sleep dreaming about what it would be like to seduce her.

"I've been a vegetarian since I was fourteen, when my ninth grade science teacher took us on a field trip to a slaughterhouse," she said. "That was sixteen years ago. That same teacher put the make on me, but I turned him down cold. He even wrote me a letter telling me he was going crazy with love for me. I burned it instead of using it to get him fired. He handed me the letter after school when we were alone in his room, and it was written in iambic pentameter. Before I finished reading it, he came up behind me and had his hands under my blouse and his lips on my neck. It was the yuckiest moment of my life. If I hadn't liked him as a teacher, I would have fried his ass and sent him to prison."

The air current in the room seemed to have shifted. It had been months since she'd shared a part of her history with him, and he was impressed with the quality of this anecdote. This one was by far the most intimate moment of her life she'd ever shared with him.

Now he had to reciprocate with a story out of his past. Was she fishing for something? "My grandfather was also vegetarian, and I sort of superficially picked that lifestyle up from him," Don said. "Since he was killed, I've been feeling guilty. When I came back from the war, I carried a truck of anger with me and dumped it all on him."

The D.J. was spinning loud music for the dancers, but silence had settled around the two of them with the comfort of a stuffed bear—the kind an abused child clings to because if offers a promise of safety and love.

"Abuse is a nasty time bomb," Lexi said, "and you never know when it's going to go off in your face. I think our friendship has hit a snag. You haven't been responding to my signals lately. Haven't you noticed that I'm interested in you now? When I want a man, it's usually easy to get what I want. What's wrong with you?"

He couldn't come up with any words for a response. Even though he was thrilled, he felt uncomfortable. Was he about to fall off the sexual sobriety wagon again? How could he justify passing this offer up?

"Don't sit there looking like you have a toothache," she said. "Either you say something, or no more tea and chats with me."

"Sounds like blackmail," he said. "You must know that I've drooled over you for years." And into his mind popped an image of Cut's naked body, in his bed and on all fours, with him behind her.

Lexi touched his arm where it rested on the table.

"Where did you just go?"

His tryst with Cut had weakened his resolve, and his hunger for Lexi revived itself with a vengeance that was eating him from the inside out. He had to admit that he did not want to sleep alone tonight. Then an image of what Lexi must look like naked flew into his mind and pushed Cut out. His lungs contracted from the shock of it.

"Don't drop the ball, Don. We'd be good together."

He doubted he could love a woman on an intimate level, and failing at real love scared him. But it was meaningless to seduce one woman after another and care nothing about who they were. He was tired of that life. Feeling suspicious, he forced himself to focus on Lexi's face.

"What?" she asked, and the tone of her voice stung him.

When he pulled his arm away from her touch, she appeared to shrink, looking frail and afraid, as if he was about to hurt her. He reached out and took her hand in his. When he did, a jolt of electricity passed from her and raced up his arm. It was the first time he'd ever had such a reaction from touching a woman.

"I think you are the most beautiful woman I've ever known."

"Bullshit! That's a stupid thing to say. You, of all men, should know how damaging a phrase like that usually is between a man and woman who haven't been intimate yet. Are you doing this on purpose?"

"For eight years, I've ached for you," he said, "and

all we've done is talk about the books we've read, the movies we've seen and the places we've been. We've rarely shared the kind of intimacy you shared with me a few minutes ago.

"Who are you, Lexi Yu? I want to know the real Lexi, not the voice. I've seen how the men in the club react to you. They lust after you just like I've lusted after you from the first time I saw you. Why are you doing this now?"

"I've also wanted to know who the real Don Juan Casanova is," she said. Her words were a gunshot. "I know you are an infamous seducer of women and that becoming one of your bed mates is like walking through quicksand and asking to be sucked under from heartbreak. But, no matter the risk, I've always looked forward to you sitting there sipping a drink and talking with me. You are the only man I feel comfortable with, and you have never hit on me. That hurts. Oh, and I want to be clear on this: I have never had a steady boyfriend, but I think it's time."

It was difficult to imagine Lexi without a boyfriend at some point in her life. "How can I believe that?" he asked, tapping the table for emphasis.

"Hey, don't think I'm a virgin," she said. "I'm not. Up until now, men have just been toys for me to play with—just like the girls have been for you. And don't take my words wrong. I don't hate men. To me, they have always just been playthings to throw away when I'm done, until you got under my skin."

The drummer started a roll, signaling it was time for

the last set. Their hands slid apart. She stood in slow motion, and, without a smile, turned and walked toward the stage so he could feast on her subtle curves, perfect proportions and the way the light reflected off of her skin.

Their friendship had just turned into a one-way street, and it terrified him.

He didn't notice Lexi returning to their table until she whispered in his ear, and, startled, he jumped. "If you try to hide from me like you do with the other women who show an interest in you, I'm going to hunt you down and kick your ass. And don't think I can't do it. I have a black belt in Tai Kwon Do, Mr. Tough Guy. I'm not going to give you long to think, either. The next move is up to you, and you have until the end of my last song to decide what it's going to be. I'm worth the risk, and you will never meet another woman like me in your life."

He was sure she was right about that. As she walked back to the stage, he thought of Giacomo Casanova's last words on his deathbed in 1798. "I have lived as a philosopher and die as a Christian."

Don had never understood what Giacomo meant by that, but now it was starting to make sense. Thanks to his mother's constant preaching, he had been tempted to return to the Church and piety several times in his life, but he had always changed his mind, because he knew that a life guided by the Church would never work for him. What Lexi was offering was what he really wanted— to have only one woman until he died. His biggest fear had always been that he was incapable of loving anyone with that depth because his grandparents had ruined him by raising him to live the life of a Lothario just like them.

Chapter Eleven

"Hey, bro, get married and have kids!" Dion said as if he were selling used cars. Dion had a cherubic body and face and was dressed in a red blazer and black tuxedo pants with sliver piping running up the legs He wore Birkenstock sandals on his bare feet full of toes that desperately needed a pedicure.

Don realized that he should have never shared with his brother what had passed between Lexi and him early Saturday morning.

He heard "When are you going to get married and have children?" from his mother every month when he visited her. He'd heard from Jonah at least once a year that he was shirking his duty as a sperm donor to ensure the family line survived. And he heard it more than once a week from Ben, who was married to one of Don's cousins. The pair had three young children still in elementary school. There wasn't much love left between

Ben and his wife, but they spoiled their children with a mountain of attention. Too much, as far as Don was concerned. Ben's wife smoked, had tripled her weight since the marriage and slept in another room. That was okay with Ben because she snored.

Now Dion had joined the pack determined to hound Don into marriage and fatherhood. As if Dion, who had five children with his wife, was a model husband.

Dion was married to a still-stunning Cuban with nitroglycerin for a temper, and she spied on him mercilessly, but that hadn't stopped him from seducing one cocktail waitress after another in the bedroom off the upstairs office or anywhere else he could bang one. He'd used a storage room more than once and had even screwed in the cellar on the thick layer of dirt that coated the floor.

One morning, he'd even waited until the club had closed and all the customers were gone before doing it on the counter in the women's restroom next to the stage. That cocktail waitress threatened suicide when Dion lost interest in her, and she followed through with a bottle of sleeping pills. Don and Ben rushed her to the hospital to have her stomach pumped, because Dion was nowhere to be found at the time.

Only Don's half-brother Ricky the Horse had never brought up the subject of marriage and having kids, but then, he'd had nine children with two wives, and seven of the kids were following in Ricky's footsteps and were monsters just like he'd been as a child. They were driving him to double his alcohol consumption from one six-pack of beer a day to two.

"Ms. Sheridan is coming in with a party of twenty in ten minutes," Don said, hoping that would distract Dion from the marriage theme.

"If only the gods would gangbang that bitch," Dion replied. "I don't know what grandpa saw in her."

"Sheridan was one of his boat bunnies when I went to live with him as a child," Don said. "She was Jonah's hot plate special at the time and the focus of many of my adolescent wet dreams. She bailed after she married a guy in his seventies who owned three McDonalds franchises. Six years later, she inherited it all when the old guy died."

"She might have been a hotty toddy decades ago, but she looks more like a Double Big Mac today," Dion said. "Oh, shit! Here she comes. I'm leaving." He hurried toward the glass door to the club and vanished in the loud, throbbing, rock and roll music. For a moment, Don heard Lexi's rich voice, and then the door closed.

Sheridan came through the main door into the lobby. She was tall and looked like a pale, Roman witch. She wore a dress that hung on her like a tent. Her hair, dyed wild-fire henna, had platinum streaks in it, and frizzed in a cloud around her head. Her complexion was the color of beer foam. She didn't look anything like the twenty-year-old she'd been more than thirty years ago. Behind her trailed a long line of older women. They were her book club, and they met here every Saturday evening to have dinner and talk about their latest weekly Harlequin romance novel. Usually, the mob of aging women dressed in the era of the book. This week, it looked like the

The setting was eighteenth-century Boston.

setting was eighteenth-century Boston.

"Is my reservation ready?" Sheridan asked the moment she stopped in front of Don.

Women kept coming through the door, filling the lobby to capacity. When he reached a count of thirty, he stopped and said, "Correct me if I'm wrong, but your reservation was for twenty."

"I made the reservation for fifty," she said, "and reserved that upstairs dining room. The one you call Fanny's Cavern."

Someone had fucked up. Don opened the reservation book and checked. The number written was still twenty, and there were no notations about the private upstairs dining room that already held a fiftieth anniversary party of more than sixty people. Don knew the sweet couple. They had been eating here once a month for as long as he could remember.

"What name did you say the party was under?" he asked.

"Are you telling me you don't know who I am?" she screeched, and lifted her chin high, revealing the wobbly rooster wattle under it. "I want to talk to Jonah now, young man."

"You don't know!" Don said after a moment of silence.

"I know that you are an incompetent, spoiled pervert," she said.

"My grandfather's dead. We buried him last week."

Her pale flesh sagged like melting butter. For a moment, she was speechless, and her lips quivered. Then she stiffened, and all that melting flesh reverted to its menacing, perpetual expression. "Is our room ready?"

"The reservation clearly says twenty people, and there is no mention of the Fanny Hill room upstairs. We have a table for twenty ready in the D. H. Lawrence room."

"Well, I never!" She sputtered, and it was obvious her temper was about to boil over. "Who's the manager?"

"We don't have a new manger yet. My brother Dion and I are sharing the position until the family makes a decision."

"I don't want to deal with Dion, that sorry excuse for a man. What are you going to do about this mess?" Her eyes hardened into two steel balls. "I demand that you seat my party immediately."

Don picked up the front desk's phone and dialed the busboy station for Lolita's Grotto, which resembled a cobbled path in the middle of a rain forest with its secluded booths hidden behind banana trees, palms and a lush forest of ferns.

Lolita's Grotto had a glass ceiling, was the third dining room on the ground floor, and was only open on the busiest nights—Friday, Saturday and always Mother's Day. The cobbled walkway was wide enough to set up a long table with chairs, and it was the only open space long enough to seat fifty.

When the busboy answered the phone, Don told him what to do. "Tell Veronica to handle this party. Let her know that the gratuity will be twenty percent. Divide her current tables up among the other waitresses."

Hanging up, he looked at Sheridan. "Wait here until I return," he said and started down the slight incline into The Lady Chatterley room.

"This is insufferable!" Sheridan buzzed behind him like a hive of angry killer bees. "And you have the audacity to call yourself a maître d'. This disaster would have never happened if your grandfather was still alive."

Don spun on his heel and returned to the front desk to open the reservation book. He turned it so she could see and then pointed at the reservation with her name on it. "This is the reservation, and it says seven-thirty for a party of twenty. You walked through the door a quarter after eight."

"Your grandfather would have held that reservation with our table ready even if we had been three hours late." She shook her head, causing the wild strands of wiry hair to resemble Medusa's snakes.

"I regret that you and your party are having this difficulty, but my grandfather is dead and the reservation says twenty—not fifty. It's quite possible that Jonah was murdered before he had the chance to change it."

She waved a dismissive hand in the air and said, "I want to talk to whoever is in charge of your family's company."

"That won't happen," Don said. "The family trust dictates that one of Jonah's children or grandchildren will always manage the Aphrodisiac Academe, and the family's corporate board has no say over how that's done. Now, if you will excuse me, I will go and see that our table is set up and ready. Wait here, please."

"You're lying." One of Sheridan's index fingers became a javelin aimed at a spot between Don's eyes. "I have never forgotten your fumbling attempts to spy on me when I lived on Jonah's yacht. You were a creepy little boy then, and you haven't changed one bit."

He hadn't spied on her or any of the other beauties who lived on the boat because Jonah had drilled it into his head to never do that. "Staring at women, son," his grandfather had said many times, "lets them know how desperate you are. They prefer men who are interested in them on several levels, but not driven by drooling, glassy-eyed lust."

"I'm going to leave now," Don said. He could have shot a few holes in her memories of Jonah. All the women who knew and had been seduced by Jonah thought he was wealthy because of the Aphrodite and his ornamental job as general manager of the Aphrodisiac Academe. The truth was, he lived off a monthly stipend from the family trust and had no wealth of his own. The boat belonged to the trust, and Jonah had lived on it—the same as Don lived in the house in La Habra Heights—for a dollar a year.

"I know all about you, young man. You were always jealous of your grandfather and wished him dead so you could take his place as head of the family."

This time, Sheridan's words impaled him on their barbs, but he didn't let it show. He had been angry at his grandfather; that much was true. But Amanda was the head of the family and, when she was gone, Don was way down the list to head the family. One of his uncles, the

CEO of the family's real estate empire, where the real wealth was generated, would get that job.

That was when he remembered Sheridan naked and on top of Jonah on the floor. Don had come home early from school due to an upset stomach and opened the door to discover them having sex. Sheridan had glared at him. The look of disgust on her face would have chilled the devil, and he had swiftly closed the door and beat a hasty retreat to the club, where he went to the upstairs apartment and took a nap. All he remembered from her nudity was that there hadn't been an ounce of fat on her toned, naked, statuesque, centerfold body.

"No, we will not stay put, young man," she said. "I want to see our table. Take me there now." She leaned over to examine the reservation book. "I see eraser marks here. Someone changed what I called in. I want to know who did that."

Don looked over her shoulder at the glass door leading to the nightclub and saw Dion standing on the other side of the glass with a grin on his face that said he'd gotten away with another one of his infamous pranks. Slipping the reservation book from under her fingers, Don closed it and dropped it in a drawer. "Those marks are for cancellations, and we just wrote over the same space for your reservation," he said.

The phone rang. "The table's ready," the busboy said. "We're setting it now."

Don hung up and said to the teenage hostess standing beside him, "Keep them here. I'll call you when we're ready to bring them down." With that, he hurried down the gentle ramp toward the entrance of Lolita's Grotto, where he discovered three busboys and Veronica filling glasses with ice water for each place setting.

There were several tables twisting and turning along the curvy walkway, leaving only a little space for the folding chairs. To serve the customers, Veronica and her busboys would have to walk among the ferns and trees atop the shredded redwood ground cover. His eyes went to Veronica's feet, and he was relieved to see she was wearing comfortable Rockport walking shoes.

"This is an insult! We cannot accept this!"

Don turned to discover that the walkway behind him was crowded with Sheridan's book club. The teenage hostess, looking helpless, stood behind her. "I couldn't stop her," she mouthed.

"I asked you to keep your party in the lobby until we were ready," Don said.

"We deserve a complimentary meal," she said, "and I also demand that our drinks be on the house."

"I regret that isn't possible," Don replied, "but you do have a choice. You can accept this table or find another restaurant."

"Sarah," said a woman dressed all in blue with tight, curly, white hair hugging her skull, "this will be acceptable. The trees and the glass ceiling are charming, and we are hungry and do not want to go anywhere else."

With that protest, the group flowed around Sheridan and started to seat themselves on both sides of the serpentine tables.

Sheridan puffed up, and her face purpled. Then she

sighed in defeat and plopped down on one of the folding chairs. Her gorilla belly was too close to the table, and she had to shove her chair back. The metal legs scraped across the stone walkway until the back two legs slid into the planter and started to sink in the soft soil hidden under the layer of shredded redwood.

The chair toppled over, taking her with it, and she landed on her back, staring at the glass ceiling. Her tent of a dress slipped down her hideous, pale, cottage cheese, clay-like legs, exposing a plague of varicose veins.

Don signaled a busboy to help lift the chair, and he offered her a hand to pull her up. Like a lobster, her claws grabbed his hand, and her weight almost pulled him off balance. That was when he saw the nose sticking out of the redwood next to the dent she had made with the back of her head. Once Sheridan was upright and her chair safely on the walkway, Don knelt on one knee beside the nose and glanced up to make sure no one was watching.

Feeling safe, he brushed away the redwood to expose a face.

Oh, shit!

All sensation and feeling inside of him went numb at the sight of Teddy's bloated face. Thinking fast, he brushed the redwood back over the face to hide it and made sure to cover the nose.

"I demand an apology," Sheridan said.

Don stood. "I'm sorry that you slipped and fell into the planter. Please accept my apology."

"No. I want you to get down on your knees and beg me for forgiveness."

"Don," Veronica said. "You don't have to listen to this. I've got the table now. Go back to the front desk."

"No, I want him to stay here," Sheridan said.

"Sarah," the woman in blue said. "We want our margaritas. Let this young man go, and have a drink to sooth your nerves."

Taking advantage of the distraction, Don pulled Veronica aside. "Make sure that you have a credit card in hand before you place the orders."

He turned to the woman in blue. "I appreciate your patience," he said loudly enough for everyone to hear. "For that reason, I'm going to comp the first two rounds of margaritas for the entire party, but the bill for the meal and any more drinks that are ordered must be paid in advance."

There was applause, and excited chatter broke out among the women.

On the way out of the Grotto, Don said to Veronica, "Make sure those free margaritas are doubles. That will take the edge off and put them in a better mood."

She smiled.

Instead of returning to the front desk, he went into the men's room off the lobby and found an empty stall. With the door closed and latched, he sat and held his head in his hands.

Maybe I'm hallucinating, he thought. But what if I'm not? What am I going to do with Teddy's corpse? I can't leave it there. Fuck! I just knocked the bastard down a week ago and took one of his girls away from him, and I did it in front of witnesses—lots of witnesses. That was enough to make him suspect number one.

He couldn't call the cops, because Jane Eyre would throw him in a pan full of smoking hot saturated fat. Not only that, but the Aphrodisiac Academe would be closed down, because it was a crime scene.

It was obvious that he couldn't report Teddy's corpse to the police. He had to remove the body from the restaurant and get rid of it. Maybe he could dump it in an alley in Beverly Hills. Teddy had enemies who did business in that area, and that might be enough to keep Don and the club out of it.

Chapter Twelve

Don drove home at midnight, and, without going in the house, switched from the Mustang to the van and returned to the Aphrodisiac Academe. It was now two a.m., and he was back in Lolita's Grotto under the soft, diffused glow of the moon and stars shining through the glass ceiling.

Lolita's Grotto had been added to the club during a major remodeling in the late 1960s that also included an attached patio for outdoor dining that hadn't been used for almost a decade now. Since the AIDS epidemic had become official in June 1981, the annual growth of revenue from the club had slowed slightly as the free love era started to exhibit more caution and less wild abandon. With fewer customers, the patio area was closed and converted to storage.

The main lights were off throughout the empty dining rooms, and Don sat in seclusion in the most private and isolated booth in the building. The recessed table was in an artificial cave behind a waterfall. The water fell from a ledge above the table and cascaded into a pool at the foot of the table, creating a sheer curtain of water that hid the booth.

To reach the table for two, you had to leave the main walkway where Ms. Sheridan's dinner party had been seated.

There was probably someone working somewhere in the building. The Academe was rarely empty. On his way through the club, he'd picked up a bottle of Scotch and a glass. He'd also left word for Lexi to meet him here when she finished her last set.

He stared at the bottle of Scotch and thought that it was probably a bad idea to be drinking, but he felt the booze might help bolster his courage to ask his official girlfriend to help him dispose of a dead pimp.

He didn't think he could pull this off on his own, and, at the moment, he trusted Lexi more than anyone else. He would've asked Ben first, but Ben was a married man with a family to support, and Lexi was single. Don thought that two single people had less to lose than a married man with children. There was also a bottle of pink champagne on ice with a waiting, long-stemmed glass.

To hell with abstinence, he thought, and reached for the Scotch.

He stopped what he was doing when he sensed a shadowy figure moving along the walkway on the other side of the waterfall and pool. He hoped it was Lexi. The size and shape of the figure was about right, but Cut was about the same size, so it could be anyone.

"Why are you sitting in here in the dark?" Lexi asked as she slid into the cozy booth beside him and leaned forward to plant her lips on his.

When she leaned back, she said, "At least light a candle if you have romance in mind."

He didn't respond. Instead, he poured an inch of Scotch and took a sip from his glass.

"Candles create a mood of romance," Lexi said. "Total darkness does not."

"Sorry." He lit the candle in the center of the table with a match, and the fragmented, flickering light danced across Lexi's exotic features. She took his right hand in both of hers and rested her head on his shoulder.

"Wow, you even have a bottle of Asti Spumante on ice for me. How thoughtful. How did you know?"

"It's the only alcoholic beverage I've seen you drink," he said. "I pay attention." He became aware of her leg pressed tight against his, and her fresh soapy scent was exciting him. She smelled like the Irish Spring Dion preferred.

"Did you take a shower in the upstairs apartment after your last set?"

She leaned closer and said, "You tell me."

Having her so close and knowing what he was planning to recruit her for was causing a lump of worry to materialize in his throat. He opened the bottle of sparkling wine and filled her glass before he leaned back, closed his eyes and sighed.

He sensed her pick up her glass and drink. When he opened his eyes, he saw her holding his glass and sniffing the contents. "I thought you'd quit the booze."

"Today was a hard day," he replied. "And considering what I'm about to ask you, I thought I'd fortify myself."

"Holy shit, Don, are you that much of a coward when it comes to making a commitment? Have you changed your mind?"

"It has nothing to do with our relationship," he said. "I'm in a fix. I thought of asking Dion, but he's an idiot with a motor mouth. I thought of a campus cop I know by the name of Gunny, but we're not that close. Then there's Ben, but he's got a wife and three kids. I even considered asking Ricky, but I don't have the time to find him. He gets paid on Fridays and then vanishes for the weekend. I even thought of asking Mandy for help."

"You thought of Mandy before me," Lexi said, and she slid away from him, breaking contact. "What the hell is going on? I came here expecting romance, and, instead, I'm listening to you ramble on, making no sense."

"I thought of everyone," Don said, "and, in the end, the person I trust the most and probably love is you."

"Say that again," she said.

"What part?"

"Right after probably."

"Do I have to?"

With lightning speed, she jabbed him hard in the ribs. "Damn you!" she said. "How much of that shit have you had?" She indicated the bottle of Scotch.

"Okay." He threw up his hands in surrender. "I said the word love. I think I'm in love with you. I've probably been in love with you for years. What else could it be? And I've always been terrified of falling in love with anyone, because when you fall out of love it hurts like hell."

"Shut up," she said, and drained half her glass of Spumante. "I like this shit, but I can only take so much of it at a time, and I've just hit my limit." She slid the glass away from her toward the center of the table. "This is the most unromantic declaration of love I've ever heard. Usually, when a man says he loves me, he only wants to get in my pants. If you were anyone else, I'd kick your butt and leave. Of course it hurts to love someone if you break up with them. I know, because I have loved you so much for so long that it hurts. I've even considered not performing here to avoid you. Instead, I made the decision to confront you and take a chance, but I don't think you will ever ask a woman to be exclusive with you."

"That's not true."

"Have you ever asked a woman to be your girlfriend?"

"You forget that I was married once."

"That doesn't count. She trapped you when she got pregnant."

He couldn't argue with that. He'd always suspected that Susan got pregnant on purpose.

"Look, you are buried so deep under my skin that every time I play at the Academe, I can't sleep for days. It ruins my voice."

"Wait a minute," he said. "Your singing hasn't diminished at all over the years. As a matter of fact, your voice gets better every time I hear you sing."

"I've been taking voice lessons, you idiot. Singing is my passion, but I don't earn enough from it to support myself. My main source of income has been as a social companion, and that sometimes means I sleep with a customer who is willing to pay."

"Really?" He was quiet for a moment as he mulled over that new bit of information about her. Then he said, "You do it for money?"

She jabbed him again—harder.

"Hey, that hurt," he said.

"You haven't started to feel the pain I'm going to inflict on you. You aren't acting like someone who sent for the woman he loves to meet for a romantic evening."

"Tonight isn't about romance," he said. "I have to do something that I can't do alone, and I want you to help me."

She slid close to him again. "Okay, what is it?"

"Thank you," he said. "I didn't plan to tell you that I'm in love with you. That just sort of escaped, but I'm so nervous about what I'm going to ask you that my guard is down."

"What is it? Are you planning to murder someone?"

Don burst out laughing, and it almost sounded hysterical.

"Now you've got me worried," she said, and she leaned away from him again.

"No, I'm not going to murder anyone." He flapped his hands in front of his face as if he were shaking off water. "I wanted your help to move a dead body—someone I did not kill, I might add. That body is buried in a shallow grave a few yards from where we are sitting. I discovered it by accident a few hours ago, and I don't want the Academe turned into a crime scene and closed. I also don't want to be arrested for a murder that I didn't commit, because there's this stupid-ass cop who thinks I killed my grandfather."

The moment of silence that dropped in like fresh concrete lasted too long.

"Why didn't you tell me this in the first place?" she asked, and moved closer to take his face between both of her hands so she could kiss him long and hard.

"Look, stupid, you better kiss me back, and with some passion, before we get rid of this dead guy, because I'm not going to move an inch until I feel your lips on mine."

"Do you plan to continue working as a social companion?" he asked.

"Once your lips meet mine one more time, I'm retired," she said. "It's all arranged. No more men for me, and there better be no more women for you."

That kiss led to the next step, which was getting naked and making love for over an hour. When they finished and were dressed again, Lexi asked, "By the way, who is this dead guy you want to get rid of?"

"A pimp," Don said, "who had the audacity to go and get himself killed here instead of where he should have been murdered."

"And where is that?"

"Beverly Hills."

"You plan on dumping him at Grauman's Chinese Theater?"

"Of course not," he said. He was starting to worry. She was taking this too easy. She should have been traumatized, a little resistant. He'd rehearsed what he was going to say to win her over, and he was a little disappointed it had been so easy.

"Show me the stiff," she said.

When she saw the face, she said, "It's Teddy. It couldn't have happened to a nicer guy." But there was no shock or sincerity in her voice, and she was smiling radiantly. Don wondered if she had killed him.

"I hate that bastard," she said. "He tried to recruit me." She laughed. "I was pulling down twenty-five hundred bucks a night with one man when I felt like working, and Teddy's girls had to turn ten to twenty tricks a night, seven days a week, and all they got out of it was about five hundred a night because Teddy kept the rest. He actually told me that, without his protection, I could get hurt. So to make a point, I broke his nose."

"You broke his nose?" Don said. "You're amazing."

"About time you noticed that I'm more than just a voice." She kissed him, and he thought about another round in the booth.

"Okay, lover boy, enough of that for now. We've got a body to move, and time is running out. How do you plan to get him out of the building without anyone seeing us?" She stood up and looked around.

"And by the way," she continued, "I'm going to be moving into your place now that we are a couple and I'm retired. If we are going to do this being in love thing, we are going to do it right and work hard at it. And remember, a wife can't testify against her husband."

He couldn't think of anything to say in reply. He'd already been married once, and that had been a real-life nightmare.

Chapter Thirteen

Don imagined hearing his mother reading Galatians 5:19: "Now the works of the flesh are manifest, which are these; adultery, fornication, uncleanness, lasciviousness…"

"Don," Lexi said.

They were squatting on either side of Teddy's body. "My mind went someplace unpleasant," he said.

"Isn't this unpleasant enough? Knock that off and stay here," she said. "Teddy looks like a naked, wooden Indian, and his whoopee stick looks like one of those little hot dogs you find in a can of baked beans. Are you driving the Mustang? How are the three of us going to fit in it? Teddy's got the rigor mortis."

"I have an old van. I'm going to have to drive it over to the kitchen's delivery door. I don't think it's a good idea to carry a naked dead man across the parking lot."

"Don't expect me to stay here alone with him." She

glanced around at the shadows and then at the glass ceiling. "That's creepy. Someone could be up there watching us."

"I have an idea. Stay here. I'll be right back."

Her protests chased him as he hurried up the stairs to a large storage room, where he found the old, rolled-up Turkish rug that had once been in the lobby.

When he returned with the flopping, 10-foot rug braced on one shoulder, he said, "This is what we're going to do." He dropped the rug on the floor, unleashing a blizzard of dust. Lexi's hand flew to cover her mouth, and she stepped back.

"You could have warned me," she said.

"Take hold of Teddy's feet. We're going to put him on the carpet and then roll him up in it."

Once Teddy was inside the rolled carpet, Lexi laughed and said, "Now he's like a hot dog in a bun. What's next?"

"We carry him to the van and load him in the back. Think you're up to it?"

"I may be small, but I'm strong," she said. "Have you forgotten, that I have a black belt in Tai Kwon Do? And I want you to know that I work out daily with aerobics and weights to keep this body toned so I look good on stage. In fact, I can bench my own weight."

⧗

The van had a dead battery, and Don called the Automobile Club of Southern California for a jump.

While they waited, Don removed the battery from the van and used baking soda, a toothbrush and a file to clean off all the gunk covering the terminals.

"This is spooky," Lexi said. "I've never been here when the parking lot was this empty. It's like living *Dawn of the Dead* or something."

A car turned into the parking lot and stopped beside the van. Don groaned when he saw its driver was Jane Eyre Patton. His first thought was to run.

"I'm surprised to find you here at this hour," the police lieutenant said.

"We're together," Lexi said. "What's so strange about that? What are you doing here?"

Don thought that, besides being a talented singer and a great lover, Lexi was also a quick thinker.

"I came in to ask the morning crew some questions," Jane Eyre replied. "I wanted to talk to all of them before they took off. Maybe one of them saw something the day Jonah was murdered." She left the squad car and looked inside the van.

"What's the carpet for?" she asked.

"It's a gift for me," Lexi said. "I've played the club for years and always admired that carpet. When I told my boyfriend Don here that I liked it, he gave it to me."

Jane Eyre inspected Lexi for a moment and said, "I didn't recognize you. I've heard you perform." She indicated the rolled-up carpet. "It looks pretty old and dirty."

"Yeah, we have to get the mothball and dead rat smell out of it before we take it to my condo."

Don discovered that he'd been holding his breath and forced himself to breathe again.

Jane reached out and pulled a corner of the carpet back to see its design. "This carpet looks like one I wanted for my house, but it costs about five thousand dollars. You're a lucky lady. If you ever decide to sell this, let me know. Now, as long as we're here together, I have a few more questions."

About then, the tow truck arrived.

"Lieutenant," Don said, "it's been a really long day. Can't this wait until later tonight when I start my next shift? I'll be here about six p.m.

"And I'll be back, too," Lexi said. "I'm performing here for the rest of the week. I start at eight."

"I'd like to catch your act," Jane Eyre said, "so I'll be here about seven." She looked at the carpet one more time, nodded and then walked toward the Aphrodisiac Academe.

"I thought I was going to have a heart attack," Lexi said. "I've never been so scared in all my life. Instead of getting my hands on that cute ass of yours again, I could have ended up in jail."

"Did you really earn only twenty-five hundred a night?" Don asked.

"Yea, and every time you get a piece of me, remember that." She jabbed his arm—fast and hard. "You deserved that, and it is going to bruise," she said.

⧗

After the tow truck left and on the way to the 605 Freeway, Don ran a red light, and a motorcycle cop shot out of the shadows.

"I get the feeling that fate is fucking with us," Lexi said.

Don had to agree, but one good thing came out of their time together as they crossed Los Angeles county toward Beverly Hills. Don learned that Lexi was born into a wealthy family and her father started teaching her martial arts when she was three. When she was seven, her family moved to the Philippines and then, a few years later, to Hawaii, where they lived in a gang-dominated neighborhood.

"The Hawaiian gangs are more dangerous than the ones here," she said. "When a Hawaiian gangbanger threatens you, that is a guarantee you can take to the bank."

By this time, her father, a black belt, had taught her everything he knew about martial arts, and she went out on her own and learned more to become literally a ballerina of Tae Kwon Do.

When she was fifteen, she made the mistake of dating a hard core gangbanger she thought was too cute to pass up. To him, no meant yes and yes meant yes. Not ready to give up her virginity, she broke his arm, fractured three of his ribs and dislocated one of his shoulders. On top of that, she pushed him out of his own moving car in front of the nearest hospital and then drove his car to her house. Naked, she weighed eighty pounds, and he was a six footer who lifted weights and benched three hundred pounds.

That was on a Saturday night. On Monday at school, two of his older sisters made the mistake of jumping her at lunch. The attack was unexpected, and they managed to crack two of her ribs, but Lexi put them both in the hospital.

Before the day was over, a friend called to warn Lexi that there was a price on her head. Her father packed up the family and moved to Little Saigon in Orange Country, where her mother and father still lived.

"Do you have any idea how long Teddy has been dead?" she asked.

"About two days," he said.

Lexi was quiet for a moment before she said, "How the hell do you know that if you didn't kill him?"

"I spent three years in Vietnam, so I've been around dead bodies before. Sometimes in combat, the landing zone was so hot that we couldn't get the dead lifted out for days. Teddy was stiff when we dug him out, but he hasn't started to stink yet, and that takes about three days. In about a week, he'll be ripe and bloated. Do you want to hear more?"

"I'm sorry I asked," she said. "Now I don't feel so good."

"And I thought you were a tough little wench."

"What if he isn't dead?"

"He's dead. Trust me."

Chapter Fourteen

They dumped Teddy in one of the most dangerous neighborhoods in Southeastern Los Angeles, and they did it in broad daylight in the middle of a residential street.

The change in plans was Lexi's idea. Before she came up with this brilliant, nerve-shattering suggestion, she crawled into the back of the van and unrolled Teddy to examine him.

"I have an idea," she said from the back, after a long silence. "He's got a shoulder tattoo that says he must have been in the Bloods at one time. This is not a jailhouse tattoo, and I doubt that Teddy was hard core. A lot of kids that live in gang neighborhoods join just to be left alone; I bet that's what he did. We should dump him in rival territory. That way, the police won't pay much attention, and it will be recorded as just another gang killing, without an investigation or news report."

"Shouldn't you be hysterical or something?" Don

asked. "You act like dumping bodies is an everyday occurrence. All I can think of is being sent to prison. I'd rather be in bed with you every night."

Lexi slipped into the front passenger seat and jabbed his arm. "You are going to miss a lot of sleep in the next few days, honey," she said, "but not over this. I'm not into murder. I just like to read mysteries, and I go to lots of movies. In fact, I always figure out who the killer or crook is before the end, and, of course, I didn't like Teddy in the first place."

She pulled off her blouse, revealing that she wasn't wearing a bra.

"You are distracting me, and I'm the driver," he said.

"I'm 32, 22, 32. I'm five foot five, and I weight lean, mean hundred and eighteen pounds."

"I've noticed," he said. In all the years they had known each other, she'd never talked this much.

"I'll have you know that this hot, sexy little body has a B.A. in literature from Irvine and an M.F.A. in film from UCLA and was number two in its graduating class. As you might have noticed, I have great critical thinking and problem solving skills."

"For God's sake, put your shirt back on. We coming up to a red light, and there are other cars."

"In my video collection, I have Mr. Moto, Charlie Chan, Sherlock Homes, The Thin Man, Bulldog Drummond and Agatha Christie. I have hundreds of films and books, and I've read or watched my favorites dozens of times."

Don couldn't remember the last time he'd been to

the theater to see a film or even turned on his TV. But he did read about one book a month.

Lexi continued. "I sing professionally maybe three or four nights a week, and I usually escort and entertain one or two nice, mature gentlemen a week. I don't go out with idiots, and I earned almost two hundred thousand dollars last year. At least half of what I've earned as an escort is invested."

"How long have you been an escort?"

"Since U.C. Irvine. Watch it!" She shouted, and he swerved and braked to avoid hitting a bus that stopped in front of them.

"You were distracting me," he said. "Do you expect me to ignore you when you start stripping?"

"Hey, cowboy, you better keep an eye on the traffic or we are not going to sample each other's merchandise again."

"Then put your blouse back on."

She stuck out her lower lip and, with a big grin, pulled her blouse back on. "I also enjoy taking long walks and climbing mountains. I snow ski. I water ski. I rock climb. I keep up with my martial arts. I really enjoy sex with sexy men like you, who know what they're doing."

She reached over and grabbed his crotch, then took her hand back. "Now, that is what I'm talking about. You must have one hell of a genetic libido, Mr. Casanova."

He groaned inwardly and wondered if Lexi was his Henriette, one of the greatest loves of Giacomo's life. Their affair started in 1749 in Cesena, moved to Parma and then Geneva, altogether lasting less than a year—still longer than any relationship Don had had. And he wanted to beat Giacomo's record. He wanted someone to grow old with, and Lexi seemed like a good candidate for that. He also wanted her to talk less.

"I know what you're thinking," Lexi said, throwing a million-megawatt smile at him. "After we dump this stiff, I want to go to my condo, get naked, take a hot shower together and have sex before and after we watch one of my favorite romantic films of all time."

"I like Grisham and James Lee Burke," Don said.

Her hand returned to his crotch and squeezed. "I see you're still interested," she said. "My favorite is Dirty Harry." She took back her hand and struck a pose. "Go on, make my day." Her laughter sounded like musical bells. She unzipped his pants and slipped her hand inside to fondle him.

He worried that he might lose control of the van, and an accident would be a disaster.

With a startled look on her face, she twisted around and stared into the back. Yanking her hand out of Don's crotch, she stared at both of her hands in horror. "Oh, yuck! I was touching you after I touched him. That's disgusting. Pull into that 7-Eleven so I can wash my hands."

"We are not stopping until we get rid of Teddy. There are some wet wipes in the glove compartment. Use one of those."

After two hours driving around residential streets and feeling out of place, they found an empty lot with a blackened concrete foundation surrounded by sagebrush and tall sticker weeds. Don started to drive up over the curb so they could leave Teddy in the middle of the lot.

"No! Stop!" Lexi said. "Back up. You can't do that! You'll leave tire tracks in the dirt. If you want to dump him in there, we have to carry him from the street."

"Our shoes might leave imprints, too," Don said.

"Then we are not setting one foot in there. We leave no clues. Look, there's a concrete walk over there. That's where the front door of whatever was here must have been. Park in front of that walkway. Do you think this house was torched during the Rodney King riots?"

Who cares? he thought, and reconsidered spending the rest of his life with Lexi. Maybe a few years would work better, unless she talked less. "You do know that anyone could drive down the street or look out a window and see us. Do you have any idea what will happen to a white guy with a sexy Asian babe helping him dump a naked, dead, black man in this neighborhood?"

"Then we better make this quick," she said. The instant the van stopped in front of the walkway, she jumped out, ran to the back, opened the rear doors and dragged Teddy out to the street.

Back in the passenger seat, she said, "Drive!"

Don stared in the rear-view mirrors as they drove away, and he could see Teddy's body in the street a few feet from the curb.

Lexi gave directions to her place on the Palos Verdes Peninsula. She lived in a two-story townhome with an attached, three-car garage inside a gate-guarded community that overlooked the ocean. When Don pulled the van into her garage, the only car there was a 1989 black Porsche Carrera Targa 911.

They didn't watch any movies, but they did take a long, hot shower together.

Chapter Fifteen

After several physically intimate hours at Lexi's condo, the couple returned to the Aphrodisiac Academe early and retreated to the upstairs apartment for more intimacy followed by another sensual shower together.

Don was scheduled to start work at seven p.m. and Lexi at eight. At six-thirty, Don said, "My body feels like rubber. I don't have much energy left."

"Me, too," Lexi said. "What I want to do is spoon with you and sleep for at least twelve hours."

"At least you get another hour before you go on stage. I have to be at the front desk in less than a half-hour. Then there's that cop who wants to talk to us."

"It takes more energy to perform on that stage than it does for you to walk customers to their tables."

"True."

Two hours later, with the dinner rush over, Don stood behind the restaurant's front desk in the empty lobby, listening to Lexi's rich voice blasting from the club. He covered his mouth with a hand to hide a deep yawn. He didn't think he'd make it to midnight and worried that he might fall asleep on his feet.

"Do you have a moment, Donald?" It was Great Uncle Abraham, Amanda's youngest brother and the only sibling of hers who still lived. He was ninety, and he looked it, but he moved with the stamina of a much younger man. Don knew that he still rode horses and played tennis weekly. He was also on his fifth wife, and she was forty years younger than he was.

Uncle Abraham was dressed in a dark gray Brooks Brothers suit; blue, long-sleeved, French shirt; and black tie with a bleeding red rose on it. Don wondered if the blood was real. Uncle had a reputation for being ruthless and demanding. He micromanaged not only Amanda's real estate business as its CEO, but also his current wife, the seventeen children he'd had with his five wives, and the flock of grandchildren and great-grandchildren Don had lost count of.

Ben, being married to one of Uncle Abraham's granddaughters, had told horror stories to Don about Uncle's fascist management style.

"We have a half-hour," Don said, and left the front desk in the capable hands of a seventeen-year-old hostess who worked nights at the restaurant. Don had hired her when she was fifteen, and he was grooming her to become his assistant after she graduated this year. If she accepted, he planned to pay for her college tuition if she would major in business. There was a good chance she would marry into the family, too, because she had been dating a Casanova since eighth grade, a distant cousin of Don's who was not a member of Uncle Abraham's family—lucky boy.

Don led the way upstairs to the office, where they could talk in private.

Once the door was closed, Uncle said, "According to the trust Amanda set up, you are the next in line to manage this place. It's time for you to step up and do your duty for the family."

"Have you located my father?" Don asked. "By right, he should manage the Aphrodisiac. He did it for several years before he abandoned my mother and me."

"A private detective was hired, but your father has not been found yet. Now, the only family member that's skilled enough to do the job is you. We can't rely on your brother. I've already talked this over with my sister, and she agrees that you are the only person we trust to manage the club."

"You talked to Amanda and made this decision without me being there?" Don said. "And Dion is not the idiot you think he is. It's time he's given more responsibility. It might be the catalyst that will force him to grow up."

The silence that followed stretched like a rubber band ready to break. Don started working at the Academe when he turned fourteen. Over the years, he'd washed dishes, bussed and waited tables, bartended, and cooked. He was the go-to guy when his superiors were out. The only job he hadn't held was general manager.

"I'm not interested. I suggest you talk to Aunt Eleanor. I know the language in the trust, and it clearly says that if I decline, she's the next candidate."

"That's not acceptable. Eleanor is too unconventional. She's an embarrassment to the family."

"Why, because she's into voodoo, crystal balls, astral travel and exploring the afterlife?"

"She would run the club into the ground," Uncle said. "It has to be you."

Aunt Eleanor was the freest spirit in the family, which made her Don's favorite. He didn't like Uncle talking about her that way. "Aunt Eleanor would be perfect as general manager."

"No. No one has your experience. We see no reason why you should decline this job."

Don wasn't about to share his real reasons for turning down the position. He was unwilling to give up his teaching job, and now there was Lexi. Being general manger meant that he belonged to the Aphrodisiac Academe first and would have to put everything else second. The general manager could easily work seven days a week, a dozen hours a day. He was determined not to lose his relationship with Lexi.

Uncle ran a finger around the inside of his cotton shirt's starched collar. His eyes glazed over, and he started to mumble.

"I won't do it," Don said. "It's either Aunt Eleanor or Dion."

Uncle's face turned the color of a brick, and Don worried that he was going to have a stroke. "Both are unacceptable," Uncle said. "We'll have to go with Trent, then. My oldest son has an MBA, and he is an excellent choice for the job. We'll put your name on the letterhead and the business cards, but he will do the actual work."

Don decided to drive the screw deeper. "How did Trent come out of his third divorce? No, Uncle Abraham. The trust clearly says it has to be a family member descended directly from Amanda or Jonah."

The brick color spread to Uncle's neck, and Don imagined his body bursting into flame.

Don wasn't through. "How many more divorces would there be if Trent worked here? He can't keep his hands off women." He decided not to mention the same was true for Dion.

"Women will not stop Trent from keeping the club running smoothly," Uncle said, his eyes narrowed to evil slits.

"Trent would drool over the women who frequent the club regularly, and he'd scare away their business with his unmasked lascivious nature. When it comes to women, he's a road filled with ruts and potholes. But Aunt Eleanor—no matter how offbeat her lifestyle—is a people person. Nothing ruffles her, and she has the gift of knowing when to listen." Don glanced at the wall clock. "This discussion is over. The general manger will be Aunt Eleanor. I expect you will tell Grandma, and she will accept my decision."

"Why…" Uncle sputtered, unable to say another word.

"That's enough, Uncle. We both know what the trust

dictates. Your branch of the family manages Amanda's real estate holdings, but not the Aphrodisiac Academe. Aunt Eleanor will make a fine general manager, and I will enjoy working with her. Do not interfere." Don started toward the door.

"Get back here, young man," Uncle demanded. "We are not through."

Don stopped and turned. "You do not want to confront me, Uncle. That would be a mistake. I'm well aware that you are a control freak, and I will not be one of your victims."

"Freak! Freak!" Uncle's eyes bulged, and his chest heaved as if his heart was trying to escape.

Don held up a hand to silence him. "I won't be bullied by you, Trent or any member of your family, and none of them will work in this club. Ever!" He went through the door, leaving Uncle to deal with his brick colored complexion and rebellious heart.

Now Don understood why Grandma had set up the trust the way she had. She'd done it to drive her younger brother crazy, and Don relished his part in making Uncle feel powerless and miserable.

Then his mother's voice inside his head reminded him of what Jesus Christ would say. "You shall love your neighbor and hate your enemy. But I say to you, love your enemies, bless those who curse you, do good to those who hate you, and pray for those who spitefully use you and persecute you."

With effort, Don forgave Uncle for being an asshole. There would be no prayers.

Chapter Sixteen

Don feared that his confidence in Aunt Eleanor's capability as general manager of the Aphrodisiac Academe was built on sand. Her only business experience was owning a metaphysical bookstore in Pasadena for several decades. It also didn't help that she claimed that her vacations were out-of-body experiences to exotic locations around other stars.

It was obvious that Great Uncle did not fear Aunt. When Jonah had been general manager, Great Uncle stayed away because Jonah intimidated him. Now that Jonah was gone, Great Uncle was a daily nuisance, showing up without warning at any hour, day or night.

What Don remembered most about Aunt Eleanor was when his father drove to Pasadena to visit his sister and took preschool-aged Don with him. Don was fascinated with the wind chimes and charms, and, during one visit, Aunt gave him a wizard-shaped candle that smelled of vanilla and cinnamon.

Don convinced himself that the job of general manager couldn't be that difficult. Basically, all the GM did was make sure everyone else was doing their jobs. How could Aunt fail at that? He ignored most of what was going on at the club, worked his shift, waited for Lexi to finish her last act, and then drove her home to make love and sleep.

Lexi and Don split their time between La Habra Heights and the Palos Verdes Peninsula. They spent Monday through Thursday at his place, so he'd be closer to his day job, and Friday through Sunday at her condo to be closer to the club.

Wanting to spend more time with Lexi, Don started using his accumulated sick days to take Fridays off from teaching. During the day on Friday, they got up early and visited the beach to surf or build sandcastles, hiked in the local mountains, cooked for each other, and had sex everywhere they went if they found the privacy to get away with it. Then they'd drive together to the club before their evening shifts started.

It turned out—to Don's relief—that Lexi wasn't as talkative as she had been when they were getting rid of Teddy's corpse. She told him that she talked a lot when she was nervous.

Their three-month anniversary marked a milestone for Don, because none of his romantic liaisons had ever lasted that long before. From that day forward, he was in uncharted territory—a Lewis or Clark waiting to be scalped.

The only problem was that, with him gone from his classroom every Friday for twelve weeks, some of his students were turning his room into a living example of anarchy. There were four computers in his classroom, and they had been sabotaged—the mice had lost their balls, and someone had squirted a packet or two of ketchup into the disk drives. One of the monitors had been etched with gang signs and colored in with black permanent marker. The keyboards were missing letters. Spit wads, gum and sharp-nosed paper airplanes decorated the acoustic ceiling tiles, while graffiti spread across the student desks like a virus.

Because the custodians seldom cleaned the room thoroughly, Don arrived early on Monday mornings to vacuum and clean up the mess.

Twice, substitutes had called in administrators and campus police to quell riots that broke out between rival gang members. The straw that broke Don's back was when one substitute let the kids take home all of the classroom's dictionaries, and none of them were returned.

"Lexi, I can't take Fridays off anymore." He explained why.

She hugged him and said she understood. "We'll still have Saturday and Sunday to be together before we go to work," she said. She never asked him why he wanted to keep his teaching job. She just accepted him for who he was.

When spring break arrived in April, they escaped to a condo in Whistler, British Columbia, and they did some helicopter skiing from the Horstman Glacier for the seven-mile run back to the lodge.

When a blizzard hit, they stayed in and cuddled in front of a blazing fire. Don was starting to worry. His relationship with Lexi was too good to be true. He expected to wake up one morning and discover that the fantasy bubble had popped and one of them had left the other.

In the dark, with her sleeping beside him, he'd strain to hear her breathing to make sure she was really there. Lexi had become his drug of choice. He couldn't get enough of her infectious laugh.

"We have disappointed a lot of people," Lexi said on their last day in Canada. They were both naked on the furry carpet in front of the fireplace, she on her stomach facing the fire and he sitting cross-legged beside her, massaging her back.

"Hearts on an assembly line waiting to be broken," he said.

"I'm serious," she replied. "Some of my most loyal customers have been sending me hate mail complaining about you, and these are not nice guys. They are criminal types or politicians with too much power."

"Is there a difference?" he asked, and laughed.

"Hey, tough guy, was that a shaky laugh I heard?" She rolled over on her side and looked up at him. "You have nothing to worry about. I was joking. My regular customers don't know about us. When I informed them I was retiring, I told them I was filthy rich and didn't need to be a working girl anymore. Besides, my old boss from the escort service said she would take care of any problems from my regular customers who miss me too much."

"I've been thinking about your previous job as an escort," he said.

A guarded look entered her eyes. "Is it a problem? Am I going to be your next broken heart?"

"Nothing to worry about. I'm hooked on you. I guess we have Teddy to thank for that. If he hadn't gotten himself killed, I might have gotten cold feet and bailed. Running away from woman has been a habit of mine."

"I didn't tell you this before, but I checked the newspaper headlines for a month," she said, "and listened to the radio until I was sick of it. I never heard anything about Teddy. I even went to the police station a month after we dumped him and saw the report about his body being found. His death was listed as a gang killing, and there wasn't an investigation."

She rolled over on her stomach again. "Don't stop," she said. "If you ever get tired of teaching or being a maître d', you can go into massage therapy. I think you have the sexiest hands alive."

"Have you noticed my Aunt Eleanor acting strange lately?" he asked—surprising himself with his own question.

"Lower," she said, and he rubbed more oil on the small of her back and further down, over her hips and legs. "Eleanor is always strange, honey," she continued sleepily, "but I love her, anyway. She's our kind of person."

"Before we left for Canada, she said that the Academe's aura was turning dark, and she suspected that someone with evil intentions was watching her. When I asked her what she meant, she said it was just a feeling she had; that she hadn't seen anyone stalking her."

"Talking about stalkers, a few of my older customers were really upset when I told them I was retiring. There was this one old man worth millions that I'd been seeing twice a month for years. He couldn't get it up. Not once. He chain-smoked cigars, and his bitch of a wife made his life hell, so he was willing to pay twice my regular fee to spend an evening holding hands with me and talking until morning."

"I don't need to hear this," Don said.

"How many women have you made love with?"

"I didn't keep count," he said. "Until you, it was all a game."

"And how many women did you have to hit on before one was willing to do the wild thing with you?"

"Maybe fifty," he said.

"Most men couldn't take that much rejection."

"I was raised by Jonah and Amanda to think of seduction as playing the lottery. If you don't buy a ticket, you can't win. Rejection is part of the game. Heck, some days, I just wanted to see how many times I'd be rejected."

He put a finger across her lips. "The fire is dying," he said. "Get your face over here and give me a kiss. That's all I want." He was beginning to really like being a couple.

"Men are easy," she said.

⧗

While waiting at the airport for the flight back to Southern California, Don called the club and discovered from Dion that Aunt Eleanor had vanished soon after they'd left for Canada. Dion said she'd been acting spooky before she pulled the vanishing act.

"You'd think she'd seen a ghost, "Dion said. "She told me the day before she left to parts unknown that she had a disturbing talk with Uncle Abraham. The next day, poof, she was gone, and Uncle put me in charge. He said that it was only until you returned. Why don't you stay up there for another week or so? It's fun being the boss."

"Bullshit," Don replied. "If you fuck up, I'm going to kick your butt. Don't do anything crazy."

"I won't do anything that hasn't been done before, brother," Dion replied.

"What is it?" Lexi asked when she saw Don's expression.

"Nothing good," he replied.

Chapter Seventeen

"Mr. Casanova, my girlfriend wants to have sex, and I don't know what to do."

Gregg was a senior in Don's Journalism class. He'd been on the school newspaper's staff since freshman year, and he was an honor's student likely on his way to Stanford on a scholarship. He hung around until the other students were gone, and then spent fifteen minutes mustering up the courage to get to the sex part.

The girl Gregg was talking about was from Thailand. She was cute, compact and probably not even five foot tall. To hear Gregg confess that they hadn't had sex yet surprised Don, because she sat on his lap and glued herself to him in a way that didn't look like someone who hadn't had sex yet. Even at fourteen, Gregg's girlfriend was centerfold material and smart, to boot.

"What exactly is the problem?" Don asked, uncomfortable, but still curious, while he heard Jonah shouting inside his head. "Tell the idiot to get a copy of the Kama Sutra and practice it all with his girlfriend before he turns eighteen. What's the big deal?"

But Don was not his grandfather.

"Well," Gregg said, his face was a study in anguish. "I'm confused. She told me she likes sex and wants to make me happy because she loves me. We've been very open with each other, and she told her life story. She became sexually active in sixth grade, and she can't understand why I won't seduce her. She thinks I'm not attracted to her, but that isn't true."

"Gregg," Don said, "Tell me what's going on inside your head. You aren't getting to the core of this fast enough, and I'm confused."

"Well," Gregg said, letting the word trail off into silence before he continued, "I sort of wanted to save myself for the woman I'm going to marry, which wouldn't happen until after I earn my master's degree. But, Mr. Casanova, this is really difficult. I don't want to lose her, and part of me wants to give in. I feel like I'm going to break apart. Last Monday, I resolved not to do it, but then, on Saturday, after we had been alone again at her house for several hours, I was in really bad shape. My hands were actually shaking, and I was having trouble breathing."

"I understand, Gregg. What was happening to you is what it means to be a man. You were fighting against your own hormones. How intimate have you been with her?"

"Her parents work twenty-hour days, and they don't

have any other children, so we've been in her bed together naked. I've even had an orgasm when she touched me down there, but I never put it in her. I was so embarrassed." He paused and looked at Don with an odd, worried expression. "You must think I'm an idiot."

"He is an idiot," Jonah's voice shouted inside Don's head. "If I was him …" Don managed to shut off the voice. What was Jonah doing in his head?

"Gregg, I admire the goal you have set for yourself. Most men would just say yes. It takes a strong man to do what you've done. She's fourteen, and you turn eighteen in a few days. I'm not sure it would be a good idea for you to continue to date her after your birthday. How do you feel about her?"

"I think I'm in love with her," he said, "but I'm not sure the way I feel isn't being influenced by lust. And I'm very aware of the risk I'm taking if I continue to see her after my birthday."

"Gregg, what do you want from me?" Don asked.

"I want you to help me make a decision."

Wow! The gears inside Don's head came to a screeching stop. In his fifteen years as a teacher, no student had ever asked him for advice on their virginity. But he had learned that you never knew what a kid was going to say or do in the next moment. He remembered the boy two years earlier who shouted out in the middle of a lesson, "I wonder what it would be like to have sex with an elephant," and there wasn't even an elephant in the story they were discussing.

"The decision isn't going to come from me," Don

said. "What do you want more, Gregg? Do you want to have sex with your girlfriend before your birthday or save yourself for the woman you want to marry? I'm going to guess that, from what you have told me, your desire to save yourself for your future wife is stronger, or you would have already had sex with your young lady."

Gregg was sitting on a student desk staring at the floor. His face was a mask of concentration. "I want to stay true to my beliefs," he said. "I'm just confused. My emotions have had me on a roller coaster for the last month. She said we have to have sex before my birthday or she will break up with me. That's this weekend." His eyes filled with tears.

Gregg heaved a breath and used a shirt sleeve to dry his eyes. "Thank you, Mr. Casanova. Talking to you has helped me make a decision. I'm going to give her up. It will be the hardest thing I've ever done. Last night, I was ready to say yes, but now I know that would be wrong for me."

Once Gregg was gone, Don filled a box with student work he planned to correct over the weekend and hurried to the office to pick up his monthly paycheck before the door was locked. On the way to work at the club, he was going to stop and visit his mother—a visit he made on every school payday.

Giacomo Casanova was lucky with his parents. They were both actors and didn't subject him to lectures on scripture that were partly responsible for Don's confusion and reluctance to continue in Jonah's footsteps.

⏳

Don's mother was more than a person obsessed with scripture. She was also a crotchetier, a darner and a needlepointer, but her hobbies never stopped her from going to church twice each Sunday—once each to two different denominations. She only agreed with half of what each preacher said from the pulpit, so it took two different churches to satisfy what Don called her craving for the Word of God.

For as far back as Don could remember, he had vivid images of his mother with metal needles of all sizes. On the wall behind the couch she was sitting on hung a quilt she embroidered called Autumn in New England, and a king-sized afghan she crocheted covered her bed. She had decorated every dishcloth and towel in her house, and there were delicate doilies on every table and on the arms of the chairs and couches.

"I saw you at your grandfather's funeral, dear," she said as her silver crochet needles blurred through looped chain stitches.

They were sitting in the cramped living room of the same house Don had lived in until he turned ten, when he moved in with Jonah on the boat. His mother's house was a two-bedroom, one-bath bungalow next to the boardwalk in Manhattan Beach, about a mile from the Aphrodisiac Academe, and it belonged to the family.

Her kitchen was a postage stamp from a foreign country. She had visited Europe a dozen times and had carried back all kinds of cheap tourist crap that sat on the counters and hung on the walls next to her framed needlepoints.

He noticed over the years that every time she mentioned Jonah, her needles moved faster and her mouth twisted into a shape that said she didn't approve of his grandfather, but the sparkle in her eyes said the opposite.

His mother lived mostly in the past. When she talked, she split the often one-sided conversation between God or her tragic memories.

"Jonah should have settled down," she said. "He could be such a sweetheart when he wanted to be. It's too bad I won't see him in heaven when I get there."

Don could see the tears start to fill her eyes like they always did. It was only a matter of time before they trickled down her cheeks.

"Your father won't make it to heaven, either," she said, "and now Dionysus is in charge of that den of inequity where you both work. It frightens me to think of him going to hell when he dies. He was so sweet and innocent. I just don't understand what happened to him."

Dion had always been a good con artist. His sins were many, but he had their mother fooled.

Her tear-filled eyes were pale, liquid moons, making her look like a tragic character out of a silent film. When she looked at Don that way, her suffering reached out and dropped tons of weight on his back. He'd start to feel guilty, and then he resented her and wanted to be somewhere else.

"My heart broke into a million pieces when your

father deserted us," she said. This was another topic that came up every time he visited.

All of the thin, aluminum blinds were closed, creating a dim, claustrophobic atmosphere inside the house. To save money, she used only forty-watt light bulbs. Don could feel the dust coating the blinds and smell it in the fabric of her sofa and chairs. She didn't like housework. She ate off paper plates, used plastic forks and spoons, and drank out of Styrofoam cups. Most of her meals were fast food, frozen or canned. For snacks, she ate bananas and the sweetest apples, and there was always a can of salted mixed nuts on the table in front of the couch.

"He was such a gentleman," she said. "We never argued. I can't understand why he ran off. Every day when he woke up, I would tell him, 'God bless you, Cupid'. I called him Cupid because he was always concerned you would never find a good woman."

Don was nine when his father vanished.

His mother's blazing fingers stopped, and she looked up at him. "It's too bad that you and that woman you married didn't last. Divorce is a mortal sin. After you did that, I knew you wouldn't be going to heaven with me. It's going be lonely when I go."

What about God? Don thought. I'm sure He will keep you company.

Her eyes darted away from his, and the needles started looping again. "I want you to go to church with me this Sunday," she said.

She always brought this up, and his stomach churned

with guilt.

"God forgives those who admit they are sinners when they change their lives to serve Him," she said. "Your father refused to join me. Don't make the same mistake. I asked your father every Sunday, and he would just go for a walk. He loved walking along the beach. Sometimes he would walk all day. At times, he'd leave at dawn and return at midnight. He could walk for miles."

Don knew the truth. He spent Sundays at the race track or playing a high stakes card game in the Academe's upstairs apartment. Don's parents had never divorced. His father had just gone for one of his Sunday walks and never come home.

He watched her hands blur as they moved the crochet needles to the sound of the church choir singing praise to the guilt living inside her head.

She felt guilt for her years as a single mother working as a teenage prostitute. She felt guilt for Don's father leaving soon after she announced that sex between them was over because she had done her duty and given God three boys. She felt guilt that Ricky, who she bore when she was just fourteen, was a former felon, drunk, drug addict and fornicator who barely survived on poverty wages. She felt guilt for Don and Dion working at the Aphrodisiac Academe.

"Dionysus is following in Jonah's footsteps," his mother said. "It will be the end of him if you don't stop him. If you fail, he will abandon his children just like your father did."

The clock on the mantle started to ring with a rich,

deep resonating sound borrowed from a Catholic cathedral in Italy.

"Mother," Don said. "I've got to go. My shift at the Academe starts in an hour."

The tears ran down her cheeks. She left the couch and walked him to the door, where she hugged him and gave him a wet kiss.

"I have hope for you, son," she said. "I've heard you have settled down with a singer. Living together out of wedlock is a mortal sin. Marry her, and do it soon."

"Where did you hear that, Mother?"

But she had returned to the couch, and her head was bent over her crochet. He could hear her mumbling scripture. "For a good tree bringeth not forth corrupt fruit; neither doth a corrupt tree bring forth good fruit."

As he went out the door, her words followed him. "Close down the Aphrodisiac Academe," she said, "and join me in church on Sunday. If you don't, I will do something about it. A mother must look after the salvation of her children."

Chapter Eighteen

It was a twenty-minute walk from his mother's house to the Aphrodisiac Academe, where his Mustang was parked, and Don first spotted the huge balloon rising into the sky halfway there.

Until he was in sight of Academe, he had no idea that the building-sized, rainbow-colored, shimmering, beach-ball-shaped, hot-air balloon was tethered to the club. When he finally made the connection, he stopped and stared in shock.

"What has Dion done this time?" he thought.

Keeping his eyes on the rope leading from the club to the balloon, he ended up on the beach side of the building at a locked gate that led into the abandoned courtyard dining area his grandmother had once called the Garden of Aphrodite's Charms. It had been locked up and forgotten for decades. The last time Don had been inside it had been before he'd left to fight in Vietnam.

Since then, the vegetation all died, and the space was turned into a junkyard for old tables; chairs; and outdated, rusting kitchen equipment.

Using his master key, Don unlocked the gate and slipped inside the garden to discover that it had been renovated. The junk was gone. The planters were filled with new trees and shrubs, and a fresh coat of paint had been applied to every surface.

The large, circular fountain that had been at the center of the patio and showcased the larger-than-life statues of Zeus and Aphrodite getting ready to copulate doggy style was gone, and a brightly colored, railed wooden platform about six feet tall had taken its place.

The rope from the balloon led to a bolted electric wench on one side of the platform, where a large, enclosed basket with tinted windows sat. It must have been ten feet square and seven feet tall, at least. The loud roar of a torch drew Don's eyes to the flat roof of the basket, where Dion knelt beside a giant propane tank. A black hose led from the tank to an opening in the bottom of the balloon, where the roaring flame from the torch heated the air inside and caused the balloon to inflate.

Don shouted Dion's name, but the roar from the torch was deafening. He climbed the stairway on the club's side of the platform and used a ladder propped up against the basket to reach the roof.

The first thing he noticed was that Dion must have gained twenty pounds since Don had last seen him two weeks ago. His brother had no idea Don was there. Leaning over so his mouth was an inch from his brother's ear, Don shouted, "What the hell are you up to?"

Dion's arms flailed, and he staggered back like a spastic windmill until he plopped on his wide butt and placed both hands over his heart as if he were attempting to keep it from leaping out of his chest.

Once he calmed, he said, "Why did you do that? Everything in my stomach leaped into my mouth."

"Dion, what is this?" Don waved at the balloon rising into the sky above the courtyard.

His brother smiled and hurried back to the tank to twist a valve and shut off the roaring flame. "Beautiful, isn't it?" he said.

"Dion?"

"It's a surprise. Here's a hint: what's next Sunday?"

"Next Sunday?" Don said. "Don't play games with me, Dion."

Dion held a finger to his lips conspiratorially. "Shhh," he said. "Don't let anyone know what I'm doing." Then suspicion flooded his face. "Wait. I'm not going to tell you. I don't trust you. If you knew what I was doing, you'd ruin the surprise."

"How are you going to keep *that* a secret?" Don pointed at the balloon.

But Dion was already on his way down the ladder. Don hurried to catch up as Dion pushed a door open in the side of the basket and slipped inside. There were red, plush, velvet cushions piled everywhere and what looked like a wet bar in one corner.

"Dion, tell me what the hell you are doing!"

"Go away."

"Whatever you are doing has upset our mother. She told me she wants the club closed. She said if we don't do it, we are headed to hell."

"What else is new?" Dion replied. "You don't talk to her enough. She's been saying that for years."

The interior of the cozy basket reminded Don of a plush, nineteenth-century whorehouse. "Oh, shit!" he exclaimed as the intended purpose of the balloon and basket hit him. "What did you do with Zeus and Aphrodite? Grandmother paid those Italian sculptors a fortune to make them out of Carrara marble and ship them here all the way from Italy."

"I had them moved to the basement. They were in the way. Besides, Zeus was damaged."

"What do you mean, damaged?"

"Go see for yourself and leave me alone."

Don decided to deal with his brother later and hurried to the basement, where he discovered that someone had snapped off Zeus's twelve-inch marble penis very close to the surviving testicles.

The first person he thought of who was stupid enough to break into the Aphrodite's garden and do this was Norman. The club's insurance policy covered this kind of desecration, and he'd file a claim.

Chapter Nineteen

With the dinner rush over, Don went upstairs to the office to take a break and get some relief from the loud music leaking through the walls into the lobby from the club. Even though Lexi was performing, he still wanted silence.

When he reached the door to the office, he stopped. Something didn't feel right, and it took him a moment to figure it out. There used to be three doors off of the upstairs hall, and now there were only two. The door to the upstairs dining room had been replaced by a wall. Turning from the office, he went to the end of the hall and opened the remaining door, expecting to see stacks of chairs and folding tables on one side of the long, narrow storage room and shelves stocked with supplies on the other.

The storage room was gone, and in its place was a dining room with tables for private parties. Cherry wood paneling covered the walls, and the window at the far end of the room that looked out over Pacific Coast Highway was gone. It had been paneled over.

The original upstairs dining room had vanished. What had Dion done with it? Giving up his moment of tranquility in the office, he went searching for his brother, but couldn't find him. Instead, he found Veronica in the Lady Chatterley room.

"What happened to the Brothel?"

"It's still there," she said. "Dion had a hidden door installed inside that new dining room. The day Eleanor went missing, Dion had a crew working around the clock to remodel the upstairs and that outdoor garden."

"Show me the hidden door."

"I can't," she said. "I have customers, and I don't know where they put the door or how to open it. No one but Dion knows."

"Son of a bitch!" he said.

"Got that right. Dion has been up to all kinds of strange stuff since you left."

"Do you have any idea what's special about next Sunday?"

She shrugged. "I think it has something to do with your grandmother. Ask Dion. A few minutes ago, he cut through the kitchen from here and headed to the club."

Through the busy kitchen, a gloomy hallway ran past the alcove with the dishwasher, the glassed-in downstairs office and one of the walk-in refrigerators. On the other side, a stairway led downstairs to the basement storage rooms where most of the beer, wine and liquor were kept.

At the end of the hall, before the door that led backstage, there was a dumbwaiter that served the basement, the ground floor and the second-floor dining room.

Don stopped at the dumbwaiter, pushed the sliding door aside and looked in. When he was a kid, he rode this elevator to the basement. He thought he might still fit, but it would be tight. At the moment, the elevator was at the bottom of the dark shaft.

The intercom next to the dumbwaiter buzzed, and the light that indicated a call for the maître d' started to flash. He pushed the button. "What is it?"

"Don, there's a gentleman at the front desk who says he knows you."

The man waiting for him was looking down the brick ramp into the Lady Chatterley room as if he expected Don to appear from that direction, and, from his profile, Don recognized him immediately. It was Dr. Ruben, the dictatorial principal who ran the high school where he taught. What the hell was he doing here?

"Dr. Rubin," Don said.

The man spun around, looking relieved. He had a receding hairline; a large nose; protruding, gapped teeth; and no chin. The high school's staff called him Hitler or The Rube. He had other names, too, depending on who you were talking to.

"Mr. Casanova," he said, "you are exactly the man I want to see."

⧗

"I'm confused," Don said to Lexi from across the table. She was on her break and sipping a cup of steaming green tea. "No, confused is an understatement. I'm shocked. Numb."

Curious, she leaned forward. "Wow, even Teddy's corpse didn't get you to react like this."

"My principal came in tonight. His wife left him a few months ago, and he wanted my advice on how to meet women. I introduced him to Debbie, that dancer from Las Vegas. Ten minutes later, they walked out the front door together holding hands. "

"But I bet Debbie dropped by the lobby to see if you were available first," she said.

"That's not important. I have no idea how the Rube knew I worked here. I thought I'd kept this place secret from the district's administration, just like I keep the teaching job a secret from my family."

"It's a small world," she said. "I'm glad you hooked him up with Debbie, though. I've been thinking of having a talk with her. She's got to stop flirting with you."

"When Debbie wakes up in the morning and discovers who she climbed in bed with, she's going to hate me," he said.

"Good. That will save me from kicking her ass." Lexi leaned forward and kissed him. "Break's over."

⌛

At closing, Lexi and Don retreated to the upstairs apartment to make love and sleep for a few hours, and now Lexi was taking a shower before they drove to his La Habra Heights home. Don planned to be in his classroom by seven a.m. to start the month of May.

While Lexi freshened up, Don searched for Dion and found him on the ground floor in the hallway that led from the kitchen to the club, struggling with something he was stuffing into the dumbwaiter. It looked like a large, canvas, draw-string laundry bag.

Unnoticed, Don slipped into the darkness of the dishwasher alcove. If he couldn't get Dion to admit what he was up to, Don would spy on him.

Just when it looked like his brother had succeeded in stuffing the oversized bag in the dumbwaiter, the drawstring slipped and the opening widened enough to allow a naked foot to escape. Dion cursed and stuffed it back inside, pulling the drawstring tight.

What he'd witnessed left Don with a brain freeze, and he stopped breathing for a moment. He questioned if he'd really seen what he thought he had. There was a chance he'd been hallucinating. Dion was an idiot, but he wasn't a killer. At least, Don didn't think he was. Maybe it was a mannequin, but what would Dion be doing stuffing that into a laundry bag? The Aphrodisiac Academe was a nightclub and restaurant—not Victoria's Secret.

Don watched Dion slide the dumbwaiter door closed and jab the button to send it to the basement. Younger brother moved to the intercom, picked it up, dialed numbers and mumbled into the speaker before hanging up and hurrying toward the kitchen.

Don slipped across the hall to the basement stairway.

He prayed it was a mannequin, but he had to see for himself. When he reached the dumbwaiter and slid the door open, there was no bag. Where had it gone? Dion must have an accomplice.

Stealthily, he searched the basement walk-in refrigerator and liquor storage. Nothing! Where the hell had it gone? There was no way a mannequin or a corpse was going to get up and walk away.

Combat, he could handle. He could even assassinate someone for the CIA. But he couldn't handle the idea that his younger brother was a killer. And it bothered him that this was somehow similar to Teddy's mysterious death. Had Dion been involved in that too?

When a voice spoke from behind him, Don—heart pumping—spun around, ready to fight.

"What you doing here this early in the morning, Mr. Casanova? You going to scare the rats away." It was Rudolf, the club's rat catcher. Rudolf was an ex-con covered in jailhouse tattoos. Even the top of his bald head was tattooed. Ricky had recommended Rudolf for the job several years ago, and Don had given him a chance. The man was a miracle worker when it came to eradicating rats, mice and cockroaches, and Don had since recommended him to other restaurants. Everyone who hired Rudolf had been satisfied with the results, and Rudolf was earning good, honest money getting rid of pests.

Rudolf had a lot of tricks, and he hated using poison. One of his favorite methods was to put out the best bait possible in the middle of a large, walk-in freezer and then sit in a chair behind the open door until he heard what sounded like a rat convention inside. He'd slam the door, and, a few hours later he'd dispose of all the furry, frozen rats.

His bait was a mix of peanut butter, sliced bananas, raisins and bacon or pork fat.

"I was looking for a bottle of wine to take home, Rudolf," Don said as he slipped a bottle from the wine rack and walked toward the stairs.

"Have a good day, Mr. Casanova."

Chapter Twenty

Ms. Sheridan appeared at the front desk on May first at seven p.m., huffing and puffing like an angry water buffalo at Eve, one of Don's hostesses. Don wasn't in the mood for this after what he witnessed with Dion earlier.

On the drive to La Habra Heights, he'd confided to Lexi, and she'd laughed. "There is no way that Dion, the wimp, is an axe murder. He's a lecherous, horrible, practical joker, but he is no killer. I vote for the mannequin. It's probably part of this mysterious surprise."

Sheridan hadn't seen him yet, so he stepped into the shadows, hoping she'd get bored and leave. But she didn't. She continued to harangue Eve, and Don felt guilty for letting his hostess suffer. He took a calming breath and fortified himself. Eve was one of his special projects. She had been recommended to him by a contact he had at the National Coalition Against Domestic

144

Violence. When Eve attempted to break up with her boyfriend before graduating from high school, he almost beat her to death and swore that, when he got out of jail, he'd finish the job. Eve was pregnant, and her fundamentalist Christian family disowned her and threw her out of the house.

Don helped move Eve from Denver to Southern California, where she was supplied with a new name and identification. At first, she lived in a women's shelter and worked full-time at the Aphrodisiac Academe's front desk. No one knew her history but Don.

Today, Eve was a single mother who lived in an apartment building the family owned within walking distance of the Academe. When Don approached Great Uncle to ask that the rent be set at half the going rate, Uncle had refused. So Don called Grandmother Amanda, who would move heaven and earth to help an abused woman in need. Some of her methods weren't politically correct or kosher, but they worked.

Don left his shadowy shelter behind the palm and walked up the gently sloping brick ramp toward the front desk. Eve had natural blond hair cut even with her jawline. She had blue eyes; soft, pale skin; and was always a cheerful sprite. Don had never heard her say anything negative or mean to a customer in the two years she'd worked there.

He could hear Sheridan the Shrew's cruel words. "I told you my party will not sit in the Lady Chatterley room. She was a whore."

Eve said, "What room would you prefer, Ms.

Sheridan?"

"The D. H. Lawrence Room, of course. No other room has the same ambience."

"Didn't you know that D. H. Lawrence wrote Lady Chatterley's Lover?" Don asked. He only counted a party of eight with Sheridan this time.

Sheridan turned to confront him.

"Wait here with your party while I get the table ready," he said, and turned to go.

"No," Sheridan replied. "I want to see our table before we sit down."

Maybe Jonah helped her marry a fast food fortune to get rid of her, Don thought. Halfway through the Lady Chatterley room, he stopped, faced her and held up a finger. "Go back to the lobby, now!"

"You can't talk to me like that." She sprayed his face with spittle.

"Management reserves the right to refuse service to anyone," Don said. "And you are not welcome here." The Lady Chatterley room was half-full of customers, and the chatter died. Every face in the room watched them.

Shit! Don thought.

Sheridan's lips became a thin, pale line on her face as she pulled them tight against her teeth. "Your mother was right. This place is a corrupting influence on our community, and I will join her in her crusade." Indignant, she stomped back to the lobby and led her party out the front door.

Don was speechless. His mother knew Sheridan, and they were cooking up some sort of crazy crusade. What was going to happen next? He wondered if the Marines would take him back.

Chapter Twenty-One

Trying to sleep wasn't easy with so many thoughts spinning inside his head. Don had seen a lot of death in his life, and those older memories were etched in the grey folds of his fatty brain. They, too, had caused some loss of sleep over the years. Lexi had done all she could to exhaust him after they crawled between the king-sized bed's cool sheets, but she was the only one sleeping now.

Damn Dion and that old crone Sheridan!

On top of everything, a voice in his head that sounded like Aunt Eleanor kept saying, "You've got to go to the club and save your brother."

Every time he closed his eyes, Aunt's face would swim into sight and push back the darkness of sleep he wanted to dive into. Why was his imagination doing this to him? Aunt Eleanor would never nag him like this.

"Okay," he said, just to shut the voice up. "I'll do it."

"What is it?" Lexi murmured, half asleep. She turned

on the dim night light. "You know," she said, "if you ask me, I'd tell you that when you've got Chinese genes, you are always going to be part Chinese. But native Chinese will expect you to speak Mandarin without an accent, and, if you can't, they will treat you like a second-class citizen. It sucks." Her eyes gave up the struggle, and she fell back to sleep.

Don watched her for a long moment before he stretched out an arm and turned off the light on her side of the bed. When making love, she lost herself in ecstasy deeper than any woman Don had known. Awake, she looked ten years younger than she was, and asleep, she looked like a teenager. He loved watching her.

The room was stuffy. He slipped out of bed; opened the French doors to the bedroom patio; and breathed in the fresh, cool air. He considered going to his woodshop to work on the redwood boxes he was building for the garden he planned to install on this patio.

Returning to Lexi's side of the bed, he leaned down and kissed her on her long neck. The silky texture of her warm skin against his lips aroused him, so he stepped back from the bed. There was enough light from the stars, moon and city lights to reveal the shape of her body under the blanket. For a moment, he was tempted to get back in bed. She slept in the nude. All he had to do was start exploring her body with his hands, and she would respond even while sleeping. She'd wake up slowly and join in totally—there would be no hesitation, recriminations or holding back.

Every doubt he'd had about his ability to fall in love

had been proven wrong by Lexi. No woman had done for him what she had done—and it wasn't just the sex. With her, he felt as if he'd finally found a partner and a home in one person.

But right now, he had Dion to take care of. Aunt Eleanor's voice reminded him of his duty. There was a big question demanding answers. Had his brother Dion killed Grandfather, Teddy, Aunt Eleanor and the young woman in the laundry bag? It couldn't be Aunt in the bag, because she'd never fit and didn't have a young woman's complexion.

Lexi had said it was probably a mannequin, and Don wanted to believe it in the worst way, but that foot and ankle he'd seen didn't look like they belonged to a mannequin. If there was a hidden space in the basement large enough to hide a body, Rudolf the rat catcher would know where it was. He was going to call the district for a substitute teacher and drive to the club while Rudolf was still working.

If Dion was a killer, Don couldn't let him kill again, but he couldn't let Dion go to prison either.

Chapter Twenty-Two

Don drove up to the club's loading dock. A twelve-foot block wall covered in English ivy bordered the drive. His Mustang would be out of sight there.

The spotlights above the delivery area were out, and that was unusual. They were always on all night, and security cameras covered the loading dock. The cameras, like the ones inside the club, fed into a bank of monitors in the downstairs office.

Other than the sound of the surf on the beach and the occasional lonely car passing, at this hour, it was spooky enough outside to trigger the paranoid alertness that came with his PTSD.

He looked in the direction of one of the cameras. There should have been a red light glowing that indicated it was working, but he couldn't see it.

What if Don was walking into a robbery in progress? What if the cameras had been deliberately sabotaged or turned off? What if Dion was inside, getting rid of the woman's body he'd stuffed in that laundry bag?

With cautious fingers, Don touched the handle of the delivery door and discovered it wasn't locked. He shivered.

He opened the door just enough to slip into the even-darker interior. At four a.m., the Aphrodisiac Academe was as silent as a tomb. The last of the night crew had left by three, and the morning crew wouldn't arrive until six. The only person who should be here was Rudolf.

It was pitch black inside the club. That could only happen if the power was turned off and the emergency backup generator was offline.

Without a light to see where he was going, the inside of the building was a minefield of furniture and equipment. It would be stupid to even attempt navigating in the dark. There was a tote bag in his trunk with emergency and survival gear. After he retrieved a flashlight and knife from his car, he decided to enter the club through the courtyard where Dion had his hot air balloon. To get to it, he had to slip through some palms and tall shrubs. When he stepped out of the brush, an old man was walking his cat on a leash. The cat easily weighed forty pounds and wore a harness.

The old man walked with his head down and his eyes on his feet. "Maurice," he said to the cat, "it's a pisser being eighty-three and not able to get it up anymore. The old man wore a plain, tweed, herringbone cap over his shrunken, bald head. Liver spots and broken capillaries spread across his face and swollen, red nose. When he spotted Don, he stopped and squinted. "Hey, don't I know you?"

"The Sunday brunch with bottomless mimosas," Don said, recognizing a regular customer now that the man had looked up.

"Oh, yeah, the nice young man who shows us to our table. I bet you think girls are easy, being all young and good-looking."

"Not really," Don said. "I have to go." He hurried to the patio gate and used his master key to get inside. As the gate latched behind him, he heard the old man muttering.

"He was rude, Maurice. Come on; let's get going while I can still walk." He made a clucking noise with his tongue and said, "The kids these days. What is to become of us with them running things?"

Skirting the platform and deflated hot air balloon, Don reached the door and was relieved to find it locked. Once inside, he placed an ear against the wall. Sometimes sounds could be detected through them.

When he heard nothing, he turned on the flashlight and, with his knife in the other hand, walked silently through the kitchen and into the club, where he imagined the ghosts of dancers, singers and DJs as if the club were a live, breathing creature with a blood-pumping heart.

After a swing through the empty lobby and dining rooms, he returned to the kitchen and the stairs that led to the basement. He turned off the flashlight and unlocked the steel-jacketed door at the top.

If Rudolf was still down there, why had this door been locked? Standing there for a long moment, he strained to listen for the slightest sound—but there was nothing. The cold, stale, dusty air flowed up the stairs and wrapped around his face, whispering for him come down. He didn't want to. He'd done shit like this in Vietnam—crawled through caves hunting Vietcong. He was getting too old to play warrior, and, with Lexi in his life, he didn't want to risk dying anytime soon. In fact, he wanted to return to the house in La Habra Heights, sleep late and make love with her for hours.

Damn that Dion, he thought. Why should I be my brother's keeper? I should let him rot in prison.

He took the first step into the well of darkness that was the basement and tensed at memories of the monsters he had hunted and killed in Vietnam. With his back against the concrete wall, he moved one slow step at a time, being careful to make not one sound. At the bottom, he smelled spilled wine and frozen rat carcass.

The dark was total here. Even when the club was empty, the refrigerators hummed a soft tune, but now, for the first time in his life, there was no sound inside the Aphrodisiac Academe except for his beating heart and shallow breathing.

Rudolf must have left, but what about the power and unlocked delivery door?

Moving slow and sliding along the wall, he touched the open door to the liquor storage room. This was wrong. That door should have been closed and double locked.

This was starting to feel like one of his search and destroy missions.

What if Dion was down here cutting up that young woman? Don waited outside the liquor storage for a long moment, listening, but there was nothing, so he moved on down the hall toward the walk-in refrigerator.

He sensed something new—the soft scent of roses, like the perfume Aunt Eleanor always wore. His mouth went dry and his muscles tightened. Was Dion cutting her up, too?

The voice in his head that sounded like Aunt Eleanor said, "There's nothing to worry about. Go back and look closer at the wine, and all will be revealed."

Inside the liquor storage, Don turned on his flashlight and discovered that one end of the floor-to-ceiling wine racks had been pulled away from the wall. On closer examination, he saw that one end of the unit was attached to a pivot that allowed it to swing out like a door. Closed, the pivot was hidden. Behind the rack, there was a narrow opening, and he could see footprints in the thick layer of dust on the floor. He could also feel a breeze rising from below.

Inside the opening, another stairway led down. He had spent most of his life working and playing in this building and never had any idea there were hidden passages. Not liking it at all, he started down the stairs. Every fifteen steps, he reached a landing where the staircase turned ninety degrees.

After six landings and seven flights of steps, he reached the bottom and guessed that he was at least eighty feet underground.

Grandmother had the Academe built and never trusted the government. She'd launched her fortune breaking the law during Prohibition.

She said there was no way to predict what oppressive law might be passed next and that you had to be ready for anything.

She had Chinese friends, business partners and customers who'd suffered because of the Chinese Exclusion Act of 1882—which made it illegal for Chinese to immigrate to the United States or be eligible for citizenship—and she'd helped smuggle wives and children into the United States for these Chinese men, supplying false identification so their families could stay until the act was repealed in 1943.

When GOP Senator Joseph McCarthy terrorized the nation in the 1950s with his homosexual witch hunts and so-called Red Scare, she'd provided a safe haven and legal support for any of her friends who were targeted by McCarthy.

Being in the porno industry, she had many friends in Hollowed who were socialists, communists or homosexual, and, to protect herself from McCarthy, she used her escort service like an insurance policy. Those high-class hookers were provided to rich and powerful men from both major political parties. If Amanda needed a favor, she had hundreds of clients she could call.

She must have built this tunnel as an escape route. Standing at the foot of the stairs, he shined the light down a long hallway that stretched into darkness. He'd lost his sense of direction and didn't know if it led under the ocean or inland. The air was cold and smelled of wet concrete.

Counting his steps, he started walking, and one hundred fifty feet later, he reached a rectangular room about twenty feet wide and hundreds of feet long. In the center, stretching as far as he could see into the darkness, were oil derricks—one after another—bobbing up and down. Pipes and wires brought power in and pumped crude oil out.

He started to giggle hysterically when he realized what his grandmother had pulled off. Now he knew where some of her billions came from.

Where the oil went, he had no idea, but he was sure Amanda owned a front company that refined the oil and sold it through a small, independent distributer—which she probably also owned.

In awe and with Dion and the dead girl momentarily forgotten, he walked the length of the chamber and counted twenty-one oil derricks pumping liquid gold out of the earth. She had been stealing from Standard Oil for decades and laundering the money through all of her ventures, which explained how the Aphrodisiac Academe could afford high-priced entertainment like Lexi and still earn impressive annual profits.

He traced the pipe carrying the crude oil to a wall, where it vanished through the concrete. It was easy to imagine the oil pipe running for miles under family-owned land—deep under shopping malls, hospitals, warehouses, theaters and apartment buildings.

How many people knew about this operation? Who maintained the equipment?

Of course! Why hadn't he figured it out? This was where Dion must have taken the young girl's body. That's why she had vanished, and that meant Dion was involved. He knew. Don felt horrible. His grandmother had never trusted him with the family secret, but evidently had told his younger brother. He wondered how many other family secrets there were.

But Don inspected the entire operation and found no body. There were no more doors or hallways leading off into the unknown, either. Where had Dion taken it?

Don returned to the Academe's basement, where he discovered that the power was back on, along with the lights. He pushed the wine rack closed and heard it click. He'd find out how to open it later.

First, he wanted to find the body, and the next place to look was the walk-in fridge. It was twenty feet deep, and its walls were lined with stainless steel shelving. Maybe it covered up another hidden doorway.

Outside the large freezer, he hesitated. If someone snuck up behind him after he went inside, they could close the door and lock him in. A few hours in there, and he'd be a Popsicle.

Taking a fortified breath, he pulled the heavy, insulated door open and walked in. What choice did he have?

Chapter Twenty-Three

The first thing Don saw when he stepped inside was the bait surrounded by frozen rats. Rudolf had not finished cleaning up, and it was almost six a.m. Employees would start to arrive soon, and trucks would start making deliveries. He'd have to move the Mustang.

Taking time to inspect the locker, he rattled the stainless steel shelving and used a broom handle to poke the concrete walls, but found no hidden doors.

He even pushed aside the table-sized butcher block to see if there was a hidden stairway under it, but only discovered more floor.

What next? he thought, staring at the meat grinders on a counter next to the door.

What a novel way to get rid of the incriminating evidence, he thought. What if his brother had turned the body into hamburger and planned to serve it to the customers to get rid of the evidence?

That would be gross, he thought, and was relieved that the only meat in his diet came from wild salmon when it was in season. Then he felt a guilty for feeling relieved.

What had Dion done with the woman's body?

"Look upstairs," Aunt Eleanor's voice said inside his head.

Halfway up the stairs, he heard voices coming toward him, and his heart raced from the rush of adrenaline. Hurrying back down the stairs, he hid in the dishwasher alcove. Across the hall, by the dumbwaiter, waited a wheeled, stainless steel cart.

The lights came on, and Don had to close his eyes against the glare. He needed a better place to hide. The dishwasher, he thought, and crawled inside.

"I tell you, she's gone." It was Rudolf's voice. "I brought the carving knives, and she wasn't where you said you left her. I checked everywhere. Maybe she wasn't dead."

"She couldn't be alive," Dion said. "I made sure before I stuffed her in the laundry bag."

Don lay prone on a belt of dull prongs designed to hold the dish racks in place, but he didn't feel any pain. Instead, he took shallow breaths and listened to his younger brother and Rudolf the rat catcher talk in the hall outside the alcove.

"How did you lose a stiff?" Rudolf asked, following up with a mocking chuckle.

"You don't believe me!" Dion's voice had gone up an octave, which was how he always sounded when his wife accused him of cheating.

"She had to be alive," Rudolf said. "How else could she pull a disappearing act like that? Dead people don't get up and walk away. There's only one way in to the pumping room, and when I checked a moment ago, the wine rack was closed and locked. Did you tell that lunatic uncle of yours what you were doing?"

"You think he took her?" Dion's voice had moved to an even-higher pitch of panic. "Hell no! I didn't tell Uncle Abraham anything about the dead girl, and he wouldn't have the strength to move the body by himself, anyway."

"Who else could it be?" Rudolf said. "The three of us and your grandmother are the only people alive who know about that pumping room. That skinny bitch couldn't have weighed even a hundred pounds, and I've heard that old fart of an uncle of yours has done some pretty kinky things with young girls like her. Maybe he killed her."

"Don't talk about my Uncle Abraham like that," Dion said. "Have you forgotten who signs your paychecks for maintaining the pump room?"

Rudolf snorted. "The old fart will have to pay a lot more if he wants to keep these lips closed."

"He doesn't know about the dead girl, and you better not tell him," Dion said, his voice now flooded with anger. "I'll pay you to keep quiet myself. How much?"

Rudolf erupted with laughter, which faded as they finally walked away. Don wanted to slap that sound out of him. It was people like Rudolf, Uncle Abraham and Dion's wife that had made Dion into what he was today:

a fumbling fool, a man with no confidence, a man who could do nothing right—someone who lost dead bodies.

Don left the dishwasher and watched his brother and Rudolf start down the stairs to the cellar.

Killers were angry, evil men, and Dion wasn't like that. Don was convinced that, at heart, his younger brother was still a child. He did goofy things to get attention. He did stupid things like the hot air balloon. He cheated on his wife every chance he got. But he wasn't a murderer. Dion didn't have the disposition. The only answer was that, if Dion had killed the girl, it had been an accident.

He had a choice. Follow them or move his car. He picked the car option and cut through the club to a service door that would lead him to the loading dock and the Mustang.

Getting out without being discovered was his plan. If he succeeded, he planned to be back in bed when Lexi woke up.

He stopped and looked up at the Casablanca fan hanging from the dance floor ceiling. It had stopped spinning, and his hair was standing on end as it did in Vietnam when he was on high alert.

"Don't leave," Aunt Eleanor's voice said inside his head. "Go upstairs, but be careful. She isn't alone. Be ready."

"Who isn't alone?" he asked the empty room. "What do you mean?" But Aunt Eleanor's voice didn't answer. He thought that he might be dreaming and would wake up any moment beside Lexi, but he had never had a dream as crazy as this one.

"Hey," he said to the Casablanca fan hanging over his head, "I could use some help here. Come on. You got me out of a warm bed, and for what? If you're going to invade my dreams, you should at least explain what's going on." When she didn't reply, he got angry.

"Fuck you!" he said, and started toward the service door. He was not going upstairs again.

The entrance to the loading dock was only a few feet away when he heard a voice he didn't recognize. "What's a car doing parked here?"

"How the fuck should I know?" It was Carl, the opening cook.

"Well, how am I going to make my delivery? Move it."

"Cool it," Carl said. "It belongs to a member of the family that owns this place."

Hell, Don had lost track of the time. It was a few minutes after six o'clock, and the morning crew was arriving, along with the first delivery. And there would be more deliveries.

"Look," Carl said, "move your truck to the curb in front of the restaurant's lobby door and bring the fish in that way. By the time you get there, I'll have the lobby door propped open. You just have to get the fish to the kitchen, and my crew will take them from there."

Not wanting to be seen, Don changed direction and decided to do what Aunt Eleanor's voice had urged him to do—go upstairs. He ran toward the club's glass door that opened on the lobby. The shortest route to the second floor was the stairs off of the Lady Chatterley room.

When he reached the lobby, a flashlight beam pinned him from outside, and he held up a hand against the glare while a dozen possible excuses about why he was here this early in the morning flooded his brain. Then he remembered that he didn't need an excuse, because his family owned the place. He could come and go as he wanted like he'd been doing for decades.

He waved for the person to move the flashlight beam away from his face, and when the man did, Don saw Dr. Ruben, his principal, standing there with his face against the glass.

Don thought he'd gotten rid of the idiot when he hooked him up with Debbie. What was he doing back here at this hour? He did the only thing he could do: he opened the door.

"I was with Debbie, and I forgot my wallet," Ruben said. "I went back to the motel, but she was gone and so was the wallet. I need to get it back and took a chance I'd find you here."

"She's probably on her way back to Vegas," Don said. "I don't see how I can help you. She dances at the Rio off the Strip. Call her there."

"I have a high school to run," Ruben said. "I don't have the time for this."

"And I do?" Don retorted.

"I called for a substitute. That means you're free."

"I'll do what I can and get back to you," Don said, and he pushed Ruben back through the open doorway into the early morning fog. "What would happen if the district administration knew about you and Debbie in that motel room? You have to be careful who you trust."

Ruben face stiffened into his Hitler mask. "Remember who writes your evaluation."

Don judged the distance to the man's throat and imagined smashing his voice box with a quick jab. He'd enjoy watching the man squirm and twitch on the sidewalk as he died from lack of oxygen. No big deal; just one more body to dispose of. He smiled, stepped back and closed the door in Dr. Ruben's face.

When he reached the upstairs office, Don sat behind his brother's desk and called the district's substitute hotline. When the clerk answered, he asked who his substitute was for the day and was pleased to hear it was a skinny, five-foot-two, seventy-four-year-old, retired, lesbian science teacher who was as mean as Bill Romanowski, the NFL linebacker. He was happy now. With her in front of his students, the room would still be there tomorrow.

It was stuffy. The air wasn't moving in the room, and that was unusual. He leaned back in his brother's expensive office chair and saw that the grill to the vent above his head was hanging loose. There were fingertips visible inside the duct.

"Oh, fuck," he said. He quickly locked the office door and braced a chair under the knob. He climbed on top of the desk and peeked inside the duct, where he discovered Debbie.

He pulled her limp body out of the duct and onto his

shoulders. Taking care not to fall, he made it to the floor and carried her into the apartment, where he dropped her on the bed. Searching her skin-tight blue jeans, he found Dr. Ruben's wallet stuffed in a back pocket.

He made space for her in the walk-in closet, covered her with a dirty shirt and placed the laundry hamper in front of her. Then he reached up to loosen the closet's bulb until the light went out.

That would have to do until he could return to dispose of her. The easiest choice would be to move her to the oil derrick chamber.

Back in the bedroom with the closet door closed, he took a deep calming breath. A lump grew in his throat and tears filled his eyes. Not all of his affairs were worth remembering, but Debbie had been a sweet, sexy, passionate young woman, and the world would be a darker place without her.

He guessed there was one good thing from this discovery. He didn't have to worry about human hamburgers being served. But Dion and Rudolf didn't know where Debbie's body had gone. That meant someone wanted the body to be discovered in the club?

Why did someone want to see the Academe turned into a crime scene and closed?

He sighed. It was time to go home and slip into bed beside Lexi. Debbie would have to wait.

Chapter Twenty-Four

How do you tell your lover that you want her to help you dispose of another corpse?

After a few hours of sleep and some early afternoon lovin', Don broached the subject. "I need your help again," he said.

"Tell me this is a joke," she said after he finished explaining his morning.

"I can't do it again. How about Ricky? I'm sure he's disposed of bodies before."

The last number Don had for Ricky was disconnected, so Lexi went with Don to Ricky's house, but no one was home. Don left a note to call him as soon as possible—that it was an emergency and he needed Ricky's help—knowing full well that only Ricky's wife and oldest daughter could read. The rest of the family was illiterate.

That night, business was slow and time crawled on

its hands and knees until three a.m., when Lexi reluctantly helped Don move Debbie's corpse to the oil derrick chamber, where they left it rolled up in a blanket mostly hidden behind the last derrick.

"We can't keep going on dates like this," she said as they drove to his house again.

"I know. I'm sorry."

"You still liked her, didn't you?"

"Are you serious? How can you be jealous of a dead woman?"

"I thought so," she said, and crossed her arms, refusing to speak or look at him for the rest of the ride home.

Once inside Don's house, Lexi said, "I'm sleeping in a different bedroom tonight."

And that was it. Don was left alone, feeling like shit, while he stared at the blinking light of his answering machine telling him two messages waited.

One was Ricky telling him how he could be reached through a friend, and the other was from Mandy, telling him that Cut was missing.

It was almost five a.m., and he had to be at school before his first class started at eight. Maybe he could squeeze in a few hours of sleep first. He didn't want to deal with Cut right now, and he hoped she wouldn't turn up dead, too.

Don stripped as he walked down the hall to the master bedroom and tossed his clothes on a chair without turning on the lights. His body ached, and his eyes felt like they were full of hot, desert sand. All he wanted was to sleep, and he was tempted to call for another substitute. Slipping into bed, he discovered he wasn't alone. There was a naked woman waiting.

He smiled. "You changed your mind about sleeping alone," he said, and pulled her naked body against his.

He found her lips, and the kiss would have aroused a dead man from the grave. His hands explored her while her hands explored him in all the right places, and what he touched felt great, but this woman wasn't Lexi.

"I'm glad you're so happy to have me back in your bed again," Cut said. "I was tired of studying how to speak properly and listening to all those book tapes. Mandy is a slave driver. I was lonely and horny, and you're the only man I trust. Why can't I live here with you?"

Don slid away from her and out of the bed to turn on the nightlight on his side. Cut saw that he was still interested, and he had to admit he was tempted. He slipped on his pants to hide how he felt.

"You can't do this, Cut," he said.

"I'd rather go back to the streets if you won't have me," she replied.

He sat on the edge of the bed, and she sat up, revealing the naked upper half of her Victoria's Secret body.

Shit, he thought, and moved to a chair against the far wall.

"If I can't be a model," she said, "I want to be a hooker. And if you don't want me, then find me a nice pimp."

"I don't think there is such a thing as a nice pimp," he said.

"Sure there is," Lexi said, as she pushed open the bedroom door and walked into the room, also wearing nothing.

Good Lord, Don thought, closing his eyes in defeat and dropping his chin toward his chest. "How much did you hear?"

"All of it," Lexi said, "and I know the perfect pimp for this delicious young thing. Cut will make a fortune with that voice and diction training."

"I want you both to cover up," Don said in desperation.

"Why?" they both replied in unison.

"I can't think."

"That might be a good thing," Lexi said. "Men are so easy." She went to the phone on the table beside the bed and made a call.

While she waited for someone to pick up, Lexi said. "If you want to keep Cut alive, I think it would be a good idea to move her to the east coast. I know there's a job waiting for someone as sensual and sexy as she is with the same woman that represented me."

⧖

With two women driving him crazier than normal, he had to get out of the house so he dressed and drove to school earlier than planned, and the day went smooth until his fourth period, right before lunch, when Brent the

Brat, a student from hell, spit on the classroom doorknob. Not just any spit, but a thick, slimy, green gunk.

Then someone knocked on the door a few minutes before the class was to end, and Don, being closest to the door, opened it to find no one there. Students with hall passes often ran around knocking on doors, and sometimes a bold one would pull a fire alarm and sent the entire school out to the football stadium.

He picked up the intercom and reached the secretary in the office, who said that the vice principal in charge of discipline wasn't on campus. The only administrator available was Dr. Ruben—the one person who wouldn't discipline a student. He asked for Gunny to be sent, instead, and hung up the phone right as the bell rang.

All his students filed out, including Brent the spitter.

Don tapped on his desktop as he thought about how he could get Dr. Ruben to transfer Brent out of his class once and for all. When Gunny got there and heard what happened, he chuckled and joked that Don would need a big bribe to get Dr. Ruben to do anything. Don sat up and quickly called the office again. When Dr. Ruben came on the line, Don explained the situation and said, "I have your wallet. I'd appreciate it if you would cooperate and transfer this kid to another English teacher."

Ruben agreed immediately and asked, "Was Debbie anxious to see me again?"

"Absolutely," Don replied. He didn't think Ruben had killed her. "But she might not be back in town for a while."

When Don hung up, Gunny said, "You got him to cooperate over a wallet? That may have been a first."

Don told him about the motel room and the dancer. He didn't tell Gunny that the dancer was dead.

Chapter Twenty-Five

It was another payday at school, and that meant another visit to Don's mother. Don wasn't working at the Academe that night, but, after visiting his mother, he planned to drop by and make sure Dion and Rudolf hadn't discovered Debbie or added to the body count.

He tried to track down Ricky by visiting the junkyard in Irwindale where Ricky worked part-time stripping parts off wrecked cars and trucks, but his brother wasn't there. The junkyard man suggested Don try a friend of Ricky's, a biker named Nick.

Nick was a retired wrestler who weighed about four hundred pounds. On one arm, which was as thick as Don's thigh, he had a Harley tattoo, and on the other arm, he had a Hell's Angels tattoo. He had long, thick, gray hair and a dark beard that was constantly matted with dried food.

He'd met Nick before and found him to be a very

mellow guy—if you didn't stumble on his dark side. Nick was also a former Marine and spent most of his time working on bikes.

He'd served in Vietnam in a tank battalion, and he'd crushed all of the bones in his hand when he'd slammed a tank hatch on it while diving for cover during a mortar attack. Ricky mentioned once that Nick also worked part time collecting for a loan shark.

Nick's 1982 Harley–Davidson Super Glide II, the pride of his collection, sat in the middle of his living room amid oil stains on the bright orange shag carpet. There were dirty clothes and Coors cans scattered everywhere.

Many of the cans would end up flattened and glued on the walls, where Nick was creating his own stylized aluminum wallpaper. He'd already finished the living room and kitchen and was working his way down the hallway to the three bedrooms and two baths.

He also used Coors cans to hold up the top of his coffee table.

The inside of the house smelled of oil, stale beer and urine. Don had seen Nick piss out of an open window once.

Nick said he hadn't seen Ricky for at least a week and had no idea where he was.

When Ricky went missing, it usually meant one of two things: either he was in jail or shacking up with a woman he'd picked up in a bar. Later, Don would learn that his assumptions about Ricky were wrong.

His mother's cottage was crowded when he arrived.

"Wait out on the porch," she said when he knocked on the screen door. "My stitching club is having a meeting, and we'll be done in a few minutes."

It was a warm evening, so all her windows and doors were open, and the screens didn't filter out the voices from inside. Don sat on his mother's covered porch and stared at the beach on the other side of the boardwalk. The sun was setting, and the horizon was turning purple and pink with splashes of orange mixed in.

Eye candy wearing a string bikini skated by on Rollerblades, and Don enjoyed what she offered until she was out of sight. Lexi looked better, but she wasn't here.

"What's our first step to close down the Aphrodisiac Academe?" a familiar woman's voice asked from inside the cottage.

Forgetting about eye candy, Don became all ears.

"We'll start picketing this weekend," his mother said. "I've already contacted the Right to Life people and told them that the Academe financially supports a family planning clinic, and they have agreed to supply signs and people."

"Will we have to help them make the signs?" a sexy voice with a French accent asked.

Careful to stay in the shadows, Don moved to a window to spy on them. He saw Ms. Sheridan and the cop, Jane Eyre. The French accent belonged to the beauty with the incredible hair and legs that he'd seen at Jonah's funeral. There were a few other women he didn't know.

"What about you, Jane?" his mother asked.

Jane Eyre said, "I'm doing my job. If I can link Jonah Casanova's death to the Academe in some way, it will help us at least temporarily close the place while we drudge up something bigger." Don decided that, by standing next to the window, he was risking getting caught, so he returned to the lawn chair.

"Gabriella," Jane Eyre said, "have you discovered anything?"

"I think one of the bartenders is selling drugs," the French voice replied. "I saw him slip a little bag across the counter to a customer."

"I'll talk to narcotics and get them to plant an undercover detective in the club," Jane said. "Which bar was it? If we have evidence that the bartender is selling drugs, that will close the place down for sure."

"It was the bar closest to the entry, where customers pay the cover charge," Gabriella replied. Don loved the sound of her French accent, but he didn't like what she was saying. He'd have to talk to Ben so they could catch and fire the bartender before the undercover narcs arrived.

"What does this bartender look like?" Jane Eyre asked.

"He's tall and thin, and he wears several earrings in each ear. He also has a tongue ring and dyes his hair a different neon color every night. His hair was blue on Saturday."

Don knew exactly who she was talking about. That bartender was an ex-con, and he would lose his job as soon as Don reached the Academe and questioned him about whether or not any other bartenders were selling.

Deciding to slip away and return later to visit his mother, Don left the porch and hurried along the boardwalk toward the Academe.

He had to leap out of the way of a guy on a bike, which almost ran him down. "Watch where you're going!" he yelled, but the guy flipped him off and didn't slow down.

Back on track, he registered the giant hot air balloon a hundred feet up in the air.

"Oh shit," he said. He knew where it was coming from, but, before he could deal with that, he had to tell Ben about the bartender.

An hour later, while Ben took care of the bartender, Don went to the garden to discover several sexy-as-hell young women in string bikinis staring up at the balloon's basket.

"What's going on?" he asked.

They looked at him, and one said, "Oh, hi, Don. We're waiting for Dion to come down so we can go to work. Our customers should be here any minute, and we don't know why he's still up there."

The rope from the balloon led to an electric wench. Don climbed the stairs to the platform and activated the wench, and the balloon started its journey back to the deck. When he turned around, he found the girls had huddled together, looking like expectant kittens.

"What did Dion promise to pay you?" he asked.

"Two hundred fifty an hour," a blue-eyed blond said.

"I'm sorry, girls, but this job is over before it starts," Don said. "I want all of you to go in the club and have dinner on me."

"Hey, we came here to party and get paid," a brunette with a 38D chest said. "We're not going anywhere until Dion tells us himself. He's the one who hired us, and he's the one who has to fire us."

A chorus of voices supported her.

The basket touched down.

"If my brother's inside, I'm going to have a word in private with him," Don said. "You will all wait right where you are standing. When we finish talking, you'll get your shot at him."

Don opened the door and slipped inside. The door was on a spring and slammed shut behind him.

"Dion," he said, but before he took one step, he could tell that his brother wasn't going to respond. Dion was on his back in the middle of the basket looking very dead.

"Dion?" Don leaned closer to examine his brother. "If this is one of your practical jokes, you are going to really upset all of the lovely ladies out there."

Dion's eyes bulged from their sockets, and his face was swollen and purple. A thick, round, white shaft protruded several inches from his mouth. Dion's lips were split, and the blood had coagulated and scabbed over. Don hesitated before he reached out and tapped the broken end of the shaft with a fingernail to confirm that it was probably stone.

"Ladies," a man's voice said from outside, "what's

going on here?"

Don stepped away from his brother's body and pushed the door open just enough to peek out. There were two uniformed police officers standing just inside the gate.

"There have been several complaints about that balloon," the older officer said. "Who's in charge here?"

"Dion," 38D said.

"And where might we find this Dion?" the officer asked.

"We think he's in there with his brother Don," the blue-eyed blond said, and several of the others nodded.

Don closed the door and latched it. His mouth went dry, and his vocal cords froze. He staggered back a step, lost his balance and fell across his dead brother. When he rolled over to sit up, he was an inch from the stone shaft protruding from Dion's mouth. The pattern in the stone looked familiar—in fact, it looked like the marble Zeus was sculpted from.

"To tell you the truth," 38D said, "we don't know if Dion is in there. When we arrived, the balloon was already in the air. But we saw Don go in. He was looking for Dion, too."

Don couldn't let anyone find Dion like this. He took hold of the marble shaft and pulled. It resisted, so he grabbed it with both hands and heaved. It came free with a sucking pop. Yep. Zeus's penis.

Why would Dion be giving that a blow job, and how had he choked to death on it? His brother was an idiot, but he wasn't stupid.

The door rattled. "Hello in there," the older cop said. "We'd like to talk to you."

"Just a minute, officer," Don said. He used a napkin from behind the bar to clean the penis, wrapping it in another napkin before slipping it inside the crotch of his pants.

When he unlatched the door and stepped out, he opened his mouth to talk, but no words came out. Instead, he doubled over and vomited on the officer's spit-shined shoes. He gasped for breath and managed to say, "Can't breathe." The world swirled around him and everything started to turn dark.

From a distance, he heard one officer telling him to put his head between his knees.

"Hey!"

Don looked up, dazed, to see several old men entering the courtyard. One of them was the old man he'd seen walking his cat.

The cat man pulled out a wad of hundred dollar bills. "Dionysus said he'd be waiting for us. Where is he? Who do I pay?" The old man stared at the girls and pointed at 38D. "I want that one."

Holy shit! Don thought. A floating whorehouse! His face went numb, and he thought he was going to throw up again. Dion had really outdone himself this time.

"Are you going to be okay?" the older officer asked as he knelt beside Don. His younger partner pulled open the basket door and went inside.

Jane Eyre Patton walked through the gate. "What's going on in here?" she asked. "Has a citation been issued for this violation?" She pointed at the hot air balloon.

The older officer looked at Don and sighed. He pulled out his pad and pen.

"Does this mean we aren't going to get paid?" the blue-eyed blond said.

"Paid for what?" Patton asked.

"To go up in that balloon thing with these old men," 38D said.

The door to the basket opened, and the young officer stuck his head out. "There's a dead guy in here, lieutenant." He pointed at Don. "And this one was inside when we arrived."

"What's this?" Great Uncle Abraham had just entered the garden from the Academe's door. "I received a call about that balloon and came to see what was going on."

When he saw Don on his knees beside the older officer, he put both hands on his hips and said, "I expect an explanation."

Don shook his head and pointed at the older cop. "Please tell him," he said.

Three other men came through the gate—two were middle-aged and the third was at least seventy.

"Officers," Patton said, "detain all of these people for questioning."

With attention diverted from him, Don saw a chance to ditch Zeus's dildo. He retrieved it from his pants and slipped it through a gap in the balloon platform, where it splashed in the fountain Dion had built over.

Uncle knelt beside him, and Don felt the old man

put a gentle hand on his shoulder. "Is the dead man Dionysus?" he asked.

Don nodded yes.

"Did you do it?" Uncle questioned.

"No. Dion has been dead for at least a few hours, and I just got here from my mother's cottage."

Patton said, "Read him his rights and take him in for questioning." Don realized that she was talking about him.

"Don't worry, Son," Uncle Abraham said. "If what you say is true, the family's lawyers will have you out on bail in a few hours, and the charges will be dismissed. Do you have any witnesses that saw you at your mother's house, other than your mother?"

Don pointed at Patton. "Her."

Chapter Twenty-Six

Don was well aware that drinking like a fish would get him drunk. For about a decade after Vietnam, women and booze had been his way to escape the caustic memories he'd brought back from the war that sometimes felt as if they were dissolving him from the inside.

And during those years, his mother had called him every Sunday afternoon at the Academe and say, "Don Juan Casanova, this is your mother speaking, and I'm praying for you. Peter 2:11 says, 'I beseech you as strangers and pilgrims, abstain from fleshly lusts, which war against the soul.' Your father, may God forgive him, left us because he could not control his lust or his avarice."

And every Sunday after he got off work, he'd flood his body with Scotch, rebelling against his mother's self-righteous belief that God and Scripture was not just her salvation, but everyone else's, too.

In those days, when he got drunk, he seldom woke up alone. To stop the endless inebriated seductions, he'd learned to control his drinking. If he could stay away from the booze, he had more success staying celibate.

Now here he was, getting tossed in the drunk tank after being read his rights.

The drunk tank was no place to spend time sober. One drunk threw up and then fell asleep in his own pool of vomit. Another pissed himself several times. A third had endless diarrhea.

The high-priced squad of family lawyers didn't arrive until the next evening, and they came to bargain. The family would get him out of jail and cover the legal expenses if he agreed to become the general manager of the Aphrodisiac Academe. It was a quick decision.

An hour after being released, Don was sitting in front of the Aphrodisiac Academe with Uncle and staring at the yellow crime scene tape. A squad car sat in the empty parking lot with two officers watching.

"The lawyers are working on getting the club open," Uncle said. They were sitting in Uncle's chauffeured, dark blue, late-model, stretch Lincoln. "You know, of course, that you are responsible for all of this."

His uncle didn't need to pound the guilt spike in any deeper than it already was. He knew it was his fault.

"You should have agreed to run the Academe when your grandfather was murdered," Uncle continued.

"Enough!" Don replied. He opened the door and got out of the car. "I'm going to walk to my car. I parked between my mother's house and the club."

"We'll have the Academe open by Friday," Uncle said. "Be ready when the call comes. Oh, and—let the police catch the killer. You are no longer a Marine."

Don leaned down and looked at Uncle. "Once a Marine, always a Marine," he said. "If I catch the killer first, I'll deal with him." He smiled, turned away from the Lincoln and started walking.

He wondered what Uncle knew. There was a look in his eyes that told Don he was holding back.

Out of sight of the squad car, Don slipped around to the secluded loading dock wrapped in yellow crime scene tape. All he had to do was slip under it, unlock the delivery door and step inside to check on Debbie's corpse.

"Don't even think about it," a voice said from behind him.

Don closed his eyes and concentrated on slowing the sudden flutter in his heart before he turned to discover the older officer from the previous day. He now also recognized that the officer was a regular on Saturday nights.

"I don't know your name," Don said, offering a hand. The officer's shake was firm, and his hand was dry. Don's was clammy.

"Call me Hal," the officer said. He glanced at the security camera. "Everything is on tape. Lieutenant Patton had the system fixed and activated. If you go inside, you'll be charged."

"Do you know how long my brother was dead when

we discovered his body?"

"About six hours," the officer said.

"And she still kept me in the drunk tank."

"Don't blame the lieutenant," Hal said. "She can be a hard ass, but she knows what she's doing. She's a good cop, and fair. I think your uncle is the one who wanted you to stay locked up."

"The son of a bitch," Don said.

"I'm sorry about your brother," Hal said. "Whenever he saw me in the club, he always remembered my name and gave me at least one drink on the house."

"Dion was like that. I will continue his tradition when I see you in the club, officer. Now, if you will excuse me, I've got to be on my way."

The Mustang was parked at a meter halfway to his mother's bungalow. The meter had expired hours before, and there was a parking ticket under the windshield wiper. He'd give it to his Uncle and let him pay for it. That bastard owed him. When he retrieved his cell phone from the locked glove compartment and turned it on, there were a dozen messages, all from Lexi, wanting to know where he was and if he was okay.

If given a chance, he would have called Lexi when he was in jail and asked for her help, but the chance to make a call was never offered. He was convinced that was Uncle's doing, too. Now he understood why he had never been officially booked—not even fingerprinted. They read him his rights and then sent him straight to the drunk tank.

Lexi picked up on the first ring. "Good God," she

said, "where have you been? The news is full of Dion's death. They say it could be a serial killer because your grandfather and brother were both killed the same way. Are you coming home? God only knows how scared I was."

Paralysis grabbed his vocal chords, and his first attempt to answer her came out as a croak. He cleared his throat and explained what had happened and where he'd been all night. "I have something to do before I come home," he said. The sun was setting, and he was determined to get inside the courtyard after dark and retrieve Zeus's marble dildo from its underwater hiding place.

"I don't know what you're going to do, and I don't want you to tell me over the phone," she said. "No telling who might be listening."

"I'll be home as soon as possible," he replied. "And, Lexi, keep the doors locked."

⧖

An hour later, Don was hidden outside the courtyard's ten-foot wall. If he was caught this time, even Uncle might not be able to get him out of jail.

He made it to the top of the wall with help from a palm tree. Glancing around before climbing down into the courtyard, he spotted the one surveillance camera moving slowly in a 180-degree arc toward him.

He scrambled back toward the cover provided by the palm trees and lost his balance. One leg went on either side of the wall. He landed on his groin, and pain exploded inside his head. His lungs seized up, and his eyes watered as he struggled to breathe. With effort, he turned his face away from the camera and lay perfectly still on the wall's narrow top.

It took a few minutes for the camera to cover its 180-degree arc, and, before the camera returned, he climbed down into the courtyard. Moving quickly, he searched for an opening in the platform's base. He found one, and it wasn't locked. He opened it and slid into the brackish, scummy water covered with dying lily pads. It took him fifteen minutes to find it in the dark.

Dripping wet and covered in dark scum, he left the fountain, but had to wait for the camera to point in the other direction before climbing to the top of the wall. Needing both hands free to climb, he tried to put the dildo in a pocket, but none were deep enough to keep it from falling out. He slipped it inside the crotch of his pants again, but it slid down his pant leg.

The only thing he could do was put it in his mouth. He forgot to wipe the dildo clean and was rewarded with a mouthful of mud and pond scum.

Once he was crawling along the top of the wall toward the palm tree he'd used to climb up, a thick gray blanket of fog began creeping in from the ocean. The temperature was dropping, too, and goose bumps broke out under the soaked clothing. He started to shiver.

Thanks to his mother's insistence that he memorize passages from the Bible when he was a child, Proverbs 6:30 appeared in his mind. "Men do not despise a thief if he steals to satisfy his soul when he is hungry, but if he be found, he shall restore sevenfold."

He wondered what Zeus would look like with a seven-foot boner.

Reaching the ground outside the wall, he stepped from the shrubs with the marble dildo still in his mouth.

"My God, a mugger from the black lagoon," said the old man with the forty-pound cat, which hissed as the hair stood stiff along its spine.

Without saying a word, Don ran across the boardwalk to the sand and sprinted toward the surf.

"Help! Help!" the old man called out, but his voice wasn't very loud. He sounded more like a leaky tire.

Taking the dildo from his mouth, Don raced toward the Pacific Ocean, planning to throw the thing as far as he could into the water. But what if the tide washed it back up on the beach and someone found it?

Shit. He made a hard left turn and started jogging on the packed, wet sand closer to the surf. A wave roared in and boiled around his ankles, and he threw himself down to let the ocean rinse him off. Standing again, he raced toward the marina. He'd hike out to the end of the mile-long breakwater and throw the dildo in the ocean from there. With the fog coming in, it would be almost impossible for anyone to see him.

He reached the breakwater, and the car-sized boulders didn't offer a smooth pathway. If the fog had been any thicker, he wouldn't have been able to see his hand if he held his arm out. A foghorn sounded in the direction of the ocean, and, inland, he heard the jingle of reindeer bells.

With the fog stealing his ability to see where he was walking, he struggled to keep his balance on the large, helter-skelter boulders. He passed a figure in a bright, hooded rain slicker. The figure was facing the ocean, and Don thought he saw a fishing pole.

Aunt Eleanor's voice arrived inside of his head like a freight train. She was so loud, he couldn't understand what she was shouting. Sitting down on a boulder not far from the rain slicker, he cradled his head in both hands and tried to get her voice to go away.

He was thinking maybe it would be a good idea to see a shrink about this voice in his head when a blow landed against the side of his skull. The impact forced him face-down on the boulders as fireworks exploded behind his eyes.

"Hey, what's this fucking shit?" Don heard someone shout, and he struggled to put a name to the familiar voice. It wasn't Aunt Eleanor, and it wasn't inside his head. He heard a grunt, a scuffling sound, and what sounded like fists hitting a slab of solid meat.

Don struggled to stand, but his knees buckled. Ricky told him once that you never go down in a fight, no matter how hard they hit you. Once you were down, you were done for.

"You want to squab with me," Don heard the voice say, "you going to get jacked up."

Don shook his head and struggled to remember where he was. The world was blurry through his double vision. What felt like an anaconda dropped across his shoulders, and he attempted to push it away.

"Cool it, little brother. I'm the cavalry, not the Indians."

"Ricky," Don said.

"Who else would it be?"

Ricky was the black sheep of the family, but Don still loved him. Maybe because he identified with Ricky more than anyone else in his messed-up family. "Help me walk," Don said.

"That fag really jacked you up," Ricky said.

"How—" Don tried to ask, but he lost the train of thought.

"Sometimes I think it's safer in the joint," Ricky said, helping Don to his feet. "I got wheels. We're going to blow this dump. That was a mean hit you took, so you'll wear my brain bucket. You need it more than me. Besides, helmets are for pussies. But I ain't saying you're a pussy, so don't take it wrong." He gently guided Don along the rough, rocky surface of the breakwater toward the street.

When they reached a raked Triumph sitting by the curb, Ricky slipped the hard, black, steel helmet decorated with skulls and crossbones over Don's head and fastened the strap under his chin.

⧗

As Ricky drove, the roar of the Triumph's engine rattled Don's brain worse than the blow on the breakwater. Because of his wet clothing, the wind chilled him to the bone and he started to tremble. He had to wrap his arms around Ricky, and he could smell metallic sweat.

By the time they reached Don's house, Don was numb from the cold, and his arms felt like they had frozen stiff. Ricky stopped the Triumph thirty yards from the gate because a car was blocking the entrance. He gunned the bike, ready to spin around and retreat if there was any sign of danger.

The car door opened, and a woman got out. She was dressed in a miniskirt that revealed great legs topped by a matching figure. "Is she one of your women?" Ricky asked. "She has a set of jugs on her that look like the headlights off of a 'fifty-nine Cadillac. I wouldn't mind some of that action, my own self."

Ricky raised his voice. "Hey babe, you looking for company? Them headlights real or plastic?" He made a vulgar sound deep in his throat and waggled his tongue.

The woman walked toward them, hips swaying with each step.

"Shake it baby, just don't break it," Ricky said.

"Asshole!" The woman had a Cuban accent. "Your mother should have washed your mouth out with soap and sandpaper." She looked at Don. "Is that you?"

As numb as he was from the cold, Don still managed to croak out, "Ricky, meet your youngest brother's wife, Maria."

Maria's features were lean. She had brown eyes, a thin nose and a small mouth with full lips painted the color of ripe plums. Her dark, curly hair fell to her shoulders.

"I didn't believe the news when they said you were a suspect in Dion's death," she said. "You loved him as much as you love his children." She pointed at Ricky. "I didn't know there was another brother. Dion never mentioned him. Why didn't anyone tell me?"

"Ricky had the same mother but a different father," Don said.

"Teach him some manners."

"What are you here for, Maria?"

"My children need a father," she said. "Dion was never much of one, but you have been when it was called for. They need you."

He was tempted to ask if she needed him, too, but getting in bed with Maria was asking for hell. "I will always be there for them," Don said. "You know that."

"Dion was an asshole," she said. "I think he got himself murdered just to make our lives miserable. Me and the kids want to stay with you until we get used to him being gone. Not that he was around all that much when he was alive."

The back door of the Mercedes opened, and Don could see her children. The youngest started getting out. Maria turned, pointed a finger at him and said, "Get back in that car and close the door. You don't move unless I tell you to."

The boy started crying, but did as he was told.

"I think you need to be with your family in Miami," Don said. "I'll buy the tickets."

She stared at Don for a long moment before she

said, "Fuck you! You're an asshole, too. I don't need a bastard like you in my life. Go to hell and take this cock-breath, garbage mouth with you."

"You want I should knock her upside the head?" Ricky asked. "A bitch with a mouth like that deserves to get smacked."

Maria gave Ricky the finger and spit on the ground in front of the Triumph. She turned her back on them and, with swaying hips, walked to her polished, black Mercedes and sped away. The children's sad faces were lined up across the rear window, watching Don as the car vanished from sight.

⧗

Ricky popped open a sweaty Coors can and drank it empty in one long gulp, immediately popping the next one right afterward. Don had taken a hot shower and changed his clothes and now sat across the table from Ricky sipping a glass of pinot noir. Lexi was asleep, and he didn't want to bother her.

"Now that I can think, tell me how you arrived at the right time to save my ass," Don said.

"I was out of circulation in the nuthouse in Camarillo. I turned myself in when my wife went to live with Rudy." He buried his face in his hands and wove his fingers through his thick, curly, greasy, dark hair.

"How did that happen?"

"His wife died of breast cancer."

"Rudolf the rat catcher had a wife?" Don said.

Ricky nodded. "And once his wife was six feet under, he had to go and steal mine." He looked up, agonized. "I had to go, or I would have killed both of them. But I can't go back in the joint. I'll kill myself first."

Don couldn't think of anything to say. His older brother probably had two or three women on the side as mistresses. He often bragged how his "thing" was getting longer and thicker from all the extra action.

"I had to talk to someone, so I called Nick, and he said you came to his house. The junkyard bull told me you talked to him, too. I got worried that you were in some sort of trouble, because you never did that before, so here I am. Nick gave me a ride from the nuthouse after I checked my own self out. I got to the Academe just in time to see you take off running down the beach. You looked worse than I feel. It almost killed me, keeping in sight of you. Then I saw this dude hit you with something and you fall down. The rest is history."

"Live here with us," Don said. "The mental hospital is no place for you."

A smile split Ricky's face, revealing his missing teeth and a few of the chipped survivors stained yellow-brown from excessive coffee and cigarettes. He had given up on false teeth, because he kept losing them on his regular weekend benders. He finished the second can of Coors and removed a third from the six-pack.

Don stiffened. He'd forgotten about the dildo, and he didn't remember what happened to it.

"What is it?" Ricky asked, sounding worried.

Don explained.

Chapter Twenty-Seven

For the first time in his life, Don felt bored, and he hated it. He'd quit his teaching job and finished his first week as general manager of the Aphrodisiac Academe. The job was everything he thought it would be—the worst.

He didn't get to interact with people like he did as a teacher or maître d'; he was basically just a watchdog, making sure everyone else did their job properly.

At least he got a huge desk and private bathroom. At the moment, he was in his private bathroom staring in the mirror. His eyes were bloodshot, and, for the first time ever, he had puffy, purple bags forming below them.

In the last seven days, he'd only taken Sunday off, but had spent more time sleeping than doing something with Lexi.

The other six days, he'd worked sixteen-to-twenty-hour days and slept in the upstairs bedroom. At the moment, "numb" and "depressed" weren't enough to describe his mind and body.

Ricky had moved into one of his bedrooms, but Don hadn't seen him once in the last seven days. If Lexi hadn't been performing in the club and staying at her condo nearby, he wouldn't have seen much of her, either.

The intercom phone buzzed and pulled him out of the bathroom.

"We got a problem, boss," said his cousin Trent, Uncle's youngest son. Trent was now the acting bar manager, and the bartenders and cocktail waitresses had a bet going that Trent wouldn't last through the month—that he would quit or get fired or Don would murder him.

Don sighed. "What is it this time?" he asked. Through the intercom, he could hear customers cheering and one lonely, sad-sounding boo in the background. It was Monday night football in the bar.

"There's a tough-looking broad selling fifty-cent tequila shots in the women's bathroom."

"Throw her out," Don said.

I'm a guy," Trent said. "She's in the lady's room."

"Fuck!" Don slammed the intercom phone into its cradle, hoping the noise would give Trent a headache. He hurried to the bar, where the dance floor, stage and DJ's booth were empty, but the bars were three deep with football fans swilling cheap booze, eating free food—peanuts, pretzels, sardines and cubed cheese—and yelling at the half-dozen televisions mounted high on the walls.

Trent was staring at a long line waiting to get into the lady's bathroom.

Don spotted Norman standing at the front and

pushed in front of him, Norman shoved him back. "Hey, wait your turn, scumbag."

In response, Don slammed Norman up against the wall with one forearm braced against his throat. Norman lifted a fist.

"If you throw that fist at me, it will be your funeral," Don said. "What kind of flowers would you like me not to buy?"

Norman looked confused, and his fist unfolded and dropped to his side.

"Get him out of here," Don said.

Trent and one of the club's new bouncers stood behind Don, who glared at his cousin. "Why did you let this idiot in? He's been eighty-sixed for months."

"I looked at his ID," Trent said defensively. "It said he was twenty-four. I didn't know he wasn't supposed to be in here."

"If you had looked at the mug shots on the bulletin board in the downstairs office, you would have known, and the ID was fake. Do you want to get the Academe closed down again? Take the bouncer with you to escort Norman out of the club, and make sure I never see him in here again, or you will both be out of a job."

Trent looked shocked, and he stammered, "My dad wouldn't like that."

"I don't care what Uncle Abraham likes. I run the Academe, and he has no say over this establishment."

Norman was sputtering about his rights. Don put his face an inch from Norman's and kept his forearm pressed hard against Norman's throat. "Shut up!" Don said.

Norman's words died on his lips while his terrified eyes darted about, looking for a way to escape the madman who had him pinned to the wall.

"What are you waiting for?" Don snapped at Trent. "Someone to come along and suck your worthless dick? I want this idiot out of the club ten minutes ago."

Trent stammered, and his face turned brick red. "You're in our way, cousin."

Don shoved Norman at Trent, and the bouncer took hold of him and dragged him away. Don glared at the few faces still standing in line. Half of them had melted away. "What are you waiting for?" Don asked. "An invitation to leave? Get out of here. This bathroom is off-limits." Once the hallway was empty, Don pushed his way into the women's bathroom, where he discovered two women and three men waiting in line in front of the sink for shots.

"I want everyone out of here but her," Don said, and they all hurried out.

The woman calmly filled a Dixie cup with cheap, drug-store Tequila and held it out for him. "It's on the house," she said. "You look like you could use one."

Don couldn't help it. His anger evaporated, and he started to laugh until his eyes flowed with tears. She was dressed in fancy cowboy boots, and she wore a leather miniskirt with a sheer, lacy blouse that revealed skin like tanned leather. She was a walking billboard for melanoma. Her face was round like a cantaloupe, and she was in good shape, with a cute figure and slender legs.

Gaining control, Don wiped away the tears and

asked, "How old are you?" Her baked-on tan made her look older than she was, but he guessed that she was younger than 18.

"You don't like my booze?" she asked.

"You can't sell liquor in here. Get off the counter and leave, or I'll call the police and have you arrested."

Don took one of her full bottles, unscrewed the cap and started to poor it down the drain.

"Hey, you can't do that," the girl said. "I paid good money for that tequila. I'm going to sue you for destroying my property."

"Why don't you do that? Find yourself a four-hundred-dollar-an-hour ambulance chaser. But what I'm going to do is count to five, and you better be out the front door of the Academe before I finish, or I'm going to drag your skinny, little ass to the freezer and throw you in there to cool off for a few hours."

She hopped off the counter and started for the door.

"Stop!" he said.

She turned with a hopeful expression.

"There's a skinny guy outside hiding in the bushes. His name is Norman. Introduce yourself to him. You two might just be made for each other."

Her mouth dropped open.

"Go, before I change my mind and put you in the freezer instead."

Alone in the bathroom, Don finished emptying several tequila bottles and tossed the empties in the trash can. Finished, he leaned on the counter and stared at his angry face. This bullshit job was getting to him. He wasn't going to survive to summer.

He heard skittering on the tile floor and looked in time to see a rat run under the closed door of a shitter. He hadn't seen Rudolf since Dion had been murdered. He'd called the phone number for Rudy's Exterminators, and there had been no answer or answering machine to leave a message on.

Maybe Rudolf was also no longer among the living.

Chapter Twenty-Eight

Not liking what he was about to do wasn't going to stop him. The door to the basement liquor storage was locked and braced shut with a chair under the doorknob. Once Don was confident that no one would easily discover what he was about to do, he knelt in front of the wine racks, felt for the hidden switch and unlatched the shelf unit. The air coming up the shaft was cool and smelled slightly rancid.

That was not a good sign. He'd hoped the cool, dry air in the chamber would slow up Debbie's decomposition.

Slipping a bottle of Cognac from the rack, and holding it by the neck like a club, he walked softly down the long flight of stairs. The deeper he went into the earth, the thicker the stench of death grew, until he had to take out a handkerchief and cover his mouth and nose.

But that didn't help, so he stopped to uncork the

bottle of Cognac and drenched the cloth with it. Breathing the brandy worked, and he went deeper until he stood in the dim light surrounding the pumping oil derricks.

When he reached the last oil derrick, the mystery of Rudolf's whereabouts was answered. The exterminator had been exterminated.

He was dead and lying next to Debbie. Someone had pulled his pants down around his knees, and his mouth was a bruised and bloody mess just like Dion's had been.

That ruled Dion and Rudy out as the killers, leaving only Uncle Abraham. But how was an old, frail man like him going to pull off so many killings successfully? And what was his motive? Had Rudy threatened to reveal the oil derrick room? Even though Don still favored Norman, the evidence suggested strongly that he couldn't be the killer.

Don didn't like the possible answer. Uncle had a partner, and Don thought it might be Trent.

The bottle of Cognac begged to be tasted, and Don took a long swallow. The liquor burned all the way to his stomach. Another generous slug spread the tingling numbness he longed for down his legs and arms.

Ricky, still agonizing over his wife's infidelity, was in no shape to help him get rid of two bodies, and Lexi wanted nothing to do with it.

That left Ben. Together, they could solve this mess. He took another sip of the Cognac, turned off the lights and made his way up the stairs and out of the tomb.

When he reached his office, his desk phone was

ringing. It was Lexi. "Come to my condo tonight," she said. "I want to see you. Do it for me."

Chapter Twenty-Nine

Lexi said, "I'm going to Europe on tour for the summer, and I leave in three weeks."

"Europe," Don said. He'd just walked into her condo from the garage. This couldn't be true.

"What about us?" he asked. This wasn't right, he thought. Since he'd been twelve, no girl had ever left him.

Her eyes shifted from his. "An old friend arranged the tour through someone who owns a record company in New York and wants to produce my second album. I'll be an opening act in Ireland, England, Portugal, Spain, Belgium, Germany, Italy, Switzerland, Greece, Sweden, Norway, Finland and Russia in front of more than a million people.

"I've added some original songs to my act. Haven't you noticed? I've been singing them at the Academe. The producer likes my material, and we are leaving for New York tomorrow morning to start recording so the record will be ready to sell on tour."

"You said *we* are leaving tomorrow morning." Don said. "Is the other half of that we me?" He didn't want to be a struggling, celibate hermit again. He wanted to be with Lexi. He loved everything about her.

"I'm glad you made it home so we could share this last night together." Her high cheekbones glowed, and her quick, hyper movements revealed how excited she was. She turned and walked to the kitchen, where she'd been cooking dinner.

He followed her, and the smells in the kitchen told him that she had put a lot of effort into the meal. "Who is the old friend?" he asked.

"I used that Moosewood cookbook of yours to plan this feast," she said. "I drove to Costa Mesa and shopped at Mothers and brought back a surprise. I've been in the kitchen for hours. I want tonight to be special."

He cupped her chin with one hand and put a finger over her lips to stop her. "Who is he?"

"I think its Billy Joel," she said.

"Not the singer," he said. "I want to know who your old friend is."

"Tell me you're happy for me," she said, and the look in her eyes spelled desperation.

He leaned down and kissed her on the lips. "I'm happy for you," he said, and decided he wasn't going to become emotional. He'd been through too many short-term relationships with far too many women to fall apart because another one was ending, even if it was with the woman of his dreams—the one he thought he'd be spending the rest of his life with. At the same time, he thought his heart was going to shatter like glass.

"You could go with me," she said. "After all, you already quit teaching, and you hate your job at the Academe. It isn't like you need it." But when she said this, she turned away from him and focused on the food she was preparing for their farewell dinner. She didn't really want him to go with her.

"I'll drive you to the airport tomorrow," he said, "but I won't be going. We both know that."

Later that night, after dinner, after the lovemaking, and when Lexi was asleep beside him, he lay awake, wondering if how he felt now was how Giacomo Casanova had felt in 1750 when he broke up with Henriette.

Chapter Thirty

Don climbed mountains to get closer to God and escape the fake world of glass, concrete and steel. It was also how he dealt with painful emotions.

Mount Baden-Powell was named after the founder of the boy scouts. It was located in the San Gabriel Mountains that separated the coastal valleys from the desert in Los Angeles County.

From where he lived in La Habra Heights, it took more than an hour to reach the mountain. It'd been a month since he'd hiked Baden-Powell, and he'd been with Lexi on that trek.

Before he left, he put the Academe's restaurant manager, in charge. He hadn't bothered to let anyone else know what he was doing, and he didn't care if an earthquake opened up the ground and swallowed the club and everyone in it.

Once he reached the Baden-Powell parking lot, he

hiked more than four thigh-burning miles of switchbacks along a narrow trail to the ninety-five-hundred-foot peak, passing old growth evergreen trees on loose shale that offered treacherous footing if you left the trail carved into the steep slope.

Above nine thousand feet, there were a few two-thousand-year-old twisted yellow pines along a narrow ridge that led to the summit.

It was a weekday, and Don hadn't seen anyone since he'd left the Jeep. That was the way he wanted it.

The mountains weren't the safest place to be alone. During winter, when there was black ice on the trails, the news would sometimes report an injured or dead hiker who'd slipped and plunged into a canyon.

One summer, Don read about a troop of Eagle Scouts hiking from one end of the sixty-mile-long mountain range to the other. One walked away from the camp at night and had never been found.

There were black bears up here; cougars and rattlesnakes; and, on rare occasions, the most dangerous predator of all: man.

Don's own close call with death here had been several years earlier, when he and Ben lost the trail because of snow, slipped on a slick spot, and skidded down the mountainside into a tree. Now Don carried a sixty-pound survival backpack with a one-man shelter, a sleeping bag, a change of clothing, food, cooking gear, water and several supplies.

He seldom hiked alone in the mountains, and had never camped overnight by himself.

At the summit, Don slipped out of the backpack, and, sixty pounds lighter, bounded around like a man on the moon. The top was about forty degrees colder than the parking lot, and he dug through the backpack for his cold weather jacket.

His intended campsite was in a hollow surrounded by bent trees that helped block the frigid night wind.

He ate lunch with the Mohave Desert spread out toward the east and the ten-thousand-foot-high Mount San Antonio to the west.

After eating and taking a nap in the sun, he shouldered the backpack and moved to the campsite, where he discovered the remains of a fire ring. He searched the surrounding mountainside for dry kindling.

With the arrival of night, he sat by the fire, soaked up its heat, thought of Lexi and felt lonely. If she had been with him, they would have zippered their sleeping bags together and cuddled through the night, making love and sleeping.

Don heated and ate his dinner, and, as the fire died, he stared into the fading flames and ached from memories of the ski trip to Canada with Lexi.

The only sound was the whistling wind. The sky treated him to a visual feast of stars that were so close, he was tempted to reach up and grab one.

Instead, his hand went to the reassuring handle of the Bowie knife in a sheath strapped to his belt. Without a weapon, he wouldn't be able to sleep.

Continuing to watch the night sky, he spotted the red and green lights of passenger jets headed toward LAX.

With the fire dead, he stood in front of his small shelter and let the sharp wind nip at his face. Inside his sleeping bag, the wind buffeted the sides of his small tent, and he lay there staring at the yellow fabric close to his face. The Bowie knife was out of its sheath and under his jacket, which he'd rolled up as a pillow.

He couldn't sleep. He felt too exposed inside the shelter, so he gathered up his knife and sleeping bag, slipped his feet into his unlaced boots, and left the shelter to find a secluded place in the nearby brush. In Vietnam, when a bunker or a foxhole didn't feel safe, he'd slip away from the others to find a more secluded place to spend the night. He had to admit that being alone spooked him, and he wished Lexi was there.

Chapter Thirty-One

The sound of cloth ripping woke him. Don had no idea what time it was. His first thought was that it was a bear getting into his tent in search of something to eat. He crawled out of his sleeping bag and pulled on his boots. He held the Bowie in one hand and turned on his flashlight, bursting from the brush and running toward the tent, waving the light around and screaming to scare the bear away.

But it wasn't a bear.

It was a big man in a dark brown down jacket, leather ski mask and black knit watch cap pulled tight over his head.

The man lifted a pistol and fired a bullet past Don's ear. Don slid to the side as he aimed the bright beam of the flashlight into the man's eyes. He then threw the light away from him and tumbled in the other direction. The man fired the pistol repeatedly at the light as it spun through the darkness.

After rolling for several yards, Don scrambled to his feet and ran. Another shot hit a tree close to his right shoulder. Don dropped to the ground, curled into a ball and rolled down the steep slope. His left shoulder hit a tree, and his body rebounded to the right. His arm went numb from the blow and he lost his Bowie knife.

He was covering distance too fast, and he had no idea where he was headed. If there was a cliff, death was almost certain. Then he hit something hard with his head.

⧖

The sun's heat and a woman's voice woke him. He hurt all over.

"Can you move?" she asked.

He opened his eyes and thought that he must have died and gone to heaven. It was the women from his grandfather's funeral—the one with the incredible hair and legs that would steal a man's breath.

Her hair was loose, and she held a crumpled canvas safari cap in one hand. Her blue jeans were tucked into high-top hiking boots. But it was her fascinating eyes that truly captured his attention. She reached out and cautiously touched his face with her fingertips. He flinched, and she jerked her hand back. "Sorry, you have a nasty cut on your cheek."

"I saw you in my mother's house, and I don't bite," he said, and closed his eyes. "Do you?" The sun felt good, and he carefully moved his limbs. Pain reported in from all over, but nothing seemed broken. He was no stranger to physical pain, but it had been a long time since he'd hurt this badly. He'd heard her name at his mother's house, but he couldn't remember it now.

On impulse, he reached up, slipped a hand behind her head and pulled her down to kiss her. She resisted at first, but then gave in and kissed him back. She tasted sweet, and his hands felt their way under her jacket and shirt to explore her warm, smooth skin.

It was nice to be alive. The kiss ended, and she rolled back onto her haunches. "Wow," she said. "I didn't expect that. I guess you're going to live." She let out a nervous laugh and pushed that incredible hair out of her eyes.

"Sorry about that," he said. "I thought I might be hallucinating and figured there was only one way to find out if you were real. Thanks for not hitting me. Are you from France, and what's your name? I should at least know the name of the woman I'm kissing."

She blushed. "My name is Gabriella," she said. "I found out you were up here from your manager at the club, and I've been looking for you for hours.

"Come here," he said. "I want another kiss. It's better than aspirin." There was nothing like a beautiful woman to help you forget about your broken heart, he thought.

"I didn't come here for that," she said. "I came to talk to you. It took me awhile after I arrived in California to get the courage to do this, and once I arrived, I couldn't risk that the fear would return, so here I am."

Seeing that he wasn't going to get anywhere, he said, "You were at my grandfather's funeral and mother's house, scheming to close the club. Who are you and what do you want?" He sat up and noticed that he didn't have his boots on. They must have come off as he was rolling down the mountainside.

"I was visiting your mother to get to know her," she said.

Why would anyone want to know my mother? he thought. "I want to get back to my camp and see what I can salvage," he said. "Did you find some boots and a knife, too, by chance?"

She held the Bowie out, and he took it. "Help me up, please," he said.

Every part of him hurt as he stood, and the headache that had been waiting to ambush him rushed into his head with a vengeance. He almost blacked out, but she let him lean on her for support.

"Are you sure you are going to be okay?" she asked. "It wasn't easy to get down here. You came to a rest on a shelf after some thick brush slowed you down enough to stop you. If the shelf and that brush hadn't been here, I don't think anyone would have ever found your body. The footing on the climb up will not be easy, and yes, I did see a pair of boots."

"Let me lean on you, and we'll take it one step at a time," he said. "We'll get there. I'm tougher than I look."

The climb wasn't as bad as he thought it would be, except that his stocking-clad feet felt every twig and pebble. All the early-morning workouts, daily walks and jogging would pay off, because he'd recover faster.

They found his boots, and he put them on after shaking them out to make sure nothing with a stinger had moved in. The camp was a disaster. The tent was shredded, the bear canister open and the food gone. His backpack was still in good shape, and she helped him gather his gear and stuff it in.

"I don't understand why you left the canister open," she said.

"I didn't. The man who attacked me did that. I think he wanted people to think a bear killed me. He took a shot at me." He pointed at the bushes, where they would find his undamaged sleeping bag. "I was sleeping over there, away from the tent."

"Someone tried to kill you?"

"It's not the first time," he said. He started to kneel so he could roll the sleeping bag up, but when his left knee touched the ground, a sudden jolt of pain paralyzed him for a moment.

"I'll do that," she said. "Do you think this person was the one who killed your grandfather and brother?"

"Maybe."

She started to roll the bag from the bottom. Something moved under it. Forgetting his pain and injuries, Don grabbed her and yanked her away from the bag. Trembling, she pushed into his embrace and wrapped her arms around him to hold on. They both stared in horror at the rattlesnake that appeared from under the bag. Its head faced them, and its tail vibrated in a blur as it vanished into the brush.

Don brushed her long hair from her neck, and he caressed her skin with his lips to taste her scent. This reminded him of Lexi. She twisted around, and their eyes met, inches apart. Lips met and hands explored. He undid her jeans and slid his fingers down across her flat belly.

She pushed away from him and stepped back. The flush on her cheeks and the wild look in her eyes said that she was as turned on as he was. He took a step toward her, and she held up a hand. "No," she said. "That's not why I came looking for you."

"But you want it as much as I do," he said.

"Of course—" Her words died.

"Why are you here?"

"I wanted to talk."

"Like you talked to my mother?"

"Something like that."

He sighed. "I don't understand."

She shrugged as if that didn't matter. "Do you want my help or not?" she asked.

☒

It was a long, painful, limping trek down the mountain to the parking lot.

"How do you want to do this?" she asked.

"I think I can drive. We'll go to my house. Will you follow?"

She nodded.

"Where are you staying?"

"A hotel."

"Save the money and move into one of my bedrooms."

She started to protest.

He held up a hand to stop her. "I'm not going to make any more moves on you unless you let me know it's okay." Then he remembered. "But my older brother Ricky is staying at my place, and he can be a bit crude."

She sashayed to her car, where she stopped and looked back at him with flirty eyes. "Your brother doesn't need to know there's nothing going on between us," she said. "As far as he's concerned, we are an item, and I'm off limits. With your history with women, that should be easy for him to accept."

"Are you sure there's nothing between us?" he asked.

"You already have a girlfriend in New York," she said.

"You sure know a lot about me."

She returned to him and touched the side his face that wasn't injured. She leaned forward and kissed him softly and fleetingly on the lips.

She stepped back, an amused look in her eyes. "It isn't that I'm not attracted to you. But I am in love with another man, and it is because of that love that I have traveled thousands of miles to find out more about you and your family.

"It is regrettable that Dion died. He was a cute man who suffered greatly at the mouth of his beautiful wife. I find her hard to like."

"You know Maria?" She kept surprising him.

"Yes, of course I have met her, too. And I know

where your house is. I will check out of my hotel and move to your house, as you have suggested. I'm looking forward to meeting Ricky, as I have heard so much about him from your mother. I'll cook dinner for you both tonight."

"What else can I offer the woman who saved my life?" he asked.

"I hardly saved your life," she said. His reward was a promiscuous smile that kept him supplied with erotic fantasies on the drive home. What a strange encounter, he thought.

Chapter Thirty-Two

The fat girl stood in the dirt with her thumb out.

Ricky yelled, "Stop!"

Without thinking, Don's foot hit the Mustang's brake pedal, and he guided the car to the dirt shoulder and came to a stop about twenty yards in front of the hitchhiker.

Ricky reached for the cold can of Coors between his feet and took a long swallow. Don thought about the fine for having an open container in the car.

"Back up," Ricky said.

Don shifted to reverse, and dust spiraled in front of the car as they backed toward the girl. He guided the Mustang to a stop beside her. Ricky opened his door and patted his lap. Smiling, the girl slid in and sat where he'd indicated.

This might not be a good idea, Don thought.

Ricky pulled another can of beer from its plastic web and popped it open for the girl. She took it and drank the can empty. Then she belched.

Obviously, this was his brother's kind of woman.

"Let's go," Ricky said.

The tires were hardly back on the road before Ricky had his hand under her short skirt, and she almost dropped the second can of beer he handed her.

"See that motel over there?" Ricky asked. "Pull in there." He nibbled the girl's earlobe as she finished her second beer, and her face flushed brick red when Ricky's hand moved further under her short dress. Her eyes turned glassy, and her mouth dropped open.

Ricky held out his free hand. "Spot me enough to pay for the room and pick me up in three hours," he said. "I'm good for it." He tapped the side of his seat as a reminder of the Glock hidden beneath it.

"I got it," Nick said from the backseat.

"Take shotgun." Ricky said, and, when he got out with the girl, Nick moved into the front.

Pulling away, Don watched the two of them French kissing in front of the motel from the Mustang's rearview mirror. Why had he agreed to let Ricky and Nick be his bodyguards? They were cheap—costing only an endless supply of cold beer and cigarettes—but he hadn't counted on their ability to drink a dozen beers each, just during daylight hours. At night, the intake doubled, and they could go through several packs of cigarettes daily.

It was Gabriella's fault that he'd caved in and hired them, and now Don understood why Ricky's wife had always supplied him with an ample quantity of beer and cigarettes. If he went without either for even a few hours, he turned into a gargoyle with attitude. The beer and cigarettes were his pacifiers.

The first night Gabriella stayed in the La Habra Heights house, the three of them sat around the table eating continental food cooked by her able French hands. After dinner, they'd gathered on the upper deck, where she pried answers out of Don about Jonah and Amanda. She didn't reveal why she wanted to meet him and his family, and avoided every attempt he made to find out.

"What are you doing?" Don asked. "Writing a history of my family?"

"Maybe," she replied.

The bodyguard idea appeared over dinner a few days later. She was ten years younger than Don, but acted as if she were his older sister.

He protested at first. "The house has an alarm system, and I can take care of myself."

"Like you did on that mountain?" She challenged.

⏳

Don and Nick returned after the allotted three hours to pick up Ricky. Pulling into the motel parking lot, Nick leaned across and honked the horn. Ricky came out of one of the bungalows, a leftover from the Route 66 era.

Nick moved to the backseat, and Ricky slid into the front. He took a warm beer from the depleted six-pack on the floor, popped the top and sucked the foam as it boiled out. There were a dozen more six-packs in the trunk. Even warm, any beer was better than no beer.

Ricky drank half the beer, and then howled like a wolf. "That was one blinkity blink hot piece," he said. "She gobbled me good."

"Does she have a name?" Don asked.

"I never asked," Ricky replied.

Gabriella had dressed the bodyguards in dark Brooks Brothers suits with black shirts and white ties. Both wore mirrored aviator sunglasses at all times. Nick carried his Colt .45 in a shoulder holster under the suit jacket. Ricky's small back holster held a compact Glock 38.

Don thought they looked like lowland gorillas dressed in suits, and he was starting to feel like a mob boss.

⌛

A week after the bodyguard routine started, the four of them gathered at three a.m. in the Academe's upstairs office. Nick had arrived with a flatbed truck and parked it by the loading dock. Lashed down on the back of the truck were a half-dozen fifty-five-gallon metal drums full of bleach and sand.

Wearing gas masks with charcoal filters, they stuffed the corpses into the barrels. Nick never said what he did with them.

Even with the constant companionship, Don was lonely for Lexi, and it wasn't easy having beautiful, fashionable Gabriella around.

"Imagine what the world would be like if we could clone you," Don said to Gabriella as they stood on the loading dock and watched Nick leave.

"You'd regret it," she said and smiled.

Don stared at her and thought he might be falling in love, but they were probably all falling in love with her.

Nick had been the first one to make a move on her, and, a second later, he found himself flat on his back with a bruised jaw. It turned out that Gabriella was a master of French kickboxing.

He never touched her again, but did shave off his beard when she asked.

"Now that you aren't hiding behind all that facial hair, you look handsome," she said.

Ricky kept his hands off of her, but flirted outrageously in his rough ghetto style. She handled him as if she had been born to his world.

Chapter Thirty-Three

It was during Sunday brunch, on Ricky's shift—his second week with bodyguards—that Ben stopped at the front desk. They hadn't talked much recently.

Ben knew who Ricky was, but he'd never met Nick, and Gabriella's presence must've really tickled his curiosity.

Ben leaned close to Don's ear and whispered. "What's going on?"

"My brother and his friends needed jobs, so I invented one for them," Don lied. He'd rather run nude across the ice in Antarctica in the dead of winter than admit that they were his bodyguards.

"That's really strange," Ben said. "Couldn't you have created jobs in the kitchen? The suits are quality threads, but Ricky and the other guy look like three-ton rhinos in ballet outfits. I'm more interested to hear about this woman with that hair and those legs. Wow!"

Don knew Ben was fishing. He decided to change the topic. "You going to improv this Tuesday?"

"I get it," Ben said. "You don't want to talk. Okay, be that way." And he left.

Eve walked through the front door into the lobby. She was barefoot, dressed in laced-up shorts and a halter top that revealed a lot of toned abdomen. This was her first day back after two weeks, and she was scheduled to start working the front desk in an hour. She stopped next to Don, close enough that he could feel the sun's heat radiating off of her exposed skin.

"I have news," she said, and leaned closer to him until he smelled the ocean in her blond hair.

"You've been on the beach," he said.

"Newport," she said, "and I wasn't alone."

Don's mouth went dry. He was afraid to ask. "Let's step into the storeroom and talk about this there," he said.

She flashed a smile that revealed perfect, white teeth. Her lips were glazed with a pale peach lipstick. Taking Don by the hand, she led him toward the recessed door in the shadows behind the front desk.

"It's okay, Ricky," Don said.

Ricky winked and smiled a lecherous, gap-toothed grin.

Once they were alone behind the closed and locked door, she said, "You owe me big time."

Oh, crap, he thought. He'd asked her to go out with his former principal and then forgot to tell her he quit.

She cocked her head at a flirty angle. "You promised

a reward if I had good news."

"You name it, and I'll do it if I can," he said.

"I managed to book a room in the same hotel on the same weekend the graduating seniors from your high school's ASB were having their end-of-school dinner party with their advisor and parents."

"You didn't—" He couldn't say another word.

She shook her head. "I didn't have to," she said. "I booked the room on the tenth floor and had my timing down perfect. It was easy. Their reservation was at the rooftop restaurant in that hotel. It just so happens that one of my friends is a senior at your high school, and she let me know when they arrived.

"I was in the hotel room with you-know-who slobbering on my neck when my friend called the room, and then I told the old guy that I wanted to eat first before you-know-what could happen. My friend had everyone in front of the elevator in the lobby when the door slid open to reveal me in his arms while I was giving him lots of tongue. He even had a hand under my blouse. You should have been there. It went down like something out of Mission Impossible."

"Holy shit, Eve!" he said. In his wildest imagination, he never expected Eve to go this far, but, after she had listened to his complaints about the idiot for so long, he shouldn't have been surprised.

Her blue eyes radiated cool sparks of excitement and pleasure. "Call someone you know who works in the district office, and you'll hear that he isn't principal anymore."

She moved closer to him until their bodies touched, and she stood on her toes. "And now, I want my reward," she said. Her pale, peach-colored lips touched his, and she tasted sweet and fruity.

Without thought, his hands moved to the exposed skin at the small of her back and slid down over the lacy fabric of her shorts. Her tongue darted into his mouth. Her hands reached for his crotch and discovered how excited he was. She pulled his zipper down and undid the belt and top button. They staggered against the shelves closest to them, and the bottles rattled against each other.

He thought about what kind of low-life he would have to be to take advantage of this sexy young woman half his age when he was still in love with Lexi and in lust with Gabriella, and the flood of guilt short-circuited his libido.

"What's wrong?" she said, her heavy, hot breath caressing his neck. They had slid down to the floor, and she was crowded between him and the shelves behind her. Half of their clothing was off.

"You are beautiful," he said, "and I love you." He kissed her forehead as if she were a child. "But I don't want to lose you as a friend."

The passion and heat fled from her eyes. Avoiding his eyes, she slid away from him and started to dress. He reached out and touched her bare shoulder, and she jerked away. "You hurt me," she said. "I feel dirty. You have no idea how long I've had a crush on you. You saved me from a rotten, murdering bastard. Why do you think I went out with that disgusting, dirty old high school principal? I did it because you're my hero and I love you."

"Eve," he said, "I'm sorry."

"Don't touch me," she said with words that were shards of ice, and her eyes filled with tears. She got up, hurried to the far end of the storeroom and exited through the door that led to the kitchen.

He sat on the floor surrounded by bottles of beer, wine and whiskey, and it was the wrong place to be to feel like a puddle of crap.

Chapter Thirty-Four

Sunday evening, Don told Gabriella about Eve. They were sipping warm wine in the cool night air on the patio outside of his woodshop.

She reached across the patio table and covered one of his hands with hers. "You did the right thing, even if she did take it wrong."

"It's going to take more than that to make me feel better," Don said. "I should have had sex with her. You have no idea how long I've fantasized about her."

"You fantasize about every woman you like. Deny that you don't think about me the same way. Men fantasize about women all the time. If you had given in, it would have turned out worse later.

"By doing what you did, I think you helped Eve grow up a little. Sure, it was a painful lesson, but this is how a woman learns to survive."

"Or jump in the ocean and drown," he said.

They sat in silence. What Gabriella said made sense, Don thought. After the incident at the Well of Purity in Vietnam twenty years earlier, he'd dreamed about being the knight in shining armor. He'd tried to play that part for abused women ever since, and it often turned sour when he ended up sleeping with them.

He wondered about Cut and how her new life as a high-class escort in New York City was working out.

"It's time for me to get some sleep," Gabriella said. "I'm on in three hours."

Ricky was already in bed, and Nick was on bodyguard duty.

⌛

That night, sleep eluded Don. Women he'd seduced and women he wanted to seduce tumbled through his mind like a troupe of Chinese acrobats.

When an out-of-the ordinary night noise creaked, clicked or ticked somewhere, his imagination put the tumbling women on hold and focused on the sound.

Ever since Lexi abandoned him, he had tossed, turned and sweated through the nights—twisting the sheets and blankets into knots and sometimes kicking them to the floor. Instead of going after the blankets to insulate himself from the cold, he would be too groggy to move and would get up at dawn, chilled to the bone and shivering.

The pitter-patter of bare feet on his bedroom's wood floor warned him that he wasn't alone, and he reached under the pillow for his Bowie knife before he slid from the bed to the floor without making a sound.

Before the intruder reached his bed, he was behind them with his knife against their throat. It didn't take long, even in the dark, to discover that it was Gabriella.

Alarmed, he stepped away from her far enough to escape the reach of a roundhouse kick. "What's wrong?" He hurried back to the bed and burrowed under the blankets, pulling them up to his eyes and wrapping them around his body.

Her answer was to crawl on the bed beside him and tug at the blanket. "It's cold," she said. "Stop hogging them all to yourself."

He had wrapped the blanket around him as if it were a cocoon. "Okay," he said, and relaxed his lock hold on the blanket. "What are you doing here?"

"I could hear you tossing and turning all the way to my room. How can you sleep like this? These sheets are soaking wet."

"Sometimes I think too much, and I sweat a lot when that happens. I don't have this problem when I'm with someone."

"Where are the clean sheets?"

He told her, and it took her a few minutes to change the bed. When she finished, she joined him again between the sheets, and his heart climbed into his throat, sounding, to him, like the drum line of a high school band.

"That's better," she said.

"That's a matter of opinion," he said.

"You said you sleep better if you aren't alone, so you aren't alone. Go to sleep."

"Yea, but I usually don't sleep much when I'm with someone, either."

She was quiet for a moment. "Oh," she said, but she didn't leave. Instead, she cuddled her body against his. "You are hot, like toast that just popped out of the oven."

An elephant had parked itself on his vocal chords, and he couldn't speak. The last time he had sex was the night before Lexi flew out of his life. That was weeks ago.

She felt his crotch with one hand, and then pulled it away. "I'm not here for that," she said. "So flip the switch. You're a big boy."

"Is this some sort of test or something?" he asked.

She chuckled, rolled over on her side and faced away from him.

He reached out and ran a hand down her back. She was naked. "Do you always get into bed naked with guys and tell them not to touch? Just in case you haven't looked at yourself lately, you look better than most Playboy centerfolds."

"Shut up and go to sleep," she said.

"How do expect me to do that?"

"Pretend I'm your mother."

"Are you crazy? My mother never slept with me."

"Not even as a little boy?"

"I tried cuddling with her once when something scared me, and she shouted scripture at me and said men were born to sin. She sent me back to my room, where I learned the hard way not to be afraid of the boogeyman."

He glanced at the glowing numbers on the bedside clock. "It's almost midnight," he said, hoping she'd either leave or seduce him. "You go on watch soon."

"Don't worry about it. Nicky said he'd cover for me. How old were you when your mother did that?"

"I think I was four or five." Don was pretty sure that if she told Nick to jump off a cliff, he'd jump.

"Then pretend you are four or five again, and do what that little boy would have done if his mother hadn't rejected him."

"I'd pee my pants, but I sleep in the nude just like you do."

"Smart ass. You know what I mean."

He decided that Gabriella had to be certifiably crazy to be doing this. He rolled over on his side so his back faced hers, and then moved so their backs touched. The smoothness of her skin and the warmth of her body was comforting. It felt good not being alone.

"I grew up with three younger brothers and a twin sister, and we all shared one bed," she said. "It wasn't until my oldest brother turned thirteen and my sister and I were sixteen that my mother made a place for us in the bathtub so we could sleep separate from the boys." Her voice started to fade as she fell asleep. "It was a small bathtub."

"Are you a virgin?" he asked.

She didn't answer, and her shallow breathing told him she'd fallen asleep.

Not wanting to disturb her, he lay there like a petrified log and listened to every sound. There was no way he was going to fall asleep with her in bed, naked, beside him. He was already imaging what her body would feel like under his hands. It was driving him crazy not to touch.

Time dragged, and one hour felt like three as he stared at the clock.

She made a noise and rolled onto her back. He turned and pulled the sheets back to stare at her.

"Al," she said, sleep talking.

"I'm here," he replied, wondering who Al was and wishing it was him. No longer able to resist, he carefully placed a flat hand on her abdomen.

"Al," she said again, breathily. Her eyelids fluttered, and her breathing grew raspy. Light from the clock and from the stars and moon came through the picture window and French doors.

Dad's name is Al, Don thought.

He stared at the flickering pulse in her neck and watched its beat increase as his hand slid toward her pubic hair. She sighed and rolled on her side facing away from him, and his hand slid to her hip.

He stopped exploring her body even though he was tempted. Something wasn't right. He'd been so focused listening to her that he'd stopped listening to everything else. He took his hand off of her and, sitting up, focused all of his senses on the house.

"What is it?" she asked, suddenly awake.

"When the house is closed up at night, the air gets dry and stale. This air is fresh, and I don't smell any cigarette smoke."

She propped herself up and looked at the clock. "It's almost three o'clock," she said. "I told Nick that he could go outside on one of the balconies to smoke. He's always smoking. Why isn't he smoking now?"

"Exactly," he said.

"I left my gun in my room," she whispered.

"Take my weapon," he said, and, leaving the bed, he knelt and tilted the two-drawer night stand and reached underneath. A hollow space underneath it kept a modified forty-five-caliber Ingram submachine gun and two fifty-round clips. He handed the machine gun and both clips to her.

"I don't know how to use this," she said.

"How about my Bowie knife?"

"No. Show me how to use that." She pointed at the machine gun.

He handed the Ingram to her and watched her explore it with her hands. "I can't find the trigger," she said.

"I removed it. You'll find a notch instead. Insert a finger in that notch and pull the bolt back. When you release, it will fire the entire clip. Aim to the left of your target, and the weapon will kick to the right. It's capable of cutting a man in half."

"Disgusting," she said, and handed the weapon back. "I'll trust my feet."

"You do know that we are both naked," he remarked.

"Hmm," she replied. "Do you have dark-colored t-shirts? I didn't bring any clothes from my room."

Don pulled on dark gray sweats, and she slipped on an extra-long black t-shirt of his that hung to her knees and made her look sexier than she already was.

He groaned.

"What?" she said.

"Isn't there anything you can wear that doesn't make you look hotter than a volcano?"

She gave him a dirty look. "Men," she said, and stood to one side of the door leading out of the bedroom. Staying to the right of the door, she opened it, and Don rushed past her into an empty hall with the Ingram ready.

Gabriella followed. The great room was empty, but the sliding glass door to the upper deck was wide open— the source of the cold air pouring in. She sprinted past Don to the patio door and put her back to the wall next to it. Don moved to the kitchen and checked behind the counter.

"Hey," Ricky said.

Don spun around, ready to pull the Ingram's bolt and fire all fifty rounds in the clip. Ricky stood in the entrance to the bedroom's hallway, wearing light blue pajamas with angels chasing cocker spaniels across a sky covered in fluffy clouds.

"What?" Ricky asked in response to the expressions on Gabriella's and Don's faces. "These PJs aren't mine. They are my oldest daughter's. She gave them to me when she graduated from high school. Where's Nick? I checked his bedroom, and he wasn't there."

Then Ricky saw that Gabriella wore one of Don's t-shirts. "Wow!" he said. "What have you two been doing?"

Then he saw the Ingram in Don's hands, and Ricky quickly moved behind the couch, where he knelt down.

Don faced Gabriella. "I'm going out first," he mouthed without sound. She nodded, and he rolled through the opening to the deck with the Ingram leading the way. He immediately tripped over Nick's body, only to automatically drop and roll away from it and come up in a crouch with the Ingram ready.

Squatting and waddling like a duck, he backed under the eaves and pressed against the prickly stucco wall.

He thought the killer was in the house or on the roof. From his peripheral vision, he saw Gabriella's face asking questions. She hadn't moved. He looked at her and shook his head. "Stay inside," he mouthed. "The killer might be in there."

Ricky appeared in the opening to the patio, and his eyes widened when he saw Nick. A breath later, he vanished from sight. He was only gone for a moment, and then he was back with a knife from the butcher block in the kitchen.

Gabriella knelt and crawled out to the patio to lay beside Nick and feel his pulse. She held up her blood-covered hand so Ricky and Don could see. Someone had cut Nick's throat.

Don jabbed toward the interior of the house and mouthed, "I think the killer is inside somewhere."

Ricky and Gabriella nodded, and Gabriella returned inside and joined Ricky.

Don crawled to the railing and looked down at the ground-level concrete deck below. One of the redwood patio lounges was broken—the padded ticking lay a few feet away on the grass. Someone had fallen on the lounge and broke it. He examined the balcony railing and found a section that was cracked.

Nick had managed to put up a brief fight, and it was obvious he'd knocked his killer over the rail to the ground below. Leaving Nick's body behind, Don went back in the house and slid the glass door closed and locked it. Nick and Gabriella were still in the great room.

"You two need your weapons and go to your rooms together," he said. "I'm going to turn on the alarm, and then we search the whole house. Once we are satisfied the killer is not in the house, I'll call the police."

"Can we dress first?" Gabriella asked. She was shivering.

Ricky held out a pair of her blue jeans, a blouse and one of her stylish jackets. She took them and dressed without removing the t-shirt.

A search of the house found no intruders, and the alarm had not been compromised.

"I need a smoke," Ricky said. He looked at Gabriella first and then at Don. When he didn't hear any protests, he shook a Camel out of its pack. He took a deep drag on the filterless cigarette and let the smoke curl out of his nose.

"It's time for me to make the call," Don said.

"I don't think that's a good idea," Gabriella said. "We should dispose of Nick ourselves."

"No," Don said. "Enough people have died. You or Ricky could be next. It's time to involve the police, regardless of the outcome."

"We have to get our story straight first," she said. "No one can know about the bodies we already dumped."

"Yea, we need to get our hustle the same," Ricky said. "I'm not going back in the slammer for anyone. Someone killed Jonah and our brother and attempted to kill you more than once. We tried to protect you on our own. We failed. That's all they need to know."

Gabriella plopped on the couch, looking resigned. She sighed. "It's time," she said. "Because when the police arrive, they will discover who I am."

Both Ricky and Don looked at her.

"I'm Don's sister," she said. "We both had the same father."

"When did you discover that?" Don asked, stunned.

"The results arrived yesterday," she replied.

Chapter Thirty-Five

"I never saw the son of a bitch who tried to kill me," Don said.

"Where the hell do you get off withholding evidence in two murder investigations?" Lieutenant Jane Eyre Patton asked.

"How am I supposed to know they were connected, and what good would it have done me to report an attempt on my life? Would the police provide around-the-clock protection for me?"

"When the alleged attempt on your life took place, was there anyone else at your house besides you and the victim, who you claim was your bodyguard?"

"No," Don lied. "There were just the two of us. Didn't you read the report?"

Ricky and Gabriella had taken Don's Jeep and driven to Lexi's condo—she had left him a key—where they would stay out of sight for a few days.

Before he'd called the police, Don, Ricky and Gabriella had cleaned the inside of the house so only Don's fingerprints would be found inside. Since Gabriella hadn't touched anything on the balcony other than the gash in Nick's neck, they didn't touch the crime scene.

"The sheriff's report says that you alleged this was the third attempt. The first was a few months ago on the King Harbor breakwater, and the second was a few weeks ago on top of Mount Baden-Powell," Jane Eyre said. "What the fuck were you waiting for?" Her jaw stuck out like a bullfrog's, and she looked like she was ready to snap Don up.

"We ran a check on this so-called bodyguard of yours, and he has a record as long as an elephant's trunk. Come on, Casanova, you're holding back. Stop thinking like a Marine. Three people are dead. Although losing a low-life like Big Nick Ogden wasn't much of a loss."

"Hey, watch it, Lieutenant. He was trying to protect me, and he was a friend."

"Why not hire your buddy Benedict Wallace? He is much better qualified than Ogden. I've seen the redacted records the military was willing to share on both you and Wallace, and, from the little I read, you two together are a killing machine I wouldn't want to stick my dick into."

Don was tempted to mention that she didn't have a dick—at least he thought she didn't.

"How many kills did you and Wallace make in Southeast Asia?" she asked. "And what did you do for those years where you vanished off the earth without a trace?"

"The answer to both of those questions is not relevant," he said. "Plus, that information is classified. Talk to the Pentagon or the CIA. I can't tell you, or I'd end up in prison." He folded his arms across his chest and stared at the wall behind her.

"I bet you wake up every night with nightmares from what you did over there," she said. "I think you like killing people. Maybe you killed Ogden for the rush?"

"Charge me or let me go, Lieutenant," he said.

⧗

A half-hour later, he was out on the street. Uncle Abraham has sent the family lawyers to get his release. It was also possible that the local police chief owed Uncle favors.

Don took the bus to the Aphrodisiac Academe and got off a block from the club, planning to walk the rest of the way. In sight of the front door, he ran into the old man with the fat cat. The old man had a portable oxygen tank strapped to his back this time, and the clear plastic oxygen line curled over his ears and into his nose.

When he saw Don, the old man started to giggle, and his flabby face trembled. He rummaged in a coat pocket and dragged out an empty long-stemmed pipe and stuck it in his mouth. He started to suck on the pipe, and the saliva that bubbled out of one corner of his mouth ran down his chin.

"How do you like sleeping alone?" the old man asked, starting to wheeze.

Don stopped and stared at him. "What did you say?"

"Lexi is gone, and you're feeling sorry for yourself. I took her away from you. When she was recording her new record, I was with her. When she flies to Europe, I will be with her. Every woman has a price."

Don felt his hands curl into fists. He took a step forward, and, like magic, two men who looked like linebackers for an NFL team appeared on either side of the old man. It was obvious that they were bodyguards.

Don stopped and eyed the old man's oxygen line. "I'm sure you can't get it up, and you probably miss your tobacco even more," he said. "Lexi told me about the old, rich guy who could only hold hands. That's you, isn't it? How much time do you think you have left? When you're dead, she'll come home to me." He walked past the old man and continued on his way to the Academe.

"Come back here," the old man tried to shout, but he didn't have enough wind in him to pull it off. "Get him!" he ordered the bodyguards.

Don spun around to face the two linebackers as they moved toward him. "You have a choice," he said. "Stop where you are or keep coming and end up in a morgue."

"And he's not alone, gents," Ben said from behind Don.

"We were a two-man killing machine in Vietnam," Ben said. "Snipers. We spent two years together on missions in the jungles of Laos, Cambodia and Vietnam. I miss those days. Come on, let's get this fight over with."

The bodyguards had stopped about two yards from Don and Ben, and they looked uncertain.

"Call off your dogs," Don said to the old man. "What does Lexi charge you to watch her strip and touch her—ten or twenty grand a night? I'm guessing that, with your heart condition, Viagra would kill you."

"You can't talk to me like that," the old man said.

"You've got money," Don said. "I know all about the power of wealth. Look around you. My family owns most of the property on this street."

He belatedly noticed two men sitting in a late-model, four-door Ford Taurus painted a dull, dark, bluish gray parked on the other side of the street. It shouted undercover police.

"Come on," Ben said. "Let's go inside. This isn't worth our time."

"Did you notice the undercover police, too?" Don asked under his breath.

Ben nodded, and, once they were inside the club, they turned around and watched through the glass. The old man and his guards continued down the sidewalk away from the club. One of the guards twisted a knob on the oxygen tank. The old man's legs wobbled, and the guards both offered him arms for support.

"I'll bet those two are counting the days until that old man dies and the fat paychecks stop," Ben said. "What a shitty life."

It was a pitiful sight. "Shoot me if I get that bad," Don said.

"As long as you do the same for me," Ben replied.

"How long has the club been under surveillance?"

"Since Dion was killed," he replied. "I've also

noticed that when you come and go, you have a tail. I'd be careful what you say and do."

Don wondered if the police had been watching his house in La Habra Heights too. Even if they had been, that wouldn't be an easy surveillance with the distance from the street gate to the house on top of the hill surrounded by several acres of trees.

"There have been three attempts on my life in the last few weeks," Don said, "and that old man might be behind them." The old man had money and was jealous of Don because of Lexi. If the man had connections to organized crime, he could have put out a hit.

"That's possible," Ben said, "but it doesn't explain Jonah and Dion. Why would he want them killed?"

"There's a police lieutenant who's convinced I had something do to with Jonah's and Dion's murders. You have time for a drink? I'll fill you in about my mother's schemes to shut down the Academe, and my new sister, Gabriella."

They went into the bar and found a secluded table, where Don relayed everything except what happened to Teddy, Debbie and Rudolf. Ben had always been a good listener.

Chapter Thirty-Six

Ben dropped Don off on Palos Verdes Drive West, and Don walked the rest of the way to Lexi's condo alone. Ben assured him that they had successfully evaded the police tail.

It was two-thirty a.m., and it had been a long day at the Academe. When he reached the gate-guarded complex where Lexi lived, he walked past the condo to the cliffs overlooking the Pacific, where he stood and watched the surf crashing against the rocks below.

There was no moon, and a thin veneer of high-altitude clouds blocked most of the starlight.

It occurred to him that standing here alone at the edge of a cliff was an opportunity for the killer to have another shot at him, and he nervously scurried back to the condo.

He'd given his key to Gabriella, so he couldn't let himself in. Standing on the small porch, he rang the doorbell and listened to the muted tune of The Pink Panther theme song.

No one came.

After a long moment, he rang the bell again. Still no response. A spot between his shoulder blades started to tingle. He glanced around at the shrubbery and shadows, looking for the killer. Had the killer followed Gabriella and Ricky here? Were they dead?

He knew Lexi kept a hidden key buried under a rock in the small, walled patio area behind her condo. Once inside the confined space of the patio area, he stopped and listened carefully, searching everywhere with his eyes. The patio didn't offer any hiding places. Satisfied that he was alone, he found the key, entered the condo from the back door and was startled by the warning wail of the alarm system. He hurried to the alarm's panel, flipped up the cover and punched in the code. With the alarm off, he went through the house, turning on all the lights and looking for bodies.

He didn't discover any bodies, much to his relief, but he wondered where the hell they had gone.

He hadn't been in Lexi's condo since she'd left for New York, and, by now, she was on her way to Europe with the old man and his cat—following her dream and singing her heart out to thousands in one city after another. No way was he going to sleep here. He could sense her in the air, and it would be worse in the bedroom they'd shared.

In the garage, he found her Porsche waiting patiently, and he knew where she hid the keys. With the push of a button, the garage door clanked open, and he backed out to the street. With Cut gone, Mandy had a spare bedroom free, and Torrance was much closer than La Habra Heights. Mandy wouldn't mind, but maybe he shouldn't include her in his troubles. She was one of his best friends, and he didn't want to make her a target for the killer, too. He could sleep at the Academe.

He ached for Lexi. They understood each other and meshed like the gears in the Porsche.

Halfway to the club, he changed his mind again, but didn't know where to go. He felt tears flood his eyes, and he hated feeling sorry for himself.

He pulled to the curb and parked in an empty spot next to a meter. There was a French restaurant across the street, and an older couple was coming out. Was that Great Uncle Abraham and Ms. Sheridan? He rubbed his eyes as if they were deceiving him and lowered the window. When he looked again, they were getting into a late-model, four-door Buick sedan. Sheridan had opened the passenger door for Uncle, and he was slipping inside. After she was behind the wheel, Don stiffened abruptly when he witnessed them lean toward each other and kiss.

"Disgusting, isn't it?"

Startled—and with his heart racing—Don jerked his head to the right, expecting to meet his killer.

A man knelt beside the passenger door, looking at Don. At the sight of him, Don's breath froze in his throat, and he couldn't think or move. The man reached in, unlocked the door and slipped into the bucket seat next to him.

"I always suspected they had a thing going, even when she was living with Jonah on the Aphrodite."

"Dad?" Don said. His father had been gone for almost thirty years.

"Sorry I haven't been around," his dad said. "I couldn't help it. Your mother drove me crazy, and I had to leave. Don't tell her that though. It would hurt her feelings."

Don couldn't believe it. The man sitting next to him didn't look like he was sixty-seven. His hair was still dark and combed straight back, and he smelled of Old Spice Classic aftershave, just like Don remembered. His dad's eyes were still amber-colored, too.

"I understand," Don heard himself reply. "Mom drives me crazy, too."

Chapter Thirty-Seven

"I met a young woman named Kelly about fifteen years ago," his father said. "She was eighteen then and already a professional dancer at the Rio in Vegas."

Don knew his father had traveled the world. Wherever there was a casino; a private, high-stakes card game; or a racetrack, he went, and he'd lived off of his winnings without taking one penny from the family trust Amanda had set up.

Once a family member became addicted to the allowance from the trust, Amanda owned them. For this reason, Don had also never dipped into his monthly share. He'd earned everything he had himself.

They were drinking decaf and eating apple pie in a 24-hour coffee shop, and his dad was doing most of the talking. It was as if his father had gone for a walk and just came back.

"Was Kelly one of your women?" Don asked.

"We ended up friends," dad replied in his usual soft-spoken voice, "but we didn't start that way. For the last fifteen years, she has kept me up-to-date about you and Dion. Her sister lives near Manhattan Beach, so I financed Kelly's trips from Nevada to Southern California. When I lived in France, we corresponded often. About a year ago, I bought into a business venture in Australia and moved there. Then, a few weeks ago, I attempted to get in touch with Kelly, but couldn't. I called her sister and her friends in Vegas, but no one knows where she is. It's like she dropped off the planet, and that isn't like her. Kelly was a social creature who loved dancing and her friends with a passion few people have."

Don was sure his dad was talking about Debbie. "What was this friend's full name?" he asked.

"Deborah Kelly Quinn," he replied.

Don was queasy. How was he going to tell his father that his friend had been murdered?

"I had to keep moving, son," he said. "If any of the casinos I worked caught me counting cards, they'd have faxed my face to every major casino in the world, and it would have been the end of my freedom from Amanda."

"I take it you did well for yourself," Don said.

"Yes, and over the years I invested in businesses. I own bars in Paris, London and Hong Kong. I won a Sydney bordello in a high-stakes card game, and then, with profits from my bars and the bordello, I bought another bordello in Macao. My girls are first-rate, and my little business empire turns a nice annual profit."

Dad stopped and watched Don's face for a moment.

"I can tell what you are thinking, and you're wrong. I don't dump my hookers like Jonah did. I set up a retirement plan for my girls, and there are cash incentives if they stay healthy and in shape for their clients. I provide a safe place for them to work, and it comes with health benefits. By the time they hit forty, they are set for life and can retire if they want to."

Don hadn't been thinking anything like that. "You said Jonah dumped his girls. What do you mean?"

"And prostitution isn't illegal in Australia or Macao."

"Dad, I'm more interested in Jonah dumping his girls. Tell me about that."

"You didn't know he did that?" he said. "After Amanda closed the bordello on the boat and let her girls go, Jonah took over the business himself. The girls who lived on the boat with him were his hookers. He sampled them often, and, when he got tired of them, he threw them out and replaced them with fresh meat. I never liked that. He recruited most of his girls in Europe."

"Europe?"

Dad nodded. "He preferred European women because he felt they were more open to sex than American women. Jonah couldn't keep his hands off of his own merchandise, and he didn't use condoms and never had a vasectomy. If he knocked up one of his hookers, he sent her back to Europe with a one-way ticket and a severance package that wouldn't last a year."

"Did he murder any of them?" Don asked.

Dad looked at him oddly. "What a horrible question. No, Jonah wasn't a killer. He was a self-centered, selfish prick with an appetite for younger women." He signaled the waitress for the check.

"During one of our last phone conversations, Kelly told me that Jonah had been murdered. It was a shock to her that the old man who called himself my father was dead, but he probably deserved it."

"What do you mean 'by the old man who called himself your father?'"

Dad looked as if he had just sucked on a bitter lemon. "I don't want to talk about that here. Let's go someplace private, and I will tell you everything."

"Your room at the hotel?" Don asked.

Dad shook his head. "No, someplace else. I don't trust hotels. It's too easy to bug them, and I've acquired a few enemies over the years—crooks that I ruined for cheating at cards."

"I have a friend who lives in Torrance," Don said.

"A woman?" he asked.

"She's one of the cocktail waitresses at the Academe, and she doesn't work until eight o'clock tonight. You'll like her."

"Is she your woman?"

"Her name is Mandy, and I'll tell you about her in the car."

⧗

Twelve hours later, Don was alone on the bed in Mandy's spare room, staring at the ceiling with his thoughts swimming around what his father had told him.

Mandy had been in the shower when they arrived. She'd appeared at the door with wet hair and wearing a knee-length terry cloth bathrobe. The three of them sat around the round Formica table in a small alcove off of her kitchen.

Dad laughed when Don told him how his mother and Ms. Sheridan were leading a group of women plotting to close the Aphrodisiac Academe.

"Never happen," he said. "Have you read the trust Amanda set up for the family?"

"I skimmed it when I was in college," Don said, "but I've forgotten most of what it said. I thought it was a lot of legal mumbo jumbo."

"Let me explain," Dad said. "I'm sure you don't know what I'm going to tell you about Amanda's childhood. Most of her children and the children of her siblings probably don't know this, either.

"Amanda wanted to make sure all of her family would benefit from the financial empire she built long after she was gone, but she also wanted her siblings to pay for the way they treated her when she was a child. Her mother gave birth to Amanda when she was fourteen, and no one knew who Amanda's father was. But all of Amanda's younger brothers and sisters had the same father, because, by then, her mother had married a door-to-door salesman who treated Amanda as if it was her fault she was born outside of marriage. He set the tone for his children to look down on her. Then, when she was twelve, he sexually molested her. Two years later, she ran away from home. I think you know the outline for the rest of her life."

"I think she carries a lot of anger with her," Mandy said. "More tea?" She left the table to bring more hot water.

"Great Uncle Abraham and the others have been looking for loopholes in the trust so they can break it after Amanda's gone and get their hands on everything— cutting Amanda's children out. But anyone in the family who challenges the trust is cut out and can't work in the family business."

"Sounds like they hate their own sister," Mandy said.

"They do," Dad replied. "But the money she pays them is enough that they can't afford to leave, because it pays for their upper-middle-class lifestyle. They are all hypocrites, and that is another reason why I left like I did. I didn't want to end up like them."

"Do you know about the oil derricks?" Don asked. Dad nodded.

"Oil derricks?" Mandy asked.

"Uncle Abraham knows, too," Don said. "Maybe he found his loophole in the family trust, and that's why Jonah and Dion were killed."

"Or maybe Abraham is blackmailing Amanda because of the oil," Dad said.

"Oil," Mandy said. "What oil? I didn't know your family was into oil, too."

"It's complicated," Don said. "I promise to tell you all about it over dinner some night soon."

"Kelly also told me you had a day job that wasn't linked to the family," Dad said.

"I talk too much," Don said.

"Get out, Son, while you can. Get out of the family business before it destroys you. Get a life of your own like I did. You'll be a lot happier."

Mandy reached across the table, put a hand on top of one of Don's hands and squeezed.

Don sighed. "I had to quit the day job," he said. "Uncle Abraham set me up, and I had no choice. If I didn't become general manager for the Aphrodisiac Academe, he was going to let me rot in jail and go bankrupt paying for my own lawyers."

"There might be a way out of that trap," Dad said, "and I can help."

Chapter Thirty-Eight

Don awoke thinking about his Dad and smelling pan-fried potatoes with onions. The old-fashioned wind-up clock ticking loudly beside the bed said it was almost one in the afternoon.

With a groan, Don pushed himself into a sitting position and struggled to pull on his cotton boxers.

The only bathroom was off the hall between the two bedrooms, and it had a chipped, white, cast iron bathtub; a toilet; and a sink—all crammed in a tight space. The sink was only large enough to wash his hands, so he knelt beside the tub, positioned his head under the tap and turned on the faucet.

The water gushed out ice cold; he stifled a gasp and held his breath until he'd had enough. He used a threadbare towel about the size of tissue to dry off and walked to the kitchen, where Mandy was standing at the Formica counter watching his dad cook the potatoes.

In another skillet, veggie sausages fried, and eggs waited in a bowl on the counter.

Mandy hadn't been a vegetarian when they'd first met, but over the years—after the rape—she adopted Don's diet. She turned and inspected Don.

"To think that it took your Dad to get your clothes off for me," she said. "I know what I'm going to get you for your next birthday—new boxers that are not stained and threadbare. I think your waist is thirty-two or thirty-four."

"Second guess," he said, and yawned. "Do you have larger towels? I want to take a shower."

"Come with me," she said, and he followed her back to the bathroom. Along the way, she opened a hall cupboard and took a sun-bleached beach towel off a shelf.

"You never told me what happened to Cut," she said.

"Lexi got her a job in New York for the same escort service she'd worked for."

"Then she's working for your grandmother."

Don froze. "What? My grandmother runs an escort service? I thought she got out of that business years ago."

"She got back in. Even offered me a job. I declined."

"Where are my clothes?" he asked. "They weren't there when I woke up."

"They're in the wash."

He took the towel and closed the bathroom door behind him. When he finished showering, he put on a white, terrycloth robe he found hanging from a hook on the back of the bathroom door.

⧗

Eating Dad's home-fried potatoes with tomatoes, onions, mushrooms and hot peppers made Don sweat and brought back memories of the days he'd gone with his dad to Santa Anita to watch the buggy races. On those days, Dad always cooked the same breakfast.

Don was six the first time they went to watch the horses run, and his mother had been angry because it was a Sunday.

"Are you mad at me?" Dad asked as he chewed and watched Don.

"No."

"I wasn't a bad father," he said. "We did things together. We went camping, hiking and to the track."

"I still remember the potato chip factory where you took me once. You placed bets with a bookie there that you said worked for the mob," Don said.

"The mob owned potato chip factories across the country and had bookies in all of them," Dad said. "A double win for them. The potato chip business offered great cover and a way to launder money."

Don smiled. "And you told me I couldn't tell anyone about it because it was the mob."

"And who played Monopoly with you and taught you how to count cards in blackjack?"

"You," Don said.

"What did your mother teach you?" Dad asked.

"She had me memorize the Bible and rewarded me once with a trip to the San Diego Zoo."

Dad reached across the table and squeezed his right hand. "Then I left," he said.

"After you left, Mother went extreme with the scripture, and I started to build walls inside my head to trap the bad memories, but it doesn't do any good. They escape when I sleep."

"I have to tell you something that might be painful," Dad said. "You are not my biological son. You were Jonah's. That makes me your stepfather, but it also makes me sort of your older half-brother."

Don felt his face flush hot, and he looked at Mandy. Her eyes were round and wide and flicking back and forth from his face to his Dad's.

"What about Dion?" Don asked after he recovered from the shock.

"Dion was mine," Dad said, "which is why Jonah left Dion with your mother when you were ten and moved you to the boat to live with him. Jonah knew you were his. Jonah didn't like children, but he put up with you and taught you everything he knew about women, because he wanted his legacy to live on."

Don turned to Mandy. "Any orange juice?" he asked. Then he filled his mouth with potatoes and eggs to avoid talking.

"Jonah was in Europe when Dion was conceived," Dad said, "and for those few months while he was gone, the passion between your mother and I heated up. She always had a big appetite for sex, tempered by crushing

Christian guilt."

A glass of orange juice appeared in front of Don.

"Did you come back after three decades just to tell Don you aren't his real father?" Mandy asked, and Don was surprised by the anger in her voice. He'd never seen her get angry before. Her chair had moved closer to him, and she was squeezing his left hand.

Don felt tears flooding his eyes—not because he'd learned who his real biological father was, but because Mandy cared. He was having difficulty breathing and swallowing.

"There's more," Dad said, looking at Mandy, "but I'm not sure I'm ready to tell him everything."

"He's not a child," Mandy snapped. "He's the best man I've ever known, and he can handle it. He deserves to know."

"She's right," Don managed to squeak out.

Dad took a sip of coffee and said, "I didn't come back to the states for this conversation. I came to divorce your mother and find the woman I plan to marry."

Don stared at the tabletop and braced his head on the palms of both hands.

"What is it?" Mandy asked. She moved closer and draped a protective arm across Don's shoulders.

"I don't know. A thought is on the tip of my tongue, but it won't come out. It's stuck in my head."

"And Jonah wasn't a real Casanova," Dad said. "When he married Amanda daughter, he took her last name—not the other way around. He is an O'Neil, and his branch of the O'Neil clan comes from County

Waterford in England."

"Does that mean Don isn't a Casanova?" Mandy asked.

Dad frowned. "Yes and no," he said. "Legally, he is a Casanova, because his birth certificate says so. There's no reason for the family to know the truth, and I don't think it would matter, anyway, because his grandmother would love him, no matter what. Don also has a sister he doesn't know about."

Don's thoughts escaped. "She's French, and her name is Gabriella. She's the woman you want to marry."

Dad slid his chair back and stared at him. "Yes," he said, looking impressed. "How did you figure that out?"

"I heard her call out your name while she was sleeping, but I didn't really think her Al was you until now."

"Wait," Mandy said, shocked. "Then that means Jonah is Gabriella's father, too. This is confusing."

"Here's the story," Dad said. "Jonah recruited Gabriella's mother during one of his trips to Europe. She was seventeen, but the ID he gave her said she was twenty. He always slept with his girls before he put them to work, and it got her pregnant. He worked her hard until her belly started to show before he sent her back to France, where she gave birth to twins. Gabriella's sister's name is Gina."

"How do you know all this?" Mandy asked.

"I was thirty and spending a lot of time with Jonah on the boat when he came back from France that year."

"Wait," Mandy said. "Isn't Jonah your father, too?

Then you two are brothers." She stared at Don. "How can you marry your sister?"

Dad shook his head. "My mother was married to Jonah, but she never had any children with him. She slept around just like he did, and they seldom slept together. She handpicked the men she slept with, and Jonah didn't fit her criteria. I have no idea who my real father was, and that secret died with her a few months after my birth. But I now know that Jonah is not my biological father. So Gabriella is not my sister. She is Don's sister."

"But she's less than half your age," Don said. "And she'll be my sister and step-mother. I think."

"It doesn't bother her that I'm older," Dad replied, "and when I'm gone, I'm going to leave her a wealthy woman. I was in France fourteen years ago and decided to find out what happened to her mother, because I had a serious crush on her when she worked for Jonah. I found her dirt poor and in bad health, living with her children in an unsafe area of southeast Paris. When I met Gabriella, she was fifteen—that was fourteen years ago."

Don didn't know what to think. He felt as if his life was a fraud.

Mandy leaned closer to Don and said softly, "I'm your family now. I won't let you down." He felt his tears break loose and start running down his face. Her hand tightened on his, and she rested her head on his shoulder.

He wanted to blurt out that he'd almost had sex with his sister. Instead, he kept his mouth shut and struggled to control the emotions running wild through him.

"What about Gabriella's sister, Gina?" Mandy asked.

"She Don's sister, too."

"You don't want her in your life," Dad said. "Gabriella is sunlight. Gina is darkness. She's crazy."

"Is she as beautiful as Gabriella?" Mandy asked.

"Yes," Dad replied. "But she plays with men as if they were toys and breaks them. She had an affair with a Russian mafia boss several years ago and left Paris with him to live in Moscow. They were a match made in hell. We haven't heard from her since and don't want to."

Breakfast was over, and Mandy started to clear the dirty dishes from the table.

"I have a few shocks of my own to share," Don said. "Sit down, Mandy. The dishes can wait."

Chapter Thirty-Nine

Searching for Ben in July was like looking for rain in Death Valley. His dad and Mandy had convinced Don to recruit Ben as a bodyguard, but Don had to find him first.

He called every phone number he had for Ben, and there was no answer at any of them. He drove to Ben's house, and it looked abandoned. Tuesday night, he dropped by Ben's improv group with no result.

Mandy still went to work at the Academe, and returned with news that Uncle Abraham and Lieutenant Jane Eyre Patton were looking for him. There was still no sign of Gabriella and Ricky.

Don became moody, uncommunicative and restless. He'd leave Mandy's house at all hours to walk the Torrance neighborhoods, often returning when Mandy was at work or asleep.

⧖

It was late Sunday evening, and Mandy had worked brunch and had the night off. She'd just come from the shower and was wrapped in a bathrobe with her wet hair in a towel.

"Are you going back to work?" she asked.

Don had mailed a letter to his Uncle Abraham and to his grandmother's PO Box that told them he would not be working at the club for an unspecified amount of time, and that he had chosen an acting assistant general manager that fit within the terms of the family trust.

A week had gone by since the breakfast of revelations, and Dad had returned to his hotel room the same day. Mandy and Don sat at the small kitchen table eating nuked frozen dinners.

A large bowl of guacamole and salsa verde sat between them. They were addicted to the combination. Mandy dipped a taquito into the mixture, scooped up a generous amount and put it in her mouth.

"To be honest, I don't know what I'm going to do," Don said. "I'm wondering where Ben is. You haven't seen him at work. No one has been at his house for a week, and no one is answering any of the family phones. Gabriella and my brother have also vanished. Where have they all gone?"

"You don't have to go back to work," she said. "Stay here with me. I like having you around, even when you're grouchy."

"That might not be a wise invitation," Don said. "Someone wants me dead, and people trying to protect me are getting killed or disappearing."

"Don't talk like that," Mandy said. She scooted her chair around the small table until it was next to his and rested her head on his shoulder. "I haven't forgotten the time I didn't want to live and you wouldn't leave me alone. You even moved into my old apartment and slept on that lumpy, old couch."

"That couch smelled like a wet dog," he said, and smiled at the memory.

"If it hadn't been for you, I wouldn't be here now in this house. Hell, I'd probably have slit my wrists."

He turned to look at her, and her lips were inches from his—the look in her eyes told him what she wanted him to do.

Fear shot through him, and he looked away. "What about you?" he asked. "Why are you still letting all those horny bastards at the Academe cop a feel?"

He and Mandy had met in front of the teachers' mailboxes at the high school, and the space was narrow and cramped. He'd excused himself and started to squeeze around her. She was on her knees, peering into her cubbyhole near the floor. She'd glanced up, and he fell into her eyes just like he was falling into them now.

The dresses she wore back then clung to her body like water, and he thought she must have been an angel. When they were dating, they'd kissed, but they had never slept together, even though the way she touched his arm and smiled at him brought his blood to a boil. The night she was raped was the night he'd planned to make his move.

And now he knew the invitation was there again, but he thought she was too good for him.

"Maybe I should fly to Europe and track Lexi down," he said, and saw the invitation in Mandy's eyes shatter. She got up, walked to the stove to pour more herbal tea in her mug and then slid her chair around the table, taking back what she'd offered.

He felt like a heel. "I used to think Ben was always going to be my best friend," he said, avoiding the hurt and disappointment in her eyes. "But now, I'm not so sure." Don reached for her hand, and she slid it away from him. He swallowed hard and felt even more guilt.

Did he want to risk losing Mandy? He wasn't sure. He'd already lost Lexi and Eve.

"And when you get to Europe and find Lexi, are you going to ask her to marry you?" Mandy asked. "You better. It's the only way you're going to get her back. We talked all the time when she was on breaks." She got up and took her rejection to the refrigerator, where she searched the shelves.

"I've lost my appetite," Don said. Half of the food was still on his plate.

"I've noticed, and you've been losing too much weight."

Mandy closed the refrigerator and turned to stare at him with that hurt and vulnerable look still in her eyes, and it made her look even more desirable.

He wondered if she was naked under the bathrobe. The first and only time he'd seen her nude had been when he discovered her in her classroom after the rape, and she had been a bruised and bloody mess.

Leaving his chair, he went to her. "I'm a fool," he said, "and I'm going to kiss you." At first, she looked stunned, and then she leaned into the kiss, and her features relaxed passionately.

They stumbled against the small refrigerator, and it rocked back to hit the wall with a thunk. Glass rattled inside. Her lips were firm and warm, and then her tongue was in his mouth and her fingers at his belt. He undid the bathrobe's sash, pulled the robe off her shoulders and let it fall to the floor.

Then time froze for an instant before he stepped back and gawked at her body. He couldn't take his eyes off of her. "Whoa," he said. "It looks like Michelangelo painted you like he did the Sistine Chapel!"

She knelt to pick up the bathrobe.

"No!" he protested. "I want to feast on your body art."

"It's cold," she replied.

He took her hand and towed her to the cramped bathroom, where he closed the door and turned on the electric heater.

"Please don't put the robe back on. I'm begging you." He dropped the lid on the toilet seat, sat and twirled his index finger in a circle, indicating he wanted her to turn in a circle. The bathroom was heating, and she handed him the robe.

"You're the first person who's seen it," she said. "In fact, I've kept it hidden from everyone but the artist."

"Why would you want to hide it?" he asked. "I had

no idea that tattoos could be this detailed, this incredible. Who's the artist?"

"A woman," she said. "Someone I trust."

She had turned until her back was to him.

"Stop!" he said, and reached out to touch the figures on her back. "This is The Rape of the Sabine Women. I've seen the original work, but I think this is just as incredible. What caused you to do this?"

"My body is my temple," she said. "After those boys beat and gang raped me, I felt ugly and dirty for months, even after you helped bring me back. My mother convinced me to join a support group, and that's where I met the artist. At one of the meetings, she talked about how ugly she'd felt after she'd been raped, and how she'd taken her skill as a tattoo artist and turned that ugliness into beauty. I asked her to do the same thing for me."

He covered his mouth with a hand and stared at her in horror. "I'm so sorry," he said. "It's because of me that you were raped and almost died. I'm responsible for all of your pain and suffering, and I'm such a bastard for wanting to make love with you."

Before she could respond, he was out the bathroom door and running through the house. The key to Lexi's black Porsche was in his pocket, and he ran to the car.

"Don't go!" he heard Mandy call from the front door.

The engine revved, and he popped the clutch to burn rubber as the car burst from the curb and almost hit the car in front of it. At the corner, he made a hard, squealing, right turn. He couldn't go back—ever.

The only place he could think of was the Aphrodisiac Academe, where he wanted to get totally dead drunk.

Chapter Forty

When Don reached the club, instead of police, there were picketers on the sidewalk holding large signs with big letters that read, "This den of iniquity must go! Close it down!"

Another sign said, "Baby killers! The Academe pays for abortions."

He saw Ms. Sheridan with his mother at the far end of the parking lot beside a fire hydrant, and his mother was talking to a young man who looked like he might be a reporter.

Don wasn't surprised. He'd been expecting something like this since he heard them plotting at his mother's bungalow. It was ironic that his mother wanted to close down the business that clothed, fed and provided shelter for her. The bungalow belonged to the Aphrodisiac Academe, not the corporation that managed the family's real estate empire. If his dad divorced her, she might lose the monthly stipend and the free housing.

Instead of turning into the parking lot, which was full of cars, Don drove slowly by the protesters. The throbbing music told him there was a DJ inside spinning records.

The Porsche's windows were tinted dark, so Don decided to risk parking in the lot. He drove around the block and returned to the parking lot, where he found a single open space in the furthest, darkest corner—the same space Teddy had parked his Jaguar the night Don had liberated Cut. He hoped it wasn't an omen.

From there, Don slipped through the shrubs and past the palm trees to the boardwalk and let himself in through the patio gate. Inside, he discovered that the hot air balloon and the platform were gone, as well as Zeus and Aphrodite.

Why was he sneaking into the club? He wasn't a thief. He wasn't a criminal. Damn his mother and Sheridan! He stalked out the gate and around to the lobby entrance to the restaurant and made sure to stop where the picketers could see him.

When he was satisfied that he had been spotted, he slowly walked toward the door. He saw Sheridan say something to the protesters nearest her, and they all turned to stare at him with unfriendly, accusing glares, as if he was a monster that tore babies out of their mothers' wombs with his fingernails.

The lobby smelled of cigarettes and booze and throbbed with loud music. He looked through the thick glass at the crowd of bobbing, gyrating dancers swirling around the giant, neon dildo protruding from the ceiling. He wanted to find a beautiful woman and take her to the apartment upstairs, and in the morning, she would go back to her life and become one of his blurry memories.

A new face stood behind the front desk. She smiled, and the wires of her braces caught him off guard. He nodded and turned left toward the dining rooms.

"Sir!" she called after him. "Sir." Her adolescent voice gave her age away. "The restaurant is closed."

He glanced to his left at the tall, cherry wood grandmother clock with its etched brass pendulum swinging behind the leaded, beveled glass. He turned to face the hostess. "You're new," he said. She was slender and cute and wearing orange-colored contacts. Her lips had blood-red lipstick on them, and her black hair was cut in a shag.

"I'm Don Casanova," he said. "The general manger. Is Ben here?"

"Oh," she said, startled, and the look in her eyes told him she knew who he was, the absent boss who was a member of the family. He wondered what gossip she'd heard about him from the cooks, waitresses and other hostesses, but figured it didn't matter, because the truth was much worse.

Mandy told him that Eve had quit—another stake pounded into his dark, brooding heart. This girl must have taken her place.

Through the glass between the lobby and the club, he saw a familiar cocktail waitress go by with a tray filled with empty glasses. Her name was Clarisse, and her big tits accentuated a long-limbed, slender body. She was also engaged.

"Never mind about Ben," he said, and walked into the loud heat of the crowded club.

Clarisse was at the bar filling an order. Don stopped behind her.

"Hi, Don," she said. "I've missed you."

Don crooked a finger at one of the other cocktail waitresses and told her to fill Clarisse's order and deliver it. Clarissa handed her the checks with the correct tables.

"What do you want, Don?" she asked.

He took her hand and led her to the dance floor. When the music slowed, he pulled her body against his. Her breasts were soft, and his hands rested on the small of her firm back. He buried his face in the space between her ear and shoulder and nibbled her neck and earlobe.

Before he kissed her, they looked deep into each other's eyes. The kiss was long and passionate, with lots of tongue. He could tell that if he took her upstairs to the apartment, she'd offer no resistance. But when he looked over her shoulder, he saw her fiancé, the accountant, staring at them.

Don wasn't alarmed. The accountant was no match for Don unless he had a pistol on him, and that was unlikely. Even if there was a weapon, Don had been in more dangerous situations with jealous partners.

The accountant shouldered over and said, "I want to talk to you, Clarissa." Without looking at Don, he made his way through the sweaty, drunk crowd toward the lobby.

Clarissa looked stunned and ready to cry. "I'm sorry," Don said, feeling cheated.

"That's okay, Don." She chewed on her lower lip and was gone, leaving him alone on the dance floor with hundreds of people around him unware of what had just happened.

He stopped at the bar, picked up a full bottle of Glenlivet and headed to the first floor office next to the kitchen, where he planned to start drinking.

In the office, Don discovered the assistant general manager, Pete, sitting at a desk checking a stack of receipts next to one of the security people, who watched a bank of monitors showing what was going on in the lobby, the dining rooms, the bar, the parking lot and the patio.

Pete nodded, and Don pulled up a chair. One of Pete's rum-soaked cigars sat in a clean ashtray.

"When you coming back?" Pete asked.

Don poured a half glass of Glenlivet and sipped from it. "I may be back for a few days in a year, and then I'll put you in charge again."

Pete stopped what he was doing and studied Don's face.

"My dad told me about an exception in the family trust." He smiled. "It allows the general manager to take a year's leave of absence and select his temporary replacement, who doesn't have to be a family member."

Pete's eyes smiled and he huffed a mute laugh. "Well, I can't complain."

"Good!" Don took another sip of the Glenlivet.

"You back on the sauce?"

"Not sure yet," Don replied. He glanced at the locked door that led to Ben's office.

Pete shook his head to let Don know that Ben wasn't in.

"When is he supposed to be in?"

"Monday morning," Pete replied. "He's been on vacation."

Don nodded. "See you later. Have fun running the place."

"I'll make sure I don't do what you'd do," Pete said. "My wife would shoot me if I did."

Don and his Glenlivet left the office for the empty lobby. Out on the sidewalk along the front of the club, he stopped and watched his mother and her ghouls walk the picket line.

Ms. Sheridan glared at him, and he lifted the bottle of booze and saluted her with it before swallowing a mouthful.

When he got to the Porsche, he took off his shoes and left them in the car before slipping through the shrubs to the beach where he walked into the foaming water and dug his toes into the wet sand as the ocean boiled around his ankles. Lifting the bottle, he took a generous swig and felt it burn all the way to his stomach. He was starting to feel the buzz.

Holding the bottle up to the sky, he looked to see how much was left—more than half. He screwed the cap back on and threw the bottle in the ocean.

Chapter Forty-One

Morning found Don sleeping on the beach against one side of a cinderblock bathroom next to the boardwalk, hidden under a giant sheet of cardboard. When he opened his eyes, he discovered that pixie-sized jockeys were racing thoroughbreds inside of his skull.

He heard himself groan and croak.

The last thing he remembered was the surf carrying the bottle of Glenlivet back to shore. The gods had spoken, so he retrieved the bottle and finished drinking what was left inside in a countdown chugalug.

After that, he didn't remember a thing. He rolled over to face the cinderblock wall and found twin dark streaks of dried blood leading to where he lay in the sand.

The throbbing in his fists and lump on his forehead revealed how the streaks had gotten there. His swollen hands ached and scabs covered his knuckles. He must have really been angry at himself.

Pushing the cardboard off, the morning light stabbed his eyes and added to his misery. He hoped he hadn't broken any bones.

A young woman walked by with a little girl holding her hand. The little girl had a thumb stuck in her mouth, and she stared at Don. The woman avoided eye contact and kept walking.

Don had seen enough winos and homeless guys to know what he must have looked like emerging from under that cardboard.

His shoes were nowhere to be seen, but then he remembered he'd left them in Lexi's Porsche. He needed some food and a beer to settle his stomach. He checked his wallet, and the money and credit cards were still there. The keys to Lexi's car were in the other pocket. Who would have suspected the bum he must have looked like was flush with cash and credit?

He groaned when he stood and decided that, considering his own stink was enough to urge him to run away from himself, he should change his clothes. Instead, he walked around the side of the bathroom to rinse off the sand, dried blood and boozy sweat with a frigid stream of water from the outdoor showerhead.

On the boardwalk, Don left wet footprints and a trail of water behind. An hour later, he was dry and dressed in new sandals, baggy jeans and a Hawaiian shirt he'd purchased from a little shop along Pacific Coast Highway in Hermosa Beach. He ate a tofu scramble at The Spot and washed it down with a bottle of organic beer that he hoped might stop the hangover drums pounding inside of his skull.

After he ate, he roamed north. It was eleven when he stopped in front of the plate glass window of a karate studio and watched a class of older women practicing blocks, blows and kicks. When he spotted Ms. Sheridan in the middle of the front row wearing a black belt around her ample waist, he thought he might still be drunk.

Not wanting her to spot him, he left, and, down the street, a copy of the *Los Angeles Times* grabbed his attention. The paper said it was Tuesday. He'd fled from Mandy's house Sunday night. He was stunned. What had happened to Monday?

Don went into the nearest bar; sat at the counter; ordered a mug of dark, draft beer; and sipped it in the gloom of the boozy-smelling place.

"You don't mind if I set here," a woman said from behind him. "I could use some company."

He turned and examined her. She was tall, slim and dressed in a tight dress that left nothing to the imagination. Long, dark, glossy hair framed her pale complexion. Bangs covered her forehead, and she had long lashes above her chestnut-colored eyes. She was attractive in her own anemic way.

"You look like you tied one on, sailor," she said. "Buy this girl a margarita, and let's party together."

He ordered the tequila cocktail and watched her run her tongue seductively along the salted rim of the glass while she stared at him. "Do you want to stay here or continue drinking at my place?" she asked.

"Is it far?"

"We can walk there," she said, and he finished his beer and felt the start of a new buzz. "I need what you look like you want. And let's keep it simple—no need for names and family histories."

Her apartment was a crowded snuffbox on the third floor of an ocean-side building. The first thing that hit him when he entered was the stench of stale urine and dog shit. The dog, a pint-sized, shaggy mutt, came running.

"Sorry," she said. "I've been away for a few days, and things didn't work out like I wanted. Wait here while I take care of him. He's probably starving."

She picked up the dog and carried him into the postage-stamp-sized kitchen. All the blinds were closed, but there was enough light to reveal several piles of dirty clothing on the floor.

She returned and took his hand. "My bedroom is this way," she said. "Watch where you step. After we're done, you can sleep, and I'll clean up and let some air in. Then we can play all day and tonight, if you like."

The bedroom was darker than the living room, and Don had a fleeting thought that maybe she was an axe murderer. He stopped in the doorway and watched her go to the bed, where she turned her back on him; slipped out of her dress; and pulled off her black, thigh-high, fishnet stockings from her long, shapely, smooth legs. Her bra came off next, and then she was under the sheets, staring at him with her large, inviting eyes.

He shucked his clothing and joined her. She fetched

a condom and reached for him, and he gasped when she slid it on. Then she rolled over and offered her back to him.

Not wanting to rush things, he spooned her back and explored her naked body with his hands. Every part of her he touched was in top physical shape. Then he slid his hands down over her abdomen to her crotch, where he discovered that she didn't have a vagina.

A jolt of electricity burned the booze from his brain, and he scrambled from the bed, grabbed his clothing and ran naked through the dark living room, where he stepped in a soft pile of dog shit. He pulled on his pants and smeared the dog shit up the inside of one full leg. Once dressed, he reached for the doorknob.

"I'm between genders," the transsexual said from the bedroom. "Come back and play. After my surgery, I'll have everything you want."

Outside, on the small landing, he pulled up his zipper and put on his shirt. Carrying his new sandals, he fled down the stairs, and, halfway to the exit, he bent over at the waist and retched his breakfast all over the rails, the wall and several steps.

Chapter Forty-Two

Don hiked the boardwalk back to the Aphrodisiac Academe to retrieve Lexi's Porsche, slipping through the shrubbery to avoid his mother and the other protestors. Lexi's condo offered a haven of privacy where he could shower and change into some of the clothes he still kept there.

In the car, he discovered his mobile phone and shoes were still where he'd left them.

Still smelling like dog shit and wearing Lexi's pink-framed dark glasses, he drove past the protestors on the sidewalk and turned right on Pacific Coast Highway.

Once he was in the condo and protected by locked doors, he activated the perimeter alarm and retrieved the gun Lexi kept in her panty drawer. Feeling and smelling shitty, Don sat on the bed he'd shared with Lexi and thought about putting the gun in his mouth.

He heard Jonah's voice in his head. "Don't let

rejection get you down, son. There's always another woman, and, eventually, one will say yes."

Two loaded clips sat on the bedspread beside him. Don picked up one of the clips, slid it into the gun and chambered a round. Then he put the barrel between his lips.

The doorbell rang.

Still holding the loaded gun, he walked, barefoot, to the front door, put an eye to the peephole and saw Gabriella.

"I know you're in there," she said.

He rested his cheek against the cool, smooth surface of the door. It would be so easy to end it all.

"Don," she said in her lilting French accent, "I love your father, and we are going to get married. I want you as my brother. Please open the door."

Don lifted the gun and placed the barrel in his right ear.

His mobile phone rang, and he slipped it out of a pocket and put it to his left ear. "Yes," he said.

"This is your mother speaking," she said.

Don said nothing.

"God is watching over you, son," she said. "Timothy 2:15 says, 'notwithstanding she shall be saved in childbearing, if they continue in faith and charity and holiness with sobriety.' I think you know who Timothy is talking about."

It was easy to turn the phone's power off. It wasn't so easy to slip the gun into his pant pocket. He opened the door. Gabriella stepped inside, and he locked the door behind her and turned the perimeter alarm back on.

"I'm pregnant," she said. "So no matter how you look at it, you're going to be an uncle."

He opened his mouth to say something, but nothing came out—not even the air in his lungs.

"Your father wants to get married as soon as the divorce is final and we return to France." Her eyes filled with tears, and she came into his arms, looking for comfort.

She made a face and stepped back. "You smell horrible."

"I'll take a shower and change my clothes. Are you hungry?"

He left her in the kitchen, returned the gun to the bra drawer and took an ice cold shower. Back in the kitchen a half-hour later, he found a bottle of white wine waiting on the table and one chilled glass half full.

"We should celebrate," he said. "Where's your glass?"

She looked horrified. "I can't drink. I'm pregnant. With twins!"

"Twins." He lifted his glass, saluted her with it, and sipped.

The table was set, and the food waited.

He finished the wine and took the glass to the sink.

"This Lexi is not right for you," Gabriella said abruptly. "From what I have learned about her, she is a woman who blows with the wind, and she will make your life miserable. I think I will pick a better woman for you."

"Do you think you're cupid, sister?" he asked.

"I'm French," she said. "Of course. I like Mandy. She is a better wife for my brother."

He opened his mouth to speak, but she didn't let him.

"Mandy came to your father—I'm sorry, your brother's—hotel room. She is very upset and worried over your vanishing. She did not say she loves you, but the French can sense these things. Americans—ah—not so much." She held out her hands, palms up, for emphasis and shrugged. "Al thinks Mandy would be better for you than this Lexi."

"You're going to be my sister-mother." Don spent a silent moment staring at her as if she were not real. "I think my grandmother might have paid Lexi to become my girlfriend," he said. "It's a depressing thought."

"I'm guessing from the expression on your face that you are beating yourself up for something," she said, and patted him on the cheek. "Look, big brother, you better pull all of those tattered strings inside of your head together and start thinking, or I will think for you."

"What did Mandy say?" he asked.

"She was crying and almost hysterical with worry, so she spilled all kinds of interesting secrets."

Don reached for the almost-full wine bottle, but Gabriella snatched it away. "No more alcohol for you. Come on, brother, I'm taking you to see Al. He's at his hotel. I think you two need to talk more."

"Hello," he said, pretending to knock on the top of her head. "Have you forgotten that someone is out there trying to kill me?"

"That's another reason we are going to the hotel."

"Am I ever going to meet your twin?"

"Never," Gabriella said. "She is triple trouble, a lunatic. I don't even trust her."

"Does she have your hair?"

She shook her head. "She always hated all of the natural highlights. She dyes it blond. I think it looks like straw."

"There's one thing we have to do before we drive to the hotel."

She cocked her head, curiosity in her eyes.

"I met a transgendered person who needs some serious advice on how to act like a woman around men so she doesn't get herself killed."

Chapter Forty-Three

After spending two days in the hotel room next to Al and Gabriella's room, it was decided that Don must renew his search for Ben and then go see Mandy.

It was early evening, and a blood-red sun was sinking into the Pacific. The protesters still walked a picket line in front of the Aphrodisiac Academe. The unmarked police car was back, parked at the curb on the other side of the street with two officers in it. The moment that Don climbed from the backseat of Al's rented, fire-red 1989 Chevrolet Camaro, the officer in the passenger seat picked up a mic and started talking.

"You better hurry," Gabriella said.

Don waved at the undercover police.

"You're a low-life," Ms. Sheridan said. She had appeared by his right side. "We're going to close this place down, you know."

Don turned slowly to face her. "Did you do the nasty

with my uncle the other night after your dinner at that French restaurant? He is a married man with children, *you know.*"

Smiling, he walked away from her shocked face and into the lobby of the Academe. The dinner rush hadn't started yet, and only the station in the Lady Chatterley room was open. Veronica was waitressing, and she had two tables with customers.

"I've never seen it this slow, even at this hour," Don said.

"It's those danged women out front with their danged signs," Veronica said. "We're losing the over-thirty family crowd, but the under-thirty singles crowd in the bar is hotter than ever."

"The wait to get into the club on Friday and Saturday nights is approaching two hours, and Pete doubled the cost at the door to get in. I want you to schedule me into the bar to hustle drinks this weekend. I've been told they need the extra help, and I'm not making enough in tips here."

"Have you ever worked as a cocktail waitress?"

Veronica shook her head.

"I'll talk to Pete, but I don't think you're going to like life as a cocktail waitress. Think about being our restaurant manager instead. We could use someone with your people skills."

"How much?"

"I guarantee that you will earn about twice what you usually take in, even with your tips."

"I'll talk with my husband."

"He's already the kitchen manger," Don said. "I think he'll say yes."

The office next to the kitchen was empty when he arrived, and the door to Ben's office was closed. Don stood in front of the blank security monitors and stared at the gray screens, and then he knocked on Ben's door. When there was no answer, he tried the knob and was surprised to find it unlocked.

He opened the door and walked in. The walls were unpainted concrete, and two light bulbs hung from cords suspended from the ceiling. A rolling chair sat behind a counter that ran along the wall facing the boardwalk. Locked, fireproof filing cabinets lined the other wall. Above his head on both sides were storage shelves crowded with dusty cardboard boxes. The place reminded him of a wartime bunker. The only thing missing was gun ports.

What surprised him was the half-dozen security monitors. Five of them were turned off, but one was on, and the quartered screen displayed different views of the outside of the club. In the upper left-hand quarter, Ms. Sheridan and her squad of smut vigilantes walked back and forth with their protest signs. The right top quadrant of the screen showed the parking lot, and the lower right scanned the loading dock. The lower left quadrant had a view of the courtyard, where Zeus and his daughter were back on their fountain pedestal in all their nude marble glory—minus the twelve-inch stone dildo.

He wondered where it was.

Now he knew why Ben always showed up at the

right time. "Get out of there!" Aunt Eleanor's voice exploded inside his head. "Do it now!" The shock of her uninvited arrival between his ears jolted him into action, and he was in the outer office questioning his sanity when Ban walked in.

"You are a hard man to find," Don said.

Ben was holding a clipboard with papers on it. He studied Don for a moment and said, "Look who's talking. I thought you'd gone to the moon. Where the hell have you been?"

"Trying to stay alive," he said, "which is why I'm here. Close the door. We have to talk." Don brought Ben up-to-date on the attempts on his life, but left out the body disposal details.

"That damn cop has been around here asking about you, too," Ben said. "I think it would be a good idea if you avoided her."

"That might not be so easy," Don said. "Did you see the undercover police parked across the street watching the Academe? They saw me."

"You leave the evasion tactics to me," Ben said. "I shook them once, and I'll do it again. I think the best thing for you to do is return to Mandy's house and lay low."

A black hole opened in his gut and threatened to suck him in. He'd planned on talking to her here on neutral ground—not going back to her house.

Chapter Forty-Four

Don waited to ambush Mandy at the time clock. When she walked around the corner to clock in, she stopped a few feet from Don, and their eyes met.

Something he couldn't identify flickered briefly in the muscles of her face before she composed her expression to hide what she was feeling.

He waited for her to speak first, and the silence stretched to the breaking point.

Another cocktail waitress came walking around the corner and had to step around Mandy to reach the clock. She glanced at Mandy and then followed her gaze to Don's face. She sucked in her breath, clocked in and fled.

What had Mandy been telling her friends at work?

Mandy's eyes broke contact first, and, like a puppet with attached strings, she stepped jerkily toward her time card in the rack, but it wasn't there. It was in Don's back pocket.

"I've already made arrangements for you to have tonight off," he said. "Veronica is picking up your shift."

She turned her back to him, stiff.

"I'm sorry," he said. "I still want to sleep in your spare bedroom if it's okay with you. If you don't want me, I'll understand."

Her shoulders trembled, and her neck muscles were taught like wires.

"Why don't you yell at me or something, so we can move to the next stage?" Don asked.

"What is the next stage?" She said in an unsteady, hushed voice.

"I have no idea."

"I thought you were on your way to Europe to be with Lexi."

Gabriella's sisterly advice about Lexi being the wrong woman for him cycled through his mind.

"You are one of my best friends," he said, "and what I did was wrong."

"Which part?"

Oh, fuck, how was he going to answer that question? "I want to rewind the tape and return to the part where I was feeling sorry for myself and you were comforting me."

"It's too late to start over," she said.

"I want to tell you about what I did after I ran away."

"I don't want to hear about it. I've heard enough about all your lusty adventures from everyone who works here."

"Don't believe everything you hear," he said.

"What happened between us happened, and you have no reason to regret anything. I was as much a part of that kiss as you were. I've had enough of you feeling guilty because of what happened to me in that classroom. There are no victims standing here right now." Her voice was louder, and her face had flushed brick red.

"I've never seen you angry before," he said.

"Shut up!" she yelled.

That's when the two of them noticed how quiet it had become. Everyone had stopped working and was staring at them.

"I guess this means I can't stay over at your place," he said.

"Men can be such children." She took a step toward him, grabbed his hand and dragged him behind her toward the Lady Chatterley room. "You are going to pay. I expect a dinner at the Inn of the Seventh Ray in Topanga Canyon before we go back to my place."

In the dining room, headed toward the lobby, Don spotted Lieutenant Jane Eyre Patton at the front desk with two burly, uniformed officers standing behind her. He tightened his grip on Mandy's hand and pulled her to a stop.

"What is it?" she asked.

"It's that cop," he replied. "Get your car and drive to that dead-end near my mother's house and wait for me there."

She let go of his hand, and he spun around and rushed through the kitchen with every eye following him. He reached the door to Zeus's courtyard and pushed it open, hoping Ben would see him with one of his hidden cameras. Ben probably already knew about Patton in the lobby.

He hurried down the boardwalk toward his mother's cottage, and his plans changed.

A big Harley-Davidson motorcycle sat on the porch of his mother's house, and Ricky rocked in the chair beside it.

"What's up, little brother?" Ricky asked.

"I should ask you the same question," Don replied.

"That sister of yours is one incredible broad. She talked to my woman and patched us both up. We're back together. Of course, it helps that Rudy got himself killed."

"Is it okay if I stay at your place?" Don asked. "I'll sleep on the couch."

"That sounds like a plan. I've been rocking in this chair for three hours waiting for our mother to come home. Let's scram."

Ricky rolled his bike off the porch and into the side street where Mandy waited in her car.

"Change of plans," Don said. "I'm going with Ricky. I think his place might be a better hideout."

"Coward," she said. "Who are you really avoiding?" She started the car and drove off.

Before Ricky climbed on his bike, he asked, "You still being hunted by the freak that iced Nick?"

"I think so, and the police are after me, too."

"You know, the way Mandy looked at you before she drove off would've boiled water. I think your sister is right about her. She's in love with you, and it hurts."

"Do you love your wife?" Don asked.

"There isn't another woman who'd put up with my shit," he replied.

Chapter Forty-Five

It was three a.m. when Aunt Eleanor started shouting inside his head. He covered his head with his musty, stained pillow, trying to drown her out and convince himself he wasn't crazy.

After he rolled off the old couch and landed on the floor, it occurred to him that maybe what sounded like Aunt Eleanor's voice was actually his intuition, and he should pay attention to what it was saying. That voice had saved his life more than once.

It was time to go, because there was no way he was going to sleep with that voice inside his head. He thought about getting Ricky up to go with him, but decided against it. Don didn't want to explain that Aunt Eleanor was inside his head shouting at him.

Lucky for him, Don knew where Ricky kept the key for the Harley-Davidson he'd inherited from Nick. Don went to the kitchen and fished around inside of a large, cracked, ceramic bowl full of hard candies. Before he left, he wrote a note and left it where Ricky's wife would see it.

The Harley was inside the garage. Don slipped on a pair of swimming goggles and Ricky's skull-covered brain bucket. Before he opened the garage door, he spent a moment spraying its springs with WD40. He opened the door and rolled the big bike down the street and away from the house so he wouldn't wake his brother and wife.

It was at the corner that he heard a voice. "Well, look what we got here. A skinny dude is lifting The Horse's wheels."

Wearing his heavy jacket, the brain bucket and the fish-eye goggles, there was no way anyone could recognize who he was, but he knew the gangbanger walking toward him. It was Black Hoodie from the scuffle at the high school, and the idiot wasn't alone. Five more thugs he didn't recognize were following him.

Don swung his leg over the seat and turned the key in the ignition.

"Hey, fucker, where do you think you're going?" Black Hoodie said.

The engine roared to life, shook the pavement and caused the nearby trees to tremble. Black Hoodie put a hand on Don's shoulder. Don buried his teeth in the hand the same instant he fed gas to the engine and engaged the transmission. The big bike leapt forward, and the front wheel came off the ground. Don let go of Black Hoodie's hand and leaned over the handlebars while his heart pounded like cannon fire. The front wheel dropped to the asphalt, and the bike rocketed down the street. That was when he discovered he was going in the wrong direction toward the end of a cul-de-sac. He managed to bring the bike to a stop before he went flying through someone's front door.

With the bike turned around, he fed gas to the engine and accelerated down the center of the street toward the six gangbangers who had spread out in a scrimmage line to block his escape. He could see they all carried bats or sections of iron pipe. At the last second, right before he hit their center, he shot the Harley up and over the curb, straight toward the individual on the right flank, who leapt out of the way to avoid being hit. As the bike raced by, Don kicked out and was sure he broke or dislocated Black Hoodie's kneecap.

At the corner, he executed a hard right turn and almost ran into a parked pickup truck sitting too far from the curb. After he left the street-gang-infested housing tract and was speeding down Valley Boulevard, he congratulated himself on his bold escape. He was soon on the freeway and headed toward Manhattan Beach. It was amazing how fast the Harley ate up the road at 100 mph on an almost-empty freeway. Before he knew it, he was off the freeway and moving much slower toward the beach.

When he arrived, the streetlights were having trouble piercing the spooky fog in front of the Aphrodisiac Academe, and the parking lot was blanketed in gloomy shadows. The dark windows of the building reminded him of empty eye sockets. He navigated the local streets, looking for a police stakeout, and didn't spot one. Once he was satisfied that no one was watching, he killed the motor and glided to a silent stop beside the secluded and mostly hidden loading dock.

He climbed stiffly off the bike and flexed his hands as he walked around the Harley, working to get his circulation going and generate some heat and feeling to the block of ice his head had become.

"Hurry," Aunt Eleanor called in a hushed voice. The door from the loading dock to the kitchen was half open, and his stomach muscles contracted in anticipation. He slipped inside the building and discovered the fog was thicker in here than it was outside. Odd, he'd never seen that happen before.

With his back against the wall, he inched along, cursing the interior fog, because visibility couldn't have been more than two to three feet.

Where was the fog coming from?

When he reached the dishwashing alcove, he heard someone behind him, and, without thinking, he climbed into the dishwasher and lay prone on the pronged conveyor as he had when he eavesdropped on Dion and Rudolph.

Inside the machine, the smell of stale soap and brackish water laced with bleach was strong and caused his eyes to water. The itch to sneeze was overpowering. Whoever the intruder was hurried past the dishwasher toward the kitchen. Don peeked out of the dishwasher, but the fog in the hallway outside the alcove was too thick, and he only saw a bulky shape glide by. Holding his breath and struggling to contain the sneeze that wanted to explode, he tried to hear where the figure was going to no avail.

Don carefully climbed out of the dishwasher and turned toward the nightclub, where he found the fog was even thicker. Visibility was down to less than a foot, and he heard the muted sound of an electric blower running.

Someone had turned on the industrial fog machine installed under the stage. He'd never seen it make fog this thick before, but now he knew what it was capable of.

The nightclub was a minefield of tables and stacked chairs. If he moved too fast, he might knock the chairs off of a table and give himself away. He had no idea where the switch was that would turn off the fog machine.

He used his master key to let himself into the downstairs office, where he discovered the room was free of fog. He locked the door and braced a chair under the knob to make it more difficult for anyone to get in.

The door to Ben's office beckoned, but it was locked, and his master key didn't work. Pete kept a toolbox under his old desk. It didn't take long for Don to pry open the hollow door, turn on the two dim lights inside and power up the monitors for all twenty security cameras hidden throughout the Aphrodisiac Academe.

Sitting in Ben's chair, he watched the monitors come alive. His eyes widened when the twenty images started to rotate, revealing more than twenty cameras. There were cameras in every room from the basement to the second floor. When one monitor flickered and revealed images of the stairwell leading down to the oil derrick room, he gasped. The images shifted again to the oil derrick room from both ends. His knee hit something, and he leaned down to discover a headset hanging from a hook under the counter. There was also a panel of switches with six rows, five to a row.

Don slipped the headset over his ears and flipped the first switch up in the top row. A red light came on in the corner image of the far left monitor. He hadn't been in the room long enough last time to see everything. On a shelf above the monitors was a recording machine, and when he flipped on the mic, the machine had started to record.

On one screen, he saw Ricky's Harley sitting beside the loading dock. Behind it was Ms. Sheridan's Buick.

That image rotated to Zeus's garden patio, and then different images of the boardwalk and parking lot.

He found Ms. Sheridan creeping along the walkway that ran through Lolita's Grotto. The fog hadn't reached that far yet. She was dressed in her karate uniform, and she looked ready to battle.

It took a moment to learn how to rotate the cameras and see different areas of each room. That was how he found Uncle Abraham chained to a pipe at the far end of the oil derrick chamber. Zooming in on his uncle's face, he could see a swollen contusion and a forehead bruise. Don feared Uncle might already be dead, but, on closer examination, he could detect that his uncle was only unconscious.

Who he saw next, sent an ice cold shiver of fear and

shock from his feet to his head. Mandy was handcuffed to another pipe bolted to the wall and dressed in her skimpy cocktail waitress outfit. He couldn't see her face because her head was hanging down toward the floor, but he knew she was alive because her body was shivering from the cold.

The urge to hurry to her side and protect her was strong, but he knew that could lead to death for all of them.

A flash of movement on one screen caught his attention, and what he saw caused him to gasp. A close-up of Aunt Eleanor's face revealed her fear and panic as she left one room and entered another one that appeared on a different screen.

A bulky figure appeared in the room Aunt Eleanor had just fled from, and it was the same person who had attacked Don on the mountain. The figure held a big knife in his glove-covered right hand.

Wait a minute, Don thought, and zoomed in on the knife to verify that it was his Bowie—the one with the red handle, the one he slept with.

On another monitor, he followed his aunt running down the hallway outside of the general manager's office on the second floor. She was headed for the stairway to the Lady Chatterley room and the lobby.

If he moved fast enough, he could cut through the first floor liquor storage and come out behind the front desk in time to help Aunt Eleanor escape safely. Without caution, he rushed from the ground floor offices into the fog and slammed into another person, who screamed.

Don's response was automatic. He used the heel of his right hand to smash the man's nose, breaking it, and then jabbed the stiff fingers of his left hand into a soft spot below the man's heart, robbing him of the ability to breathe for a moment. His last blow was a knee to the man's groin that doubled him over and caused him to vomit.

It was Norman, the pimply pest. What was wrong with this kid, who was now, thank God, unconscious? Norman's nose was severely broken and gushing blood. Don pulled tissues from a pocket and stuffed both nostrils so Norman wouldn't bleed to death.

"Who invited you to the party?" Don asked, and then raced to the locked door to the liquor storage room and found that he'd dropped his master key in the scuffle with Norman.

Reversing direction, he ran through the kitchen toward the stairs, where he hoped to find Aunt Eleanor.

He did.

She was on her back on the floor at the base of the stairs, kicking at the bulky figure in the ski mask who was trying to stab her with Don's Bowie knife. She had been slashed several times on her arms and legs, and there was blood everywhere.

Don wasn't about to let this monster butcher his favorite aunt "Try *me!*" he shouted.

The scene froze for a brief instant, and then the ski mask reached down, grabbed his aunt by her hair and yanked her head up so he could easily slash her throat from ear to ear.

Ms. Sheridan appeared out of nowhere, let out a karate yell and flew feet-first through the air to attack the figure wearing the ski mask. The knife went flying, and the two of them traded a volley of blurred martial arts blows.

Ms. Sheridan went down and was struggling to get back on her feet when the figure in the ski mask pulled out a pistol.

"Drop it," a voice said from behind Don. It was Norman, and he had a pistol in his hand. Ski mask got off the first shot and hit Norman in the shoulder, causing him to spin around and drop his weapon.

"Where's my Hammy?" Ms. Sheridan demanded. "If you've hurt him—" She was already back on her feet and moving toward ski mask, who swiveled to shoot her next. Don leapt forward, grabbed the back of her karate gi and pulled her out of the line of fire. The bullet intended for her head buried itself in the wall behind her.

Don put his mouth next to her ear and said, "I'll distract him, and you slip off to the side and disarm him." He pushed Ms. Sheridan away from him. He noticed that his aunt was crawling down the hall away from the stairs.

"You stupid fool," the killer said from inside the ski mask. "Why couldn't you stay out of my way? I didn't want to kill you, but you wouldn't stop sticking your nose where it didn't belong. Neither would the pimp, that Las Vegas dancer or the rat catcher. A few more months, and I would have had enough money from my drug venture to vanish. I was going to retire to Thailand."

"Ben?" Don said, stunned. "You killed them?"

"They all found out I was selling cocaine through the ex-cons I hired to tend the bars. They tried to blackmail me."

"What about my brother and Jonah?"

"I have no idea who snuffed them."

"And why do you have Uncle Abraham and Mandy shackled to pipes?"

"I thought you'd be at Mandy's house. When I got there, I only found her, so I took her as bait to get you. I figured once I had her locked up, I'd call your mobile phone and lure you here. But when I got here, I ran into your snoopy, old uncle and had to take him, too. Then your aunt appears from out of nowhere."

"He's not an old man," Ms. Sheridan said. "And he wasn't snooping around. He was here to help his niece Eleanor escape so we could hide her someplace else from whoever has been trying to kill her."

"You wanted to kill my aunt?"

"No, I didn't," Ben said. "I had no idea she was even hiding in the Academe. But when she discovered what I was doing with Mandy and your uncle, I had to kill her, too."

"Freeze." It was the voice of Lieutenant Jane Eyre Patton. Don looked over his shoulder and saw her braced in a firing position, ready to shoot. She wore a bulletproof vest, and behind her were two uniforms in body armor with short-barreled assault rifles.

"Put your weapon on the ground," she said to Ben. "Do it slowly. Don't be stupid."

Ben fired, and the police returned fire, slamming

Ben's body against the wall behind him and riddling him with bullets.

More police swarmed into the room. Don saw DEA and FBI agents mixed in with the local police.

"Are you okay?" Patton asked. She was standing beside him and had placed a comforting hand on his shoulder.

"I don't know," Don said. "I'm numb. I knew Ben most of my life. He was my buddy."

"And he was the killer."

"That, too," Don replied. He gestured toward Norman, who was being treated by paramedics. "What about him?"

"He works for the DEA," Patton said. "One of their undercover agents. We knew there was a major drug ring in the city, but we had no idea it was headed up here in the Academe and would never have guessed it was your friend behind it if we hadn't heard it from his own mouth. Who are all of those people that Ben said he'd killed, and didn't I hear him say he didn't kill your brother and grandfather?"

"Yea, I did hear him say that," Don replied. "The others were club patrons and employees. I had no idea that he'd killed them. And if that's true, I have no idea what he did with the bodies." He wasn't lying.

"What about your uncle and Mandy? I heard you two talking about them."

"I don't know where they are," he said. "Ben died before he said where they were. They might be in a room upstairs." How could he let the police discover the underground oil derricks? He looked at Ms. Sheridan, and her eyes told him that she knew the secret.

Don mouthed, "Go to them. Help them." Sheridan nodded. He turned back to Patton. "What about my grandfather and brother. If Ben didn't kill them, who did?"

From his peripheral vision, he saw Ms. Sheridan slip away unnoticed toward the stairs down to the basement. He hoped she knew where the hidden door was.

"Don," his aunt called. She was strapped on a gurney, and two paramedics were working on her wounds to stop the bleeding.

"We'll talk more later," Patton said, and Don hurried to his aunt's side and leaned in close.

"There's a hidden apartment upstairs with a secret stairway that leads to the basement," she whispered in his ear. "That's where I was hiding. Amanda had it built during the Academe expansion back in the 1960s."

"Does Uncle know?"

She nodded. "After Sheridan frees them, they will go there," Aunt said. "After enough time passes, I'll let the police know about that room, where they will find Uncle and Mandy."

"What about Jonah and Dion's killer?" he asked. "You're still not safe."

"I'll have police protection, and the family will provide bodyguards," she said. "And when I get out of the hospital, I'll go live with Amanda."

"I don't want to know where she is," he said.

"And I wouldn't tell you. Amanda enjoys her

seclusion and privacy."

Chapter Forty-Six

There was a large, metal tool chest in the oil derrick room, and Ms. Sheridan used bolt cutters to free Mandy and Uncle Abraham. Then she helped them climb the stairs to the hidden second floor apartment, where the police found them.

Don rode with Mandy in the ambulance on its way to the hospital.

"Are you rescuing me again?" she asked.

He was holding her hand. "Maybe it's the other way around," he said.

"What?"

Don glanced at the paramedic sitting on the other side of Mandy's gurney monitoring her vital signs. "Well, this isn't exactly a romantic atmosphere," Don said. "Your favorite restaurant would have been better, but I'm not going to wait—I might talk myself out of it."

He paused and took a fortifying breath. "Will you

marry me if I quit working at the Academe and find myself another teaching job? You could stay at home and raise our children."

Mandy stared at him as if she were hallucinating. "Run that by me again," she said. "I want to make sure I heard you right."

"You heard me," he said. "I'm asking you to marry me, and if you say yes, we are moving to San Francisco so I can find a teaching job in the Bay Area."

"Before I answer," she said, "I want to know why you want to marry me."

"The instant I saw you chained to that pipe, I thought I might lose you."

"What about love?"

"I've been running away from serious relationships since I was twelve. But of course I love you."

"What about Lexi?"

"She's in love with her music and her fans," he replied, "and that makes her history. All I did was ask you to marry me—I didn't ask for the third degree."

"What about my flashbacks from the rape? There are nights when I wake up in a panic, drenched in sweat," she said.

"What about my flashbacks from Vietnam?" he countered. "I can't sleep unless I have a loaded pistol within reach."

"Kiss me," she said.

The paramedic was smiling, but managed to look away as they kissed.

When their lips parted, Mandy said, "Yes, Mr.

Casanova, I'll marry you."

"Wait a minute," Don said. "Are you just marrying me for my money?"

She punched him gently in the arm and laughed. "Stupid. I've loved you since I came out of that coma in the hospital and saw you sitting beside my hospital bed, holding my hand. Now, kiss me again."

"Answer one question first," he said. "Are you an expert in any martial arts?"

"Of course not," she replied. "Why do you ask?"

Don smiled and looked relieved. "I'll explain later. How about that kiss now?"

⧗

Hours later—the same day—Don, Mandy, Uncle Abraham and Ms. Sheridan met in the Aphrodisiac Academe's upstairs private banquet room behind a locked door.

"Why did you hide Aunt in that secret apartment without telling me what was going on?" Don asked. "And how did you know someone wanted to kill her, too?"

Uncle reached for Ms. Sheridan's hand, and she took it in a show of support. "Jonah kept an office in the building where the family manages its real estate investments," Uncle replied. "After Jonah was killed, I went through his papers and discovered that he'd been receiving nasty letters for more than a decade, first from France and then Russia, threatening to punish him and other family members for what he'd done to one of his

French hookers after he got the poor girl pregnant.

"Amanda was mentioned in many of the letters, too. Eleanor and me in a few. I thought it best that Eleanor go into hiding, but I couldn't, because I was the CEO of the family's real estate holdings. I couldn't trust that job to anyone else. That's why Cookie," he glanced at Ms. Sheridan with fondness, "decided we'd spend more time together, and she'd protect me."

Uncle was 90, and she was in her 50s—almost forty years younger than he was.

Why does he call her Cookie? Don thought. And during her fight with Ben, I heard her call him Hammy. What will Mandy call me?

"Mandy," Don said. "We have to talk to Gabriella and Al as soon as possible. I think I know who killed Jonah and Dion."

Later, Uncle Abraham told Don that Amanda had used the hidden apartment originally as an illegal bordello during the years she'd been general manager. When she retired into seclusion, Uncle had refused to keep the bordello open, and the hidden apartment had been furnished, but vacant, for more than twenty years.

"What's confuses me," Don said, "is why your girlfriend wants to close the Aphrodisiac Academe."

"That was a ruse," Uncle replied. "We hoped the picketing would scare away the drug dealers. We knew drugs were being sold out of the nightclub, but I had no idea Ben was behind it. We even asked him to help us. I was afraid if the police discovered the drugs were being sold out of the Academe, we'd lose our liquor license. It was Cookie's idea. Now that the drug ring is out of business, the picketing will stop."

"I find it hard to believe my mother supported your plot," Don said.

"She didn't," Ms. Sheridan added. "I needed her help to garner adequate support. I lied to them. But now that I'm not feeding them, they'll go back to their routines."

"Did you mean any of the things you said to me?" Don asked.

"Of course not," she replied. "It was all part of the act. That was Hammy's idea, and he got Dion to erase the reservation so I could make a scene. Pretty good acting, huh?"

When Don called Gabriella's mobile phone, she answered. She told him to meet them at the La Habra Heights house the following day.

⧗

When Don and Mandy stopped the Mustang outside the closed gates of the La Habra Heights house the next afternoon, they were no longer single. That morning, they'd waited over an hour in line at the Los Angeles County Clerk's Office to get a marriage license and have a civil ceremony.

But the day had started with a disagreement.

"Why don't you want to wait and have a big wedding?" Don had asked.

"Because I don't," Mandy replied. "They're overrated and cost too much. Plus, I'm not about to give you time to change your mind."

"There will be no wedding photos to show our children. No memories to cherish," Don protested. "No gifts from friends and family. Don't you want a bachelorette party with some buff guy stripping in front of you while your friends hoot and holler?"

He wanted all of that and more. He wanted the fancy marriage and an average, normal life—at least what he thought was normal.

"If you want a big, fancy wedding, we'll wait until we have already survived a year together as man and wife, and that is my last word on this subject," Mandy said. "What's more important to you—a fancy wedding, or me?"

"I think I know who will be wearing the pants in our house," he said. "I have to warn you, I look horrible in a dress."

⧗

Don pulled the Mustang close to the keypad box on its post and punched in the code that opened the gate.

When Don parked the car in front of the house at the top of the hill, Gabriella was waiting outside the front door. "We expected you several hours ago," she said. "What took so long?"

"Our wedding," Mandy replied, shooting her hand out to show off her Tiffany wedding rings. "He proposed in the ambulance on the way to the hospital."

Gabriella's eyes sparkled, and she hooked arms with

Mandy and Don and led them inside the house. "In a few months, when Al's divorce is final, that will make us sisters," she said. "I like that. I'm getting a big family to call my own. I've always wanted a big family."

"Hey," Don said, "how about we have a big, fancy double wedding together?" Don stopped when he spotted the open panel in the living room wall that hid the stairs that led to the basement.

"It's okay," Gabriella said, and patted his arm. "That's where we're going—to your nightclub museum and Amanda's torture chamber."

"What torture chamber?" Don asked. He'd forgotten that Amanda had built the house and lived in it for more than a decade. He'd never seen a torture chamber down there.

"Al will explain everything," she replied. "Follow me."

At the bottom of the stairs, Mandy looked around in awe at the thousand-square-foot basement room full of hardwood tables topped with thick, Plexiglass display cases. Inside the cases were flyers, mailers, photographs, menus and napkins from famous nightclubs. Each case held a display for one nightclub. Framed posters and original paintings hung on the burled wood wall panels. The floor was covered in plush, cushy, white Berber carpet.

"Keep moving. We don't have time for this," Gabriella said.

Mandy looked at Don. "Did you do this?"

"Yes," he replied. "This is what I've been making in

my woodshop. I was ten when I started collecting. My nightclub memorabilia goes back to the 1920s from nightclubs across the United States. I've recently started a European collection, and I'm going to put it over there." He pointed to the far end of the dignified room, where there were empty spaces for future displays.

Gabriella took Don's hand. "You will have plenty of time to show this off later. Right now, we have a killer to confront, and we are keeping her in Amanda's torture chamber. Don't worry. Nothing in your museum has been disturbed. Al was impressed when he saw what you had done with the room. He said when Amanda lived here, the basement was all mirrors and red velvet."

"It was grotesque," Don agreed.

Gabriella led the way to the far back wall, where a door opened to a small storage closet. She opened the door, stepped inside and tapped a spot on the back wall near the floor with the toe of her shoe. With the sound of gears meshing, the block wall started to roll back away from them.

"I never knew this was here," Don said.

"Al says this was Amanda's sadomasochism room. Men paid a lot to enter that room and have Amanda or one of her girls."

When the wall stopped moving, Gabriella ushered them inside, where Al waited with a shackled prisoner.

"My God," Don said. "This place looks like a dungeon from the Spanish Inquisition."

"Don't be alarmed," Al said. "Most of these things were only used for atmosphere. No one's been on this rack until now."

The rack was an oblong, rectangular, wooden frame, slightly raised from the ground, with a roller at both ends. The woman on the rack, who was Gabriella's mirror image except for the hair, had her ankles and wrists strapped to ropes that went to the rollers. Her body was stretched tight, and there was duct tape over her mouth. She wore shorts and a halter top.

Mandy had covered her mouth with a hand and looked horrified. "You're torturing her?" she asked.

"No," Gabriella said. "I wouldn't do that to my sister. After we found her and drugged her, we felt this was the best place to keep her restrained until we decided what to do with her." She pointed at the duct tape. "She has a gutter mouth. Always has. And she wouldn't shut up. She hates me because I'm not like her."

"I think she killed Jonah and Dion," Don said.

Al nodded. "She admitted it, and she was planning to hunt Amanda down and kill her, too. You were not on her list, Don. She said that Dion wasn't, either, but he tried to seduce her, and that made her mad."

"My sister has a bad temper," Gabriella said, and stepped over to the rack to pat her sister's cheek. "Isn't that true, sister?"

Gina's face turned brick red, and she made angry, muffled sounds under the duct tape. The look in her eyes was lethal.

"What's this mafia boss's name?" a woman's voice asked from the entrance to the torture chamber.

Don turned. "Grandmother," he said, shocked.

Amanda entered the room, followed by two bodyguards. Don would learn later that they were former Navy SEALs.

"I called her," Al said. He turned and pointed at Gina. "She killed Jonah and Dion."

Amanda's face revealed her age, but her body was slender and upright, and she was elegantly dressed in a dark, sleeveless front-zip dress with a V-neck. She wore silk-lined, elbow-length, black, Italian leather gloves. Around her neck, she wore two strands of pearls that Pierre Cartier had made in the 1920s. Her legs were covered in black leggings from Victoria's Secret.

"Yuri Petrov, mother," Al said.

Amanda looked at Don. "I'm proud of you, Peaches. Call your contact at the CIA and ask if they want to get this Yuri Petrov."

Don wished she'd stop calling him Peaches. She'd done it all of his life. Then he glanced at Mandy, worried that she'd take it up.

Amanda went to Mandy and took both of her hands in hers. "So, you are the one who tamed my favorite grandson. You have to be very special. I've already called Abraham and told him to sign this house over to the both of you as my wedding gift."

"Grandmother," Don said, "We only got married a few hours ago. How did you know?"

She learned forward and offered her cheek to Don, who kissed it. "Peaches," she said, "I keep a close eye on the family at all times. You don't have to know how I do it. No one does. Now, go call your friend at the CIA. We will turn this young lady on the rack over to them, and they will take it from there."

"Grandmother, I'm worried about a friend of mine who works for you."

"Are you talking about Cut?"

"Yes."

"I can answer that question," Al said. "Don, your grandmother has never treated the girls who worked for her the same way Jonah treated his hookers. I know, because I learned from her how to run a proper bordello and escort service. Don't worry, Don—Cut will be well taken care of and compensated for her valuable services, and no one—no matter how wealthy or powerful—will abuse her in any way. Your grandmother would never allow that to happen."

Amanda said, "Peaches, Mandy, where do you two want to go for your honeymoon? My personal jet is waiting to take you anywhere in the world."

###

Books by Lloyd Lofthouse
My Splendid Concubine
http://www.mysplendidconcubine.com/

Finalist in Fiction & Literature: Historical Fiction:
The National "Best Books 2010" Awards

Honorable Mentions in General Fiction:
2012 San Francisco Book Festival
2012 New York Book Festival
2012 London Book Festival
2013 DIY Book Festival

"My Splendid Concubine is packed cover to cover with intriguing characters and plot, a must read for historical fiction fans and a fine addition to any collection on the genre." - Midwest Book Review

Running With the Enemy
http://lloydlofthouse.com/WhereToBuy_RunningWithTheEnemy.htm

Runner Up in General Fiction:
2013 Beach Book Festival

Honorable Mentions in General Fiction:
2014 Los Angeles Book Festival
2013 San Francisco Book Festival
2013 Hollywood Book Festival
2013 New York Book Festival

"Obviously drawn from the author's first-hand experiences as a Marine serving in Vietnam, *Running with the Enemy* is a rough but occasionally heartfelt war story.

… The book is sometimes too obviously drawn from his experience. But ultimately that's a small complaint about a book that, on the whole, is quite good and has a lot to say about the nature of the conflict ." – 21st Annual Writer's Digest Self-Published Book Awards commentary from an anonymous judge

"This book grabbed hold of me. It has left me knowing just how horrific conditions were for those who fought in Vietnam, and I applaud those who survived." - Lisa Binion, The News In Books

Crazy is Normal: a classroom exposé
http://crazynormal.com/

Runner Up in Biography/Autobiography:
2015 Florida Book Festival

Honorable Mention in Biography/Autobiography:
2014 Southern California Book Festival
2014 New England Book Festival
2014 London Book Festival

"Public school teachers will relate well to this book, as well other professionals who work with teens in challenging situations. This book is perhaps a strongest fit with college students who are interested in the teaching profession; it gives a sense of the challenges ahead and how to face them." - Judge, 2nd Annual Writer's Digest Self-Published eBook Awards

"His portrayal of life in the class room is stunning,

realistic, and even a little scary. You really get the feeling your are that little fly on the wall." - Dr. William L. Smith, Professor Emeritus status, Emporia State University

REVIEWS

Reviews are incredibly important for most authors. If you enjoyed any of Lloyd's work, please consider leaving a review where you purchased it such as on Amazon or Barnes and Noble.com.

If you are not sure how to write a review, I suggest visiting SCHOLASTIC and following their five step plan. Before you know it, you will be writing better reviews than most media professionals.

http://teacher.scholastic.com/writewit/bookrev/

ABOUT THE AUTHOR

Lloyd Lofthouse is a former U.S. Marine and Vietnam Veteran who worked as a maître d' in a 15 million dollar nightclub for a few years. He also taught English literature in the public schools for most of 30 years.